A Wonderful
Use for Fire

Hayden Gabriel is a graduate of the creative
writing MA at the University of East Anglia
and author of *The Quickening Ground*.
She lives in the south-west of England.

Also by Hayden Gabriel

The Quickening Ground

HAYDEN GABRIEL

A Wonderful Use for Fire

PAN BOOKS

First published 2004 by Pan Books
an imprint of Pan Macmillan Ltd
Pan Macmillan, 20 New Wharf Road, London N1 9RR
Basingstoke and Oxford
Associated companies throughout the world
www.panmacmillan.com

ISBN 0330 48980 1

1 3 5 7 9 8 6 4 2

A CIP catalogue record for this book is available
from the British Library.

Typeset by SetSystems Ltd, Saffron Walden, Essex
Printed and bound in Great Britain by
Mackays of Chatham plc, Chatham, Kent

All Pan Macmillan titles are available from www.panmacmillan.com
or from Bookpost by telephoning 01624 677 237

to Frances

Bright Star

Bright Star, would I were steadfast as thou art—
Not in lone splendour hung aloft the night,
And watching, with eternal lids apart,
Like nature's patient sleepless Eremite,
The moving waters at their priest-like task
Of pure ablution round earth's human shores,
Or gazing on the new soft-fallen mask
Of snow upon the mountains and the moors—
No—yet still steadfast, still unchangeable,
Pillow'd upon my fair Love's ripening breast,
To feel for ever its soft swell and fall,
Awake for ever in a sweet unrest,
Still, still to hear her tender-taken breath,
And so live ever—or else swoon to death.

JOHN KEATS

Part One

South-west Wales

The soft slap of his trainers on the track; feet fielding dusty ruts where the winter tractor gouged. Place feet, pace, breathe. Place feet, pace, breathe. Sun hot on his back. Flies buzz. Heady scent of heated foliage: oak leaves and campion. Can't be long now till – yes, there – the dark gash of the path into woodland. Turning, he dives into wooded coolness, like sliding into the coolness of sheets that settle round him. Memory flickers: his wife last night, the tautness of her back turned towards him, feigning sleep.

Branches scratch his shoulder. Place feet, pace, breathe. Place feet, pace, breathe. His eyes adjust to sun-dappled darkness, his ear to birdsong – linnet – and to the trip and trickle of water – the stream he runs beside. His body draws coolness from the air at his neck as his feet follow rising ground, splashing across the water. Place feet, pace, breathe. Lungs draw deeply now, in response to the hill. Unbidden comes a soft grunt of satisfaction, acknowledging that moment of connection, of correlation: the moment the landscape begins to dictate his breathing, challenging his body. It's a little sooner today. The heat.

Half a mile of this before the trees thin and trail and he is sent into the sun again. Topping out: a sense of triumph he knows is fatuous, but still somehow good; his body strong, even the troublesome calf muscle pulling full weight today.

The ground levels, a mile more. Place feet, pace, breathe. He feels the thumping of his heart subside. A current of air moves with him here, at his back to ease him along.

Hand dropping to the top rail, he leaps the stile to the coastal path. Light on the sea spangles and sparkles. Without missing pace, he flicks his shirt over his head; feels sun and breeze on his sweated body, circling his shoulders to ease the muscle, slowing now as the path loses height. Place feet, pace, exhale. Carefully here, where the path descends, narrow and infringed by rock; placing his feet, picking his path, the half-mile descent to the sea. When he gets to the beach, he'll take a moment to look for shells for Sebastian. He knows how the boy will receive them: silently, the steady look of steady eyes, the curling of fingers around new treasure to add to his trove.

Surrounded by the sound of breaking waves, Greg's body settles to a sense of well-being – the hard work done; this glorious sun; some of the day's stresses sweated out; his body loosened with exercise. Beneficence. And, living this moment, he lets his gaze stretch out along the beach, so that at first, the rounding of the inert body blends into the rounding of rocks and, for a few seconds, the silly yap of the terrier is about a cause unidentified.

Not another one, Greg's subconscious offers.

'Oh *what?*' he murmurs.

Stopping, he lifts a hand to shield his eyes against the glare of sun on water. Still he has to squint. It looks like Len Curry with his terrier – and at their feet . . . It is. Greg's mouth tightens. It is. Another one. The fifth this month. And this one practically at his door.

Ignoring the waved shouts of its owner, the white dot of the dog circles and backs away from the corpse.

Greg lets out pursed breath, flings his shirt over his shoulder; picks his way among the rocks to see.

Usually the stretch home is cool-off time, a steady jog along the valley floor from coast to cottage. Today he sprints it.

Nearing home, he sees movement through foliage: Ella in the garden, the white of her shirt visible in interstitial glimpses.

'Oh – there you are,' she says, as he turns into the little pathway and stops to double up, catching his breath. Secateurs in hand, she regards him. 'Whatever's the rush?'

'Another dead stranding,' Greg pushes out, smearing sweat from his eyes.

Clip, clip. Her secateurs, dead-heading roses.

'Really?'

'Common dolphin. I'll have to go down and pick him up.'

The secateurs stop. Then start again.

'Can't Tony deal with it?'

'Normally, yes, but you know he's away.'

Clip.

'I'm going out, Greg. I need to go and get in the shower now. You said you'd look after Seb.'

'I will. He can come with me.'

'I don't think *that's* a good idea,' Ella says quietly, laying dead-heads in the shallow basket on her arm, stooping to pick up petals from the lawn. 'You know how he hated going to the last one. Can't it wait till I get back?'

Greg shakes his head.

'Not in this heat. The dolphin's fresh enough for post-mortem, but it won't be for long, and besides, I've left Len Curry down there guarding the thing. Seb won't mind this one. It's very prettily dead.'

'And then what?'

'I'll have to get it to London.'

'*Tonight?*'

'Yes. Tonight.'

'I'm sorry, but I *don't* want you dragging Seb all the—'

'I'll get babysitters.'

'I don't know *who* at this short notice,' she says, placing the secateurs in the basket.

'I'll sort it, Ella,' he says as she turns towards the house. He sees her shrug as she leaves. 'OK.'

'Where *is* Seb?' Greg calls after her.

'In the shell pit,' her voice drifts back.

Blond-haired boy in the blond sand pit; particular shells in particular places in Shell Town, where the sand streets weave.

'Hi, monster,' Greg says to Sebastian, pulling on overalls he's grabbed from the pickup. 'How are you doing?'

'I'm OK. Listen.'

The boy lifts a large shell up towards his father.

'Hey, yes, the sea,' Greg says, listening briefly, taking the boy's hand to pull him up. 'Coming down to the beach? I could use some help. Bring the shell if you want to.'

'No, no,' the boy says, whisking his hand away. 'The shell goes here.'

'OK, but be quick,' Greg says, knowing that arranging shells in the shell pit can take all evening. 'Quickly now. Dead dolphin to pick up.'

Seb looks swiftly up at him.

'It's all right,' Greg says, squatting next to the boy. 'This dolphin's very beautiful.' He rests a finger on the shell he knows is Seb's favourite among his outdoor collection. 'Even more beautiful than the *Strombus listeri*.'

The boy studies his father's face.

'Come on, Seb. We have to hurry.'

It's only a calf, this common dolphin. Such an ordinary name for such an extraordinarily beautiful creature. Freshly dead, the yellow flush is still on its skin, rosing against the sleek grey. So freshly dead, even the eyes have not been taken.

'Didn't I say he was beautiful?' Greg asks Seb as they crouch side by side to see.

The boy nods seriously; reaches out towards the dolphin. Greg catches his hand.

'Mustn't touch, Seb, remember? He might be carrying bugs.'

'Gulls would have had 'im if I hadn't been here – and them two little buggers,' Len Curry interjects, indicating two boys further down the beach.

'You've done a good job, Len,' Greg says, straightening and turning to drop the pickup's tailgate. 'I owe you a beer.'

'No, you don't. Pleased to do it. Poor little sod.'

'Let's get him in, then, shall we?' Greg says, pulling on gauntlets.

'Can you lift 'im?'

'Yes.'

'What'll you do with 'im?'

'Send him to the path lab for post-mortem – where they

all go if they're fresh enough. London or Liverpool. London this time, I should think.'

He pushes the bucket of old towels towards Sebastian.

'Take these down to the water and dunk them in for me, will you, Seb?'

'Can you do it with me?'

'In a minute. Perhaps Len would give you a hand.'

'Course I will.'

Greg watches them walk towards to the sea, the terrier racing ahead over wet sand, barking. Then, his attention once more on the dolphin, carefully Greg turns the body over so he can see the underside, looking for any tell-tale signs. There's a little abrasion from the beach on the belly and the leading edge of the tail fluke. Apart from that, nothing. The flesh is plump and pliant and whole. He's been fooled before, though: thinking an animal looks well covered when it's beached and the bodyweight is compressed and displaced into an appearance of good nourishment; but even when he trial-lifts the front end of this one from the ground, the healthful rounding of the body is maintained.

Changing tack, Greg examines the face more closely and the long pointing of the dolphin's beak. Still nothing superficially. Oh, but here, some damage on the underside. From the corner of the mouth a single incision. Gently he separates the jaws. And there it is then. The clue he's been looking for. Pathognomic. Indisputable. He goes back to the tail fluke and, oh yes, the signs *are* there too when he looks more closely: fine incisions he'd missed, disguised by the beach abrasion.

He looks up at Seb's shouting from the sea's edge. The boy is holding something aloft and jumping in his excitement. Another treasure. And Greg cannot help but smile. It's only at the water's edge like this that Seb seems able to forget himself.

Squatting again at the dolphin's side, Greg shuffles nearer the head, gauges where the weight will be equal, wedges the toes of his wellies beneath the dolphin, crouches to push his gloved hands under; feels the weight ease onto his arms. Drawing breath, he straightens his legs to lift.

Turning, he finds Seb has run back again. A starfish in his hand, the boy stands silently watching his father, who towers against the sky, his arms draped with and full of dead dolphin.

He had thought he might be late for the rendezvous – a queue onto the suspension bridge and then heavy traffic beyond Bristol – but he arrives first, in fact, turning off the motorway and doubling back till he faces the setting sun. Deep ambers and orange seep richly into clouds.

The evening is still warm as Greg gets out of the pickup and goes to check the dolphin. The towels that cover it are drying and he unstraps the container of water, letting much of the twenty gallons play over the towelling. Refrigerated transport would be good if only he could find the funding. At least once the field centre with its cold store is finished, it will be possible to chill an animal before the journey to London.

He goes back to the cab to escape the noise of traffic beneath him, drinking coffee from the flask he's brought. Tuning the radio he hops channels, settling for jazz. Neon lights flick on against the reddening sky and he wonders what Ella is doing in this sunset, wonders whether or not her story of an evening out with girlfriends is to be believed. It might have been the short-notice need to find a childminder that made her tetchy earlier this evening. It might have been.

Suddenly there are lights in his mirror: the Land Rover he's been waiting for. Iain has brought his new girlfriend with him. *If we're going to have our evening wrecked, at least we'll still have each other's company,* he'd said to Greg on the phone. And meeting her, Greg can see why a man would want her along. Emma. Quickly engaging and beautiful to boot, lucky man.

'Why did he die?' she asks once the dolphin is in the body-bag and transferred to the Land Rover.

Greg spreads his hands in a shrugging gesture of ignorance. 'Don't ask me,' he shouts over traffic rumble. 'I only know about them when they're alive.'

'But you can guess,' she persists, her words promptly swamped by a juggernaut's thunder.

'You're right, I can. I can be pretty sure, in fact, with this one.'

'What then?'

'By-catch.'

'What?'

'By-catch. He got himself caught up in fishing nets,' he yells.

'So how can you . . .' she begins, but her words are quite lost this time.

Greg catches her elbow, speaks in her ear. 'Emma, it's not really the place to talk and we've both got long journeys back.' He nods towards Iain, who is emerging from the back of the Land Rover. 'Ask the man from the Natural History Museum. They'll have the post-mortem results in a day or two.'

'You're right,' she laughs.

'I'll be in touch, Iain,' Greg says, fastening the tailgate. 'Well met this evening.'

'Oh, it's pretty well rehearsed by now.'

'Fifth time this month for you, isn't it?'

Iain nods. 'And I had three in the back last time.'

'Let's hope that's an end of it for a while.'

'What's the betting?'

*

Driving back into the fading sun, letting the sax riffs lift him home, he estimates the journey time; reckons on a one a.m. arrival and he's due into work at eight.

Inside the porch door, there are leather mules, precisely moulded to the bareness of his feet. He has sluiced the back of the pickup out, disinfectant and running water, in darkness, under thin cloud and starlight and light from the open garage; as if the task couldn't wait until morning.

He takes his overalls and the towels into the tilly room, shoves them in the washing machine, clicking the dial to the hottest setting. By the sink there's Hibiscrub and a brush that bites deep to his nail beds as he scrubs hard. There's the thought of the woman, his wife, who lies asleep; the space next to her he must fill. Hot water stings. There's the clean towel to dry his hands on, the rail to hang the towel upon, beneath the ordered storage of his dive gear: cylinder, BCD, regulator, mask, fins, wetsuit, drysuit, undersuit – neat, ordered.

There's his body, heavy with lack of sleep. There's time, sliding into the depths of night. There's whisky, in the sitting room, half a tumbler full, the heat of it in his throat; his body held by the sofa; one foot on deep carpet, the other ankle held on his knee, then released as his hands move to pour more whisky as he feels the push of its power in his veins. There's the thought of the woman, his wife, who lies asleep.

The woman, his wife, who lies. Does she lie to him, he wonders. There's the rub. Not knowing what to believe any more.

The burn of the whisky spreads across his chest and is comforting. He takes another draught, his mind reaching back to his run this evening – the way the sunlight was on the water. And it was good he was able to shift the dolphin; to fill in while Tony is away. He'll be pleased the animal made it into the system: one more to add to the weight of evidence and the gathering statistics. And Greg thinks of it: the dolphin he transported, the back teeth shorn off to the gum by the gill net in his flailing to get free; the powerful thrust of the tail fluke only driving his beak further through, taking the teeth, slicing the incision from the corner of the mouth, the taut trap of fine monofilament cutting through flesh like wire through cheese; the panic of no breath left; the fierce fight snaring him tighter, holding him under, no access to air. No air. Greg heaves himself out of his chair. He shouldn't drink at this hour, he thinks, taking the drained glass through to the kitchen. It overstimulates. He rinses the tumbler under the tap. *Don't* imagine. Wait for the post-mortem report. He already knows, though, what it will say. Dry-drowning. The alcohol in his blood shakes his head at the phrase. Dry-drowning brought about through by-catch. Suffocation.

Looking up, the night-dark window reflects his face: haggard, for all his running in early-evening sunshine. And, oh yes, the two new observers to deal with in the morning – in a few hours' time. Bed, Greg. You'll probably be asleep in moments.

Sober enough to be mindful of his head on the sloping ceiling of the landing, he looks in on Sebastian. The boy is sleeping, his bedside lamp still on, the little device rotating slowly, so that light plays round the room: the turning of underwater blue behind fantasy fish and sea horses.

At the door of their bedroom, Greg hesitates, peering into the darkened room, trying to make out the shape of Ella, seeing the rise of her back beneath the duvet. He rests his head on his arms folded against the door frame and wonders if she really is sleeping – this woman, his wife. And though he knows he should sleep now, from the corridor he closes the door so the sound of the computer booting up won't wake her.

In fact he finds the machine already up and running. Brought into action by the demand of an underwater microphone a few miles out to sea, the computer screen glows in the darkened room. He picks up headphones, plugging them in to hear what the hydrophone is relaying to the computer for notation: the underwater whistling calls of dolphins. Common dolphins, like the one he transported this evening. He listens with eyes closed, through his exhaustion and the whisky haze, to this otherworldly sound, the high-pitched bubbling whispered whistles, the sudden abrasive trains of clicks as the dolphins echolocate their prey. He sighs, wishing

he were out there now, in the calmness of this night, underwater, to see them feed, to witness the gymnastic acrobatics.
He tries to identify the numbers of individuals. The software
is better at that than he is and he pulls himself back to the
reality of the keyboard, punches in numbers to get to the
program, then catches sight of the boy at the doorway:
Sebastian, silhouetted against the light in the corridor, where
he stands and watches his father.

'Come here, monster,' Greg says, dropping the headphones down round his neck, and holding his hand out to the
boy, so that Seb comes forwards, his face in the computer
light, bleary with sleep, hair spiked askew.

'Can I hear thed-olphins?' Seb murmurs.

Greg draws the boy onto his lap, gathering the little body
to him, taking the headphones, twisting the things so they
have one earpiece each. For a minute they listen, Greg's head
nestling lightly near Seb's. Sleep begins to take him.

'Come on now. Bed,' Greg says, standing with the boy in
his arms, untangling the headphones, leaving the computer to
do its stuff.

'Can I play the tape, then?' Seb asks as Greg carries him
to his room.

'You'll wake your mother,' Greg protests, but he closes
the door and, after pulling back the covers, starts the tape for
him anyway, so that – as Seb clambers into bed – the underwater calls of dolphins come into this underwater room in

the blue, moving light of the little lamp. Greg tucks the boy in.

'You didn't tell me a story.'

'When you came to bed this evening? I wasn't here, Seb. I had to take the dolphin.'

The boy's eyes watch him. No excuse. They watch him, waiting. Greg has never known a child who will wait as Seb will – quietly, for treats or answers or promises to be kept or sometimes – as now – while conscience does its work.

'Listen, monster, shove over.' Greg kicks off the mules and falls into bed beside the boy, who lies across his father's arm and shoulder, hugging him round the neck. His little fists clenched tightly, he hugs so fiercely Greg marvels again at it, brings his forearm up to hold him, the other hand to rest at his ribcage; and the little form is quite enfolded.

'Listen. It's the middle of the night and I am *not* about to tell you a story.' He smiles, his eyes closed. 'Or at least I might start one—'

'The *dragon* one?'

'OK – the dragon one, but I can't guarantee I'll get very far,' he says, as he feels sleep coming, hearing the dolphin whistle; his idling mind sliding up its ascending scale, playing unrequested images of the spectrograph the sound would make. He senses Sebastian waiting.

'Far, far away in the middle of an ocean, there's an island . . .'

'A *magic* island,' Seb corrects, his face snuggled in the dip beneath Greg's collar bone.

There's the sound of dolphins and a wave of sleep.

'A magic island . . .'

Seb's little body sighs and slackens, bathed in blue lamp-light and the story's warm waters and the rich smell of whisky on his father's breath.

'A magic island where there's one little town and not many people . . .'

There's dolphin whistle transformed to a spectrograph.

'. . . and deep forests and green hills and – by the sea's edge – there are deep water caves where a beautiful dragon lives.'

Seb struggles with sleep and loses, then wins a moment, fights to engage his ears to catch words, receives only an awareness of motion, the rise of ribs in breathing – the small movement of his own and then his little body lifted by the larger range of his father's breathing beneath him, lifting him like the rhythmic roll of saltwater waves at the entrance of the cave where the beautiful dragon lives. No words to hear, just the water and the dolphins and the slow beating of his father's heart.

Canada

It's as the wheels touch down in Vancouver that she remembers she had the dream again last night; the one she often has of her brother coming home – the jolt of wheels touching down triggering dream memory: the jolt of seeing him come home in a wheelchair. For sure her parents will have warned her, and she'd seen him often enough during his months in hospital, but still it was a shock – Richie in a wheelchair in the garden where – until the accident – she and her brother had always played.

As the plane taxies, she tries to remember which version it was she dreamt last night. Reinholdt will want to know. She can remember that – as always – the setting was the same: the garden at home at the beginning of fall as the leaves are turning and the big red ball is in her hands as their father wheels Richie through the gate; his face one of concentration as he learns this new manoeuvre. Sometimes the dream just follows memory – or what she's fairly sure is memory. She throws the ball to her brother in the wheelchair—

Sophie looks out of the cabin window, eyes catching at rhythmic breaks in the concrete.

She throws the ball to Richie in the wheelchair and it hits him hard in the face.

It had taken her quite a time to be able to say that to Reinholdt – her childhood action, one which still makes her flush scarlet with shame. Reinholdt had been typically non-judgemental, had left her his usual gentle silence.

'He couldn't react any more, of course,' she'd said. 'I suppose – aged seven – I was trying to bring things back to some semblance of normality. I suppose I thought, if Richie could still play ball—'

The plane turns towards the terminal.

Which version did she dream last night? Face it now, Sophie and then forget it for the duration of this visit home. She runs through a few familiar options: the wishful-thinking version where Richie *does* catch the ball; the version in which she goes to the chair and tries to lift Richie out, standing behind him and struggling and struggling; and the version where she *can* lift him to a standing position, just, only he's the same weight as her and when she tries to walk him she finds she cannot move.

She sighs, unsure of last night's version – or perhaps she dreamt some different ending altogether. No matter. Reinholdt will have to do without it, she thinks as the seatbelt sign switches off and she goes through the little miracle of standing.

Quite quickly she's checked onto the bigger plane for the two-and-a-half-hour flight to her parents' home. The face of the man in the aisle seat lights up when he realizes the striking blonde just boarding has been allocated the seat next to his. He smiles as he gets up to let her in, raises eyebrows, invites prolonged eye contact.

'Thanks,' Sophie says, sliding her eyes away, sliding herself between the seats; dropping lightly down and getting out papers to mark straight away: student essays due back to them next week. She does gaze out of the window, though, soon after take-off, as they fly over the snow-streaked Columbia Mountains and on over the Rockies. Before the accident, they used to go to meet her father's friends and the New Year in the mountains. Richie and she in the back of the car for the two-day drive west; waking outdoors, in bundled rugs in her father's arms, taken from the dozy warmth of the car out into ice – *Look, sleepyhead* – iced crags towering hugely over them, a shock to this child of the prairies that land could be vertical, till her mother said – *It's like the palace in the story, Sophie, the great ice palace of the Snow Queen.*

Her father is there to meet her at the airport, his face thinner, his hair thinner, his hug as warm and strong as ever. She feels the pressure of tears as he turns her, strolls with her, his arm through hers, his head – in that way he has – tilted towards her.

The talk is easy on the drive out of town: how his patients are; how Marilynn – one of the practice nurses Sophie knows well – is retiring after all these years; how Sophie's own work is going. And it's good to have him to herself for a while – a sense again of childhood, safely in the car, through childhood landscape: prairie stretching out under a translucent gold and rose-fading sky; grain elevators at the edge of the highway, huge and lit at their height and outline like so many vast rockets on their launch pads.

Nearing home and turning onto smaller roads, there's the double silhouette of a grain elevator and the church steeple reaching up; the grain store the higher, nearer to the heavens.

They have to wait where the railroad crosses for the grain train to clatter its steady load. Memories of childhood counting games: how many hopper cars is the grain train pulling? *Sev-en-ty-one, sev-en-ty-two, sev-en-ty-three, sev-en-ty-four.* Some rust-streaked. Some pristine. The long monotone wail of the whistle heard now and from her bed, all the nights of her growing up.

'How has Richie been?'

'He's been doing pretty good.'

'I've brought him some pictures of binary stars.'

'Well, I hope I get to see them too.'

Her hand brushes the nape of his neck. 'Sure you do.'

'It's been so good for him over the years, Sophie.'

'The astronomy?'

'Yeah. Wonderful the way you've shared it with him.'

'Even though it means you have to stay up nights and freeze?'

The train rattles its last trucks past and he drives on over the track.

'Worth every shiver. And it's better these days. Wait till you see the changes we've made. It's no ordinary backyard observatory we have now.'

She smiles, peers out at the darkening sky, at the stars appearing.

'Anyway, the astronomy's all your fault,' she tells him.

'Is that right?'

'Sure. All those star stories you used to tell us.'

The two children snuggled together in the same bed for storytime. *Saves me telling it twice*, her father used to say, but they knew it was about closeness for Richie: Sophie's hug a perceived if unfelt nearness; their father's hand resting against Richie's feeling face.

Sometimes she'd lie as still as Richie and make believe her body was as helpless as his. She could still feel, of course, but it was curious to be so very immobile, even for a few minutes, listening to her father's story. It made the story fill her head more. It made her wonder if this was what stories felt like in Richie's head. She remembered wondering if they

23

might swap; if one day – when she'd stayed very still – the story would end and Richie would be the one to get up and go to the other bed and she'd be the one left behind.

'Is that how you saw it,' Reinholdt had asked, during one of their early sessions, 'you leaving Richie behind?'

With the best of intentions, how could she not? At school and socially, all the things kids normally go through that he physically couldn't – or only in a limited way once he'd found the will to try. And next, university. The stars had become very different to her then, of course. She thinks back to her first vacation, coming home full of new knowledge and excitement and wanting Richie to be able to see the stars differently too, wheeling him out under the night sky's spangle. *Can you believe it, the age of starlight, Richie, taking years to reach our eyes, so that we see the stars tonight not as they really are now, but as they were years ago, so that looking out at the stars is like looking back in time. And even the very nearest star, apart from our sun, of course, even the nearest star – we can't see it from here, we'd have to go to the southern hemisphere, but anyway, it's Proxima Centauri and it's about 4 light years away, which means it's taken the light 4 years to reach Earth, and as light travels at about 6 trillion miles a year, Proxima Centauri is about 24 trillion miles away, do you see?*

Oh, and there, Richie – she'd said, spinning his chair, dipping her head next to his to make sure he could see – *that thing we always used to think of as a star in the blade of Orion's sword, the middle one of the three, it isn't so much a star as a nebula: a giant cloud of gas and dust falling in on itself and forming new stars. And when the new stars get dense enough, thermonuclear reactions start up and give off energy we call light. It looks so near, doesn't it, but it's sixteen hundred light years away, so we're seeing it tonight as it was sixteen hundred years ago.*

Oh, and this band of stars, Richie, you know – the Milky Way – stretching right out across the sky, we never knew as children, did we, it's our galaxy and the star – our sun – is part of it, our sun just one star of billions in a spiral galaxy. It's like a dinner plate, Richie, viewed edge on – the galaxy of the Milky Way. From Earth we get the edge-on view and then over here – she'd spun his chair again – *over here, if you follow the right-hand V of Cassiopeia – got it? – over there we might just be able to see a whole other galaxy with billions more stars. On a good night like this we might just – yes! – can you see it? That elongated smudge of light, yeah, that's it, the Andromeda galaxy. And I can't really begin to grasp this, Richie, but it's over 2 million light years away, so we're seeing light that's taken 2 million years to get here and there are billions of galaxies, Richie, all with billions of stars. We should get you a telescope so that you could see—*

Headlights sweep across the familiar building, lighting up the pale façade, and the plants in tubs her mother tends.

'We've been hunting out colliding galaxies,' her father says, turning the car into the driveway.

'Aha. *Have* you now?'

'We have, Sophie,' he says, smiling as he switches off the engine.

Richie comes to meet his sister in the hall.

'Hey! New wheels!' Sophie says.

'Nothing but the best,' Richie says, pirouetting his chair for her.

'Let's see!' She laughs, wanting to look at the finger-touch control that Richie in e-mails, has told her about, only he doesn't stop, goes into a circle around her in the hallway so that she becomes a traffic island as his wheels squeak softly on the wooden floor.

'Here we go, chaos already,' her father says as her mother comes through from the kitchen and Emily emerges from Richie's rooms.

'Would you *stop*?' Sophie cries. 'I want to say hi.'

And so Richie does stop, big man bringing the chair to a halt with a grin and that guttural, broken laugh of his, for Sophie to kiss the side of his face before he slickly puts the chair into reverse using the electronic pad on the chair arm, drawing his finger across it: the middle finger of his left hand, the most agile of the three he can move.

'Fantastic, Richie.'

'Good, isn't it?'

'Just have to mind you don't get mown down,' Sophie's mother, Simone, says as her daughter kisses her cheek in hello.

Emily stays to dinner. Working now supplying lifestyle aids to the disabled, she's been a friend of the family since early school days, so that it's a little like old times, the five of them round the dinner table; Richie's assistant not there for the early evening, taking some time out, due back at ten thirty, when the nurses come to get Richie ready for bed.

'Emily's redesigning my shower room,' Richie says.

'Shower room is something of an understatement,' Simone teases. 'Only hope you'll let your father and me use it when it's done, Richie.'

'Absolutely not.'

'State of the art?' Sophie asks.

'Just multiple shower heads over a trolley,' Emily says.

'For supine showering?'

'Mmm. And we're upgrading the ceiling-track hoist system.'

'I *like* the sound of a taking a shower lying down.'

'So do *I*,' Simone agrees.

'You're just going to have to keep on imagining,' Richie drawls, so that they laugh and Sophie glances across at him – at this new tone of his she hasn't heard before. She notices the support items he's using for eating – ones that are unfamiliar to her – his left arm strapped diagonally across his body in a brace; his plate held in a frame at the side of his face so that this way he can feed himself once everything's in place and his food has been brought through bite-size. Emily's influence again, perhaps, this new, more helpful gadgetry.

There's talk of the changes since Sophie was last home: old school friends – Cheryl from Richie's year, pregnant with her third, her *third*, Sophie's mother tells her, and then Lance from Sophie's year has come back from America and there's going to be a wedding in the spring. Richie and Emily will be going.

Sophie looks up. 'Will you?'

'We will,' Richie says.

'Well, that's wonderful.' She looks across at Emily. 'Wonderful.'

'They've been out to quite a few things lately,' her mother continues.

'Richie e-mailed me about going to the movies.'

'And the hockey—'

'Mum.'

'And a meal at Luka's—'

'Mum, Sophie doesn't want to hear all that.'

'And we all went to the Astronomy Society meeting the other week,' her father gently interjects.

'Oh – it was *fabulous*,' Emily says. 'A star party just near the Qu'appelle Valley, such a beautiful night – the stars were *wonderful*.'

'See anything special?' Sophie picks up gratefully.

At least her mother had the decency to leave it till later, Sophie thinks as she opens the back door to go and find her father. At least she'd waited until there were just the two of them clearing up in the kitchen before she'd said it.

'You decided not to bring Tom to meet us after all, then.'

Clearly, Sophie had almost snapped, *clearly I haven't brought him with me, given that he isn't here*. She'd bitten her tongue in time, got on with stacking plates in the dishwasher.

'Only you did say you would bring him, Sophie, and your father and I would just love to—'

'Mum, it's *over* with Tom. Weeks ago now.'

Months, in fact.

'Oh, *Sophie* . . .' Simone had stilled herself to look across at her daughter, then resumed her cleaning; her cloth wiping and rewiping the same little area. 'I'm sorry to hear that. Perhaps you'll get back together again, will you? Sort things out a bit, then perhaps . . .'

Sophie had pursed her lips up tight.

Her mother had looked down at the cloth in her hand, spread it carefully out to dry.

'It just wasn't working. I've been really busy and . . .'

'Of course, dear,' her mother had said.

'I'll go and tell Dad his coffee's ready, shall I?'

She closes the back door in relief. It would almost be better if her mother would say what she really thinks – *Oh, Sophie, not again, not another dwindling chance of grandchildren gone. Not another relationship dead in the water. Your brother manages better than you do, for heaven's sake. Only you know there's no chance he will ever have children. You're thirty-two, not eighteen.*

Stepping out into the darkness, she sees the dull-red pathway lights are lit – her father must still be in the observatory – and she follows their snaking guide down the garden towards the lakeside, loving this little habit he's maintained over the years: ten minutes peace on his own after dinner.

She breathes in the cold night air. Below freezing by the feel of it. Not many weeks now till the big freeze hits here and the lake starts to ice over. She wonders if skaters still come; if someone else's father now rigs up lights at the edge of the ice so that the after-school kids can skate, gathering together to be rink-rats as she did with the children from across the frozen water; sweeping the icy surface smooth before speeding through the freezing air: games of tag and skills to practise and rotating star formations to make; till her mother would bring cinnamon toast and hot perogies and – for a little while – her father would bring Richie out: bundled up, but cooling; his pale face floating at the lakeside; threatened by the same air's coldness she has relished on her heated cheeks. Even as her blood still sang, he would have to be taken back indoors, leaving her staring at the deep, shadowed tracks his chair wheels had made among footprints in the snow. The solo game, then. Perogies suddenly heavy in the stomach. Going off to skate at the end of the lake at the edge of darkness around reeds that poke through; staring at tracks her skates make in ice: mesmeric figures-of-eight.

She sees the red glow at the bottom of the garden from the opening of the observatory door – her father on his way out.

'Your coffee's ready,' she calls, not wanting to startle him in the darkness.

'Sophie! Won't you come and see?'

She hesitates, then says, 'Love to.'

Settling that night into her childhood bed, she looks back over the evening in the light of things Reinholdt has said. There's no doubt since she's been home she's been reminded several times of the things Reinholdt said. Deflection strategy for one.

She'd been talking to Reinholdt of how fair her father was; how he always strove to give his children equal time.

'And how was it,' Reinholdt had asked, 'when your father gave his attention to you?'

Excruciating – the word which had leapt into her mind. She hadn't known that. When her father gave her his time, she'd found it excruciating – in the garden, perhaps, in the place of Richie, where Richie could see them through the window together: playing, running. Or sometimes her father would help her with her schoolwork; schoolwork Richie – in the same room and mentally as able as she – would never physically do for himself and couldn't psychologically bring himself to tackle for years. And then there were Richie's teenage silences: days of brooding silence that would build, give way to hurtful, resentful behaviour until at last he would scream, their father brought from his surgery by Richie's screaming, the whole building filled with Richie's screaming; Richie inexorably inert apart from his face, horribly con-torted and crimson, his mouth wide-screaming, his wanting to die screamed out through his spasming.

Her father sedated Richie at such times, the silence of his drugged sleep almost worse; the house still full of shock and distress.

Richie would cry when he woke, silently, tears running down his cheeks, their mother sitting by him, stroking his face. A week or two or three's respite. And then the pattern would repeat itself.

There were times when he'd tried deliberately, Sophie realizes now, to bring on an attack of autonomic dysreflexia – the sudden, unchecked rise of blood pressure. The rage would do it, but so could the commonplace: the bruising of a limb; too tight clothing; sexual arousal; the failure to pee on time. Easily triggered and, if not immediately dealt with, just as readily fatal.

'Can you say why, Sophie?' Reinholdt had gently prompted. 'Why you wished your father wouldn't give his time to you?'

'Because it was so hard to take it, Reinholdt. Richie needed it so very much more.'

Reinholdt had given his slow nodding, said some stuff about the changes caused by having a suddenly disabled child within a family – changes in patterns of attention and activity; changes in the psychological dynamic.

'I'm wondering if perhaps, over time, it made things easier for you if you habitually diverted the course of your father's attention away from yourself.'

'Perhaps. I . . .'

Deflection strategy. She'd caught herself falling back into the habit only this evening. Her first thought when her father invited her to look at the observatory: *Richie should be here with him, not me.* Simple to overcome it this evening; simple not to background herself this time, now she's aware; now she's her grown-up, professional self.

She settles further beneath the covers. It must be late; she'd spent so long with her father in the observatory. She sighs. Lovely to spend that time with him; like they used to in the summer garden when she and Richie were very young, at the end of their father's working day: therapeutic for him, his shoulders moving with his steady tending; or in the fall, the stain of saskatoon berry on her shirt as they gathered fruit for their mother's baking; or in early summer, the damp warmth of soil on her fingers – *Look, Daddy, look!* – the miracle of new growth she has planted coming up and then toads to search for under stones by the stream, her father's big hands turning over rocks. In winter they'd find toadsicles, toads frozen in the rock-solid ground; the miracle of hibernation learned. And it's wonderful, her sleepy mind wanders, that the observatory is there now for Richie and her father – minuscule compared to what she's used to, but impressive by amateur standards: a computer-controlled scope with a good CCD and some really clever software to handle the images; the red-lit control room separate from the telescope dome and warm now that solid doors divide the two; the dome's opening newly motorized, operable remotely as the telescope is; all in order to keep Richie cosy. She sighs again, pleased for them.

Through half-sleep she registers the soft footfall in the corridor, the soft padding of careful feet – the same sound here, twice every night: Richie's assistant going in to turn him.

South-west Wales

There are grey clouds over a slate-grey sea, but no wind to speak of and not enough swell to hinder them, so the powerful outboard on the orange RIB makes light work of the distance out to sea: three miles to the first underwater microphone, a half-mile more to the second that's faulty. They fix it quickly – or rather they replace the waterlogged thing, then run a check on the laptop Greg has brought, hooding a jacket over his head and the computer – like an old fashioned photographer – as the swell slops the hull.

Greg has the company of Peta and John. Of the fourteen-strong observer team due to go out on boats from Milford Haven, these two will be his especial responsibility. He'd invited them down early, a day before the induction meeting, so he could get to know them. He's been testing them out a little, he acknowledges now to himself; finding that he watches closely how they handle being at sea.

He'd been at a conference when the interviews for the observers were held and so – having had to let others make the selection for him, there'd been no room for manoeuvre when he'd been told that one of the observers chosen was a woman. Sending a woman to sea for a week at a time with a bunch of lusty fishermen would not have been his choice, but in fact he's found Peta knows how to handle herself, adapting quickly to this trip and – before setting out – interacting with the builders at the field centre so well: putty in her hands, even crabby Patrick brought to whistling as he worked.

She is good on the transect survey too: standing now, the three strong points of contact she needs – two braced feet and good hand grip as she and John scour the sea for the movement and fins of dolphins as Greg steers the boat along the routine course. She'll do nicely. And John will too: quieter and more serious as he searches with binoculars.

There's a sighting of harbour porpoises – about six of them, but brief and distant. No actual encounters until they leave the survey grid and – on the way home – are positively mobbed. John sees them first, honing in on the boat like city kids on skateboards: bottlenose dolphins, jostling and pushing their way to the bow wave. Me! Me! Me! *I* want a ride.

'Hoodlums,' Peta laughs.

'Photographs,' Greg insists, flicking open the metal case wedged by his feet and passing the camera to her. 'Dorsal fins only. Aim to get each individual side on. Both sides if you can manage it. And paperwork, John. Could you note these down? That looks like B57 – haven't seen her for a while.

B71. B73 with calf. Nice if you could get a photo of the calf's dorsal fin, Peta. Haven't managed to get that yet.'

'Little sod keeps going under,' Peta says, taking another perfect shot of water.

'Yep. They do have that tendency.'

'Why just the dorsal fin?'

'It's how we identify them.'

'Like fingerprinting.'

'That kind of thing. Each has its own characteristics. Shape, marks, notches, scars.'

'What size population have you documented here?'

'Bottlenose? About a hundred and thirty.'

'How should I note this behaviour down?' John asks, reading from the pro forma. 'Socializing, feeding, travel, rest or play?'

'What would you think?' Greg returns.

'Play!' Peta laughs, dodging spray. 'Chase, tag, BMXing.'

'Play it is.'

The bow wave is busy with their forceful swimming: slick bodies sleekly through the water slipstream; pale grey through the pale grey-green; the running air busy with the sound of their surfacing: their punched-out breath as they break from the water, quick gasps of air as they slide on in.

Nothing more once their pod has gone, just the sea to search, to send his gaze out over; the boat to steer in the rolling lift of water, hands countering the waves in the push of a suddenly bigger swell that wants to bully the boat broadside.

There's the course to check on the GPS; the thought of the course to run tomorrow; Graham Taylor to impress that the new field centre is up and running. He must sort the projectors out this afternoon and the VHS; check the bedding is out in the bunkrooms.

Through crackle on the VHF comes the voice of a skipper calling up the coastguard before shifting to another channel.

Just the sea to search, the sky to check for changing weather and, if the builders have finished, there's the computer and paperwork to pick up from home.

Home.

Ella.

He drops his gaze a moment to saltwater on the boat deck: a shiny patch in which a strand of seaweed rolls to and fro to the motion of the boat; greenly glossy. His eyes unfocus as the thought comes before him again – his recent wondering if Ella and he have reached the point – he flicks his eyes back to the GPS – the point at which marriage becomes unsalvageable. He corrects the steering. It's his fault of course. In hindsight it's so easy to see it. Mistaken belief. *His* mistaken belief. So badly burned by Rachel, Ella's coolness had seemed like something solid, something to admire;

something to contain him sensibly. And now? He corrects the steering. It's his fault, he thinks as he scans the rise and dip and rise of waves, grey-green, steering round the lift of swell to the steady thrub of the outboard motor.

'How was the library?' Greg asks as he helps Ella unpack groceries.

Her back is to him as she places fresh salads in the fridge and she doesn't answer straight away, giving him time to think – it's happened again. She's arrived home again at six thirty. She finishes work at one on a Wednesday. Even allowing for the shopping she's done and the travel time home, there are still hours unexplained.

'Oh, you know,' she says as if wearily. 'Gearing up for the start of term.'

'Many postgrads in today?'

'A few,' she says.

'You're back late.'

'There's been a lot to do,' she says, her words monotone. 'And then I got stuck in traffic.'

He lets it pass.

'Peta and John seem good value,' he ventures.

'Yes?'

'Really ready to help out. They came back here after lunch and helped me take the last of the gear to the field centre ready for tomorrow – the projector for Power Point and the OHP and the filing cabinets – all the stuff that was in the study. And they helped set up the seminar room. Took the bubblewrap off the chairs – that sort of thing. They both seem really willing to muck in, which bodes well for their time out on the fishing boats.'

'I suppose it does.'

He looks across at the shoulder she has turned to him.

'What is it, Ella?'

Her hands still themselves, then take up their task again, placing eggs now, one by one in indentations in the refrigerator door.

'Nothing, I—'

'There's something bothering you.'

'OK.' She turns and glances at him, then takes more shopping from the bags on the floor. 'I don't think it's a good idea for you to sleep with Seb,' she says, her back once more to him.

'Last night? He woke. I was tired.'

'You know what a struggle it's been to get him out of the habit.'

'I don't suppose the odd night makes much difference, does it?'

'But it isn't just the odd night, is it? There have been several nights lately,' she says, placing milk behind its holding rail. 'Last night was the second time this week.'

'Was it?' He thinks back and finds she is right – he slept there too after Seb came downstairs late on Monday.

'And there were at least three nights last week.'

'Were there?'

She leaves a silence.

'Well. I'm sure you're right. It's probably not a good idea.' He folds an empty carrier bag – the plastic he wishes she wouldn't use – placing it in a drawer where there are already many others. 'I'm sure you're right.'

She clicks the refrigerator door closed, reaches down a glass storage jar and he moves; rests back against the work-top next to her so that he may see her face in profile, at least.

'I should try the spare room next time, should I?' he asks quietly, moving a strand of hair from her downturned face, letting the weight of his wrist drop onto her shoulder. He feels her muscle flex with the movement of opening a packet of fusilli; with the movement of unscrewing the jar's lid, before he drops his hand away. With a sound like grit from a tyre's fast spin, pasta hits the filling jar.

'You movin' to the town, then?' one of the fishermen at the bar asks Peta.

'Just for six months anyway,' Peta says. 'I'm one of the observers due to go out on the fishing boats.'

'You never are!'

'Well, I'll be—'

'You can come out on my boat any time you like, darlin'.'

'Might take you up on that,' Peta says.

Greg has to laugh. 'You've changed your tune, Don. When I was looking for boats to send observers out on, you didn't want to know.'

'Well, you never told us they were gonna be gorgeous!'

'Whose boat you goin' out on, then?'

'Now that *would* be telling,' Peta says, not sure the skipper wants it known.

'We'll find out soon enough,' Don assures her.

'Mine,' says a stocky young man, getting up from a seat in the corner. 'She's comin' out on my boat.'

'Well, *you're* a dark horse,' a fisherman rags.

'Wait till his missus finds out.'

'It's only his nets I'll be looking in,' Peta says, going to shake hands with the skipper.

'I'm Mick,' he says.

'Peta.'

'That's a bloke's name,' one of the men calls after her.

'Not in this case, it isn't.'

'This your boyfriend, Peta?'

'No. This is John. He's another observer.'

'He's not as pretty as you are.'

'Which boat you going out with, John?'

'The *Emma Louise*,' John replies.

There's a split second's silence before the fishermen burst into roars of laughter.

'What?' John asks, glancing at Greg. 'What is it?'

One of the fishermen draws breath. 'You'll be all right there, boy. Dolphin-fin soup every day at sea.' And the fishermen start their laughing all over again.

'Catch a lot, do they?' John asks.

'Did I say that?' the fisherman says, slapping him on the back amid the laughter as the two other observers Greg has come to meet walk into the pub, bags slung over their shoulders, their faces wide in wonderment at the racket.

It's good to drive from the port, to return in darkness to the tiny fishing village and find the lights of the field centre on and the place with people in it – a minibus parked outside. Graham Taylor's arrived from the university, then, bringing the other ten observers and Sheila Turner, the health and safety officer. It's the first time the centre's been used after eighteen months of planning and building work and Greg feels the buzz of it: seeing the project come to fruition. And then Graham is there before them, striding up to shake Greg's hand.

'We've made ourselves at home. The facility looks excellent, Greg.'

'Here's to some good work,' Greg says, grinning.

*

'"One day, a hot and cloudless and windless day, the beautiful dragon came from his cave and swam out to sea to catch fish for his dinner."'

'Are dragons good swimmers?'

'It's the middle of the night,' Greg says, wondering why Seb should suddenly ask that now on this umpteenth reading. 'You're supposed to be going to sleep, not asking questions.'

'Are they, though?'

'Yes. Especially this one with the webbing between his toes and nostrils he can close up, like a seal, for swimming underwater.'

Greg shifts his weight where he sits on the floor beside Sebastian's bed, determined he won't fall asleep with him tonight.

'"The dragon swam and ate and swam and ate,"' Greg continues, '"until he was quite full of fish. Then, lifting his head above the water, he saw a ship. It was the biggest ship the dragon had ever seen, but in the windless air, the sails hung about the masts and the ship wasn't going anywhere."'

Seb fingers his drawing of the ship among the thumbed-through pages.

'"The dragon could see – on the deck of the ship – a little man was pacing backwards and forwards."'

'The king!' Seb interrupts.

'It was. "– the king of a faraway land in purple robes and with a golden crown on his head. The king was pacing up and down and looking very worried.

""Whatever is the matter?' the dragon asked.

""Who said that?' the king asked, jumping in surprise.

""I did,' the dragon said, just as the king looked at the sea and saw him.

""Who are *you*?' the king asked – rather rudely, the dragon thought. 'And what are you doing loitering around my boat?'

""I came to see if I could help,' the dragon said.

""Well, you can't,' the king snapped. 'Not unless you can blow us home. There's no wind, don't you know.'

""Well, I could *try*,' the dragon said doubtfully. 'Perhaps if I just blew gently.'

""Don't do it!' the fishermen called, hauling in their nets, for they knew the dear dragon well.

""Don't do it!' the children called from their games upon the beach; for they knew the dear dragon well.

""Don't do it!' the villagers called from the quay, for they knew the dear dragon well.

""Be quiet!' the king said. 'Unhelpful lot. Get on with it, won't you?' he said to the dragon." So what did the dragon do?'

'He huffed and he puffed,' Seb says.

'That's right. "He huffed and he puffed and he blew the

45

ship along, gently at first and then a bit faster. And the king was very pleased, until something terrible started to happen."'

Greg looks at Seb's face, the picture of concern.

'The fire,' Seb says solemnly, pointing to his drawing of shooting reds and oranges.

'Yes, Seb, the fire. "Dragons breathe fire . . ."'

'*Do* they, Daddy?'

'Well, this one does. "And – even though he didn't mean them to – little flickers of flame would keep slipping out and one of them caught hold of a sail and, before he knew it, some of the sails started to burn.

""Stop! Stop!' the king cried, jumping up and down with fury. 'Look what you're doing to my lovely sails. All hands on deck and kill that dragon!' Suddenly there was a great commotion –" What's a commotion?'

'Lots of noise.'

'Lots of noise and fuss. "– as the sailors came running.

""The little princess, who'd been watching all this, sighed. 'Oh, silly, silly, silly,' she muttered to herself, and – standing on the boat's railing – she took a huge leap overboard and landed on the dragon's nose," and what happened next will have to wait until tomorrow,' Greg says, leaning to kiss the boy on the head, then putting a finger to his lips as a sign for silence.

Seb looks up at him with doleful eyes.

'But won't you—'

'Sleep well, monster.'

There's the boy to leave to his sleep, the last glance to give him over the shoulder: little bump in the bed in the underwater room, sleep well, monster, sea monster, sleeping in his lair.

At the door of the spare room in darkness he hesitates. Spare room. No bed made up, but it wouldn't take a moment. It would make a statement, though. Moving out. Too much of a statement, perhaps. Perhaps there's more talking to be done before making such a move.

In darkness he goes into their room. In darkness – he undresses soundlessly and soundlessly slides into bed beside his wife only to brush against the bare skin of the arm she has flung wide. His heart hurries its beating: Ella never sleeps unclothed unless she means to let him take her. He freezes, listening for the sound of her breathing. There, long, slow. He hasn't woken her.

Avoiding contact, he eases himself down beneath the duvet, lies on his back and draws deep breath, trying to ignore the quickening of his penis. Her timing is bloody immaculate. Again she's done it – just when he's reached a state of resignation, an acceptance of separateness under one roof, finally she offers herself. He tries to slow the thudding of his heart. She must be sleeping – wouldn't otherwise leave this arm unguarded. As he thinks of waking her, impressions of their last coupling flood him and he grits his teeth at the thought of it: her lying there for him, inert; Ella, this woman, his wife, who lies; he wanting warmth and some evidence of welcome; she so evidently wanting it over with, at one point even turning her face from him so that he'd thought of protesting that's what prostitutes do, isn't it? Offer flesh, not intimacy. He grits his teeth. Forget it, Greg. Yet his body rolls towards her, onto his belly, pressing his hardness against the mattress and she stirs too – a long, slow intake of breath in darkness, a moment's silence, then the crumple of bedding as she turns her body away from him; stretches her buttocks back till their warmness touches him. Really she means to let him take her. He reaches out a hand in the darkness, runs it from her shoulder to her waist, over the curve of hip to her thigh, where she catches it, brings his finger, lengthways to her mouth, puts it, lengthways to her teeth and nips it, presses her buttocks back against him.

Just get on with it.

In the dark he fumbles for the jar beneath the bed. His hand feels only carpet. He gropes further, locates the jar. It's down to him to lubricate the process so he does – she so silent in the silent, dark room he could be there on his own, daubing himself, and inwardly he curses again his cursed need.

It doesn't take long to take her. She and his body both

demand it is quick – a momentary thrusting that wrenches seed and relief from him: a shipwrecked sailor's floundering deliverance through dumping surf to the hardness of wet sands, so that he cries out – oh God – to find himself saved and – oh God – again, even though he believes in none.

There's a moment of recovering breath when she reaches back an arm; holds his head against hers in a gesture of what could be tenderness, so that a wave of some unnamed thing sweeps up through him, gets held in check by his frown in the dark; by his voice saying, *Ella, I—* But, *ssshh*, she smooths and *ssshh*, she smothers. *It's really late, Greg.* And it is, really late, and even as he fights it, he feels himself falling, plummeting deeply beneath the drug of sleep. Shipwrecked sailor all washed up.

Canada

'You've done it again,' Sophie laughs, taking morning orange juice in to Richie and meeting his gaze where it waits to contact hers at precisely the right height as she comes through the door.

Richie smiles. 'Plenty of practice.'

'I could tell you where to put a marker on the door frame,' he had said, years ago, 'at the eye level of everyone who comes through that door.'

'I don't believe you,' she'd teenage-challenged, so that they'd spent the early morning putting names and markers on the wood and calling bemused people in to see if he was right; delaying getting Richie out of bed until they'd done.

'Stand there! Stand there!' Sophie imperious with her father's spirit level, pronouncing on Richie's degree of accuracy. He was right in every case except for the little daughter of one of the nurses who had grown since Richie had last seen her a couple of months before.

'I might be wrong about Barbara,' he'd said. 'She never looks right at me.'

But he wasn't. They'd lain side by side – at the hysterical laughter phase by then – and waited for her to come through the door.

'Yes!' they'd cried out as she'd bustled in – immaculate uniform; hair scraped back; her eye level matching exactly her mark on the door frame – Sophie and Richie on the bed howling in fits of unexplained laughter.

'Wait! Wait!' Sophie had said, leaping up to stop Barbara by the door. 'Got to make absolutely sure.'

He's good, too, with the sounds doors make. And with footsteps on the polished wood floor. In doorways widened for Richie's chair, the doors which open onto the hall are on swing hinges which lets them be pushed from either side – and when someone passes through a door, it swings a little before it stills. There's a lot to be learned, Richie had told her, from the way the doors swing. Not just who passes through, which, in any case, he can usually gauge from the footsteps, but also something of the person's mood and purpose. Between the sweep of two doors, their father, for example, can cross the hall in six long, steady strides from kitchen to consulting rooms, or seven strides if he's come from the dining room. Then swoosh, swoosh and the door is still. No matter how busy he is, Richie had told her, their father never

– not even in a medical emergency – makes the door swing more than twice.

The practice nurse has quick, light footsteps; produces a less-prolonged door swing as she scuttles between the consulting rooms and their father's study; or towards the kitchen to get the coffee. The study and the kitchen might be difficult to tell apart, Richie had said, their doors close together, except that the study door squeaks.

'*Does* it?'

'It does,' he'd said, and she'd charged out into the hall to see, swinging the doors in turn, calling out, 'Which one is this, then?' and 'Which one is this?' to Richie as he lay in bed. He was right about those, too.

Their mother's footsteps, Richie had said, are slower than the practice nurse's and quieter, and sometimes she steadies the doors to stop them swinging.

Then there's the host of carers and Richie's assistants who come and go throughout the day. They like Jennifer Collingwood the best. Her footsteps are light and she makes the doors swing gently twice; except the one into the washroom which is stiffer on its hinges. Barbara's footsteps are staccato-hard; the doors banged open against the wall; pushed to fast and frantic swinging and, Richie said, when she goes into the washroom she always farts, loudly. He does know voices, too, Richie had protested to Sophie: the deep tones from his father's rooms, words indiscernible. He can't hear the patients in the waiting room, blocked by another room between them and the hall. Lots of women's voices, though, his mother's, often in the kitchen; the nurses and the carers who come. And then voices and footsteps from the rooms above him – rooms he cannot access any more.

Sophie never stayed while the carers tended Richie. She knew that – as soon as Jennifer arrived she would touch Richie's right hand and his feet as they all did, to check the temperature of parts he couldn't feel, but then Sophie always left the carers to it, as her mother and her father did, once Richie was a teenager and told them to. She had stopped in the hall, though, one teenage day, suddenly needing to know after all, watching through the crack in the door by the hinges as Jennifer Collingwood turned the bedding down and Barbara put on thin rubber gloves. Like guiltily watching a peep show playing out through narrowed vision, she saw the figures go through the daily ritual, wondering – as she did it – *why* she did it. Her father would have told her about it if she had asked him. Richie would have told her. Still she watched the two-woman, well-rehearsed team: Jennifer talking to Richie as they worked; the bag of piss to empty and replace; the upper body to sit up and hold steady; the flop of arms to arrange; the pyjama jacket to take off; the torso to lay down again; the penis to check for infection; the catheter to readjust; the body to manoeuvre, to strip and check for pressure marks, to roll over for Barbara to manually evacuate the bowel. Jennifer stood at Richie's head at this point, massaging his feeling head and neck as the room filled up with his stink; chattering as she massaged – domestic stuff: her little boy learning to skate now, her husband and she debating the moment to let him go to proper classes.

They'd moved arms and moved legs and turned and bed-bathed and checked and dried and creamed and powdered and put clean clothes on him; then the hoist she'd witnessed often enough; the manoeuvring into the chair. On silent feet Sophie had slid away.

'I've brought you some pictures,' Sophie says, once she's put the juice in its holder and put the tube in place for him.

'Not the binary stars I asked you for?'

Sophie grins and kisses the side of his face, nodding her head in confirmation.

South-west Wales

'Do I have to go?'

'You do, Seb. Yes, you do. You'll enjoy it. You'll see Andrew – and Daniel.'

Sebastian watches his mother. His father has gone early to the field centre and so his mother is looking after him this morning; putting things in the lunch box for him – the blue lunch box with the dolphin on it. He supposes that's one good thing. He'll be able to take his new blue lunch box.

Sebastian watches her hands folding the silver paper round the sandwiches.

'Will I have to stay all day?' he asks, although he already knows the answer.

'Not today, no. Just for the morning and for lunchtime.'

He watches as she rinses an apple under running water and wipes it. 'Have you finished your breakfast, Sebastian?'

He looks at the toast he has left on his plate.

'Don't want any more,' he says, pushing his plate away.

'Go and clean your teeth then.'

He watches as she takes a small chocolate bar from the cupboard and adds it to the lunch box.

'Go on.'

As he scrabbles down from the chair, Ella puts the boy's packed lunch in his rucksack with his gymshoes and his pencil case. Really it shouldn't be a problem for him – this first day at school. He knows several of the children already and he's been for two half-days last term *and* it's only a short walk from home along the lane into the village. And then, of course, he's so used to going to playschool – and to the childminder. Really it shouldn't be a problem.

She hears the post van; hears Sebastian's feet rushing down the stairs.

'Mummy, *I* want to get the post,' he squeals out, but she makes sure she's there ahead of him.

'Here you are,' she says, sorting through and quietly slipping into her pocket the little package that's arrived. 'You can put these on Daddy's desk. And look, Sebastian, there's a letter for you. I expect Grandma's sent you a card to wish you good luck at your new school.'

As Seb goes to his father's desk, she allows herself a peek into the package; sees the glint of gold through a little glass jar. Excellent. Excellent. She tucks the package behind a calendar that's standing tall on a high window sill.

'Ready?' she asks as Sebastian returns. 'Come on then. Exciting day for you.'

Once the boy is safely delivered to school, Ella returns, fills the washing machine; clears up the breakfast things; sweeps the kitchen floor; gets into the shower. Something of the touch of the water on her shoulder evokes a memory of Greg last night – their fucking in the darkness – and she tilts her face into the force of the water; pummelling the shampoo and the thought from her head, as – taking up the loofah – she begins to scrub her shoulders. They're two of a kind, Greg and Seb. Always wanting more of her. *You probably should have married Rachel,* she's said to Greg before now in that time when they used to bother to argue about it. *Rachel liked all that constant physical stuff, didn't she? Too intense, you said, didn't you? Making you the more intense. In fact, isn't that why you wanted me, Greg – precisely because I am less emotional, less demonstrative. That was a good thing, you always said.* She turns and sluices soap from her body. At least last night's coupling should take the pressure off her for a while and Seb will be busier now with school. Just think. Next week this day will be hers – for most of the day. No work at the library on a Thursday and Seb will be at school until three thirty. Stepping from the shower, she dries herself quickly. She must be quick now, if she's going to make good use of the time, but she needs to be calm, too. The discipline of the thing demands it.

Dressed and downstairs, she picks up the car keys, resisting the temptation to hurry. She takes the package down from the window sill; takes a long, slow breath. That's better.

Her footsteps are light on the path as she leaves.

There's a state she reaches, once she settles to the rhythm. It's one of the first skills to learn: knowing when the time is right to transfer from practice piece to the real thing. A moment too soon and her hand may yet hurry; she may not yet be calm enough. She's come to realize, that as much as anything it's physiological, so that she doesn't allow herself coffee within four hours of coming here and she has not to let herself be troubled by anything: no thoughts allowed of Seb or Greg. That last is a prerequisite that has subtly shifted in time to become a raison d'être for this facet of her life – the chance to escape absolutely. She has it down to a fine art: deftly deflecting her family's enquiries and – during her escape – blocking all thoughts of them, imagining instead – during the drive over – being already immersed in the peace of his morning room: the cool air; Jonathan's peripheral, unobtrusive presence as he works calmly, steadily, too, his head of steely-grey hair bent to his vellum; the rhythmic flow of ink from a finely trimmed quill; the slow ticking from the antique clock; the clock's slow ticking, her heart's slow beating. Timing is of the essence. There's no possibility of being late as this would delay – disturb – Jonathan, too, and this agreement of theirs is mutually considerate. He never asks about her family now. Picked up quickly not to bother, so that they've fallen into the routine of exchanging a few sentences about the progress of their work, the work of others in the group – this morning it was the arrival of gold they talked of, smiling as she placed it on the desk next to the brushes, something to think about carefully before using – and then they'd settled to work and silence. She has her work there, now, in front of her: her months and months of work building beautifully; separate utterly from the rest of her life. She focuses on each letter at a time and only perfection is good enough. At intervals she draws back, to balance the effect of the whole image, the word picture, the word symbol, the exquisitely written, interwoven, complex Celtic cross.

'As you're probably aware,' Greg says, beginning to sum up, 'John Gummer stated in Parliament that he would close any fishery proven to be catching dolphins. Dolphins are protected in European waters. It's illegal to catch them. In theory all we have to do now is gather proof that it's happening. So – it's your vital job to document and quantify by-catch.'

'But it already *has* been proven,' John interjects. 'That study off Denmark that showed by-catch of six – or was it seven – thousand harbour porpoises in a few months.

Anyway, far more than the 2 per cent take which the population could withstand. We already know it's not sustainable.'

'You're right, John, but that's there, not here. We have to prove what's happening here before the government will act.'

'But the fisheries are the same, the porpoises are the same. Of course it's happening here.'

Greg nods, remembering his own days of fierce indignation. 'We have to gather local proof. That's one of the reasons or at least one of the outcomes of the strandings project, where every dolphin we find that's fresh enough is sent off for post-mortem and the results are logged on a central database.'

'Is anyone actually taking notice of the data?' another observer asks.

Greg's lips form a half-smile and he nods his recognition of the point.

'For certain it's a slow process, but the point is it's the *only* thing that stands a chance of getting any political action. They can't get tough on a fishery, close it, reduce it, without evidence and you guys on the observer programme are a vital source of indisputable evidence, that's why your work is going to be so crucial. We are convinced that the animals which wash up here represent only a small percentage of the total number caught. Most of the corpses will sink out at sea and be eaten by scavengers long before they can reach the shore. It's only when strong on-shore winds bring in any float-ing corpses that we catch sight of them, so in the last few months, for example, the eighty or so which have been documented off the south-west coast of Wales plus the 200 or so off Cornwall and Devon represent only the tip of the iceberg, which is where you lot come in.'

He gives a wry smile.

'Fishermen will argue with most things, including a pathologist's report on the strandings we do gather, so we need a count of what's coming up when nets are hauled in. A count at the beginning of the process, not just the tail end of it – so to speak – which is what the strandings project necessarily deals with.

'Now, as you saw in the presentation, not everything we pick up has been by-caught. But. Mostly it *is* fishing gear that gets them. Around 80 per cent of the animals which strand here do so as a result of by-catch, but we just don't know what that means in terms of totals being caught, hence we need you to monitor numbers at source.

'OK. In some ways I apologize for the more gruesome parts of the video I showed you.'

A murmur of agreement runs round the room.

'And in other ways I don't. While you're very unlikely to find yourself faced with a live dolphin which having its dor-sal fin and tail fluke hacked off, you might. I did. It's how I got the footage you've just seen. Hopefully it's a worst-case scenario, but you need to be aware that it's a possibility. More likely the cetaceans that are hauled aboard will be dead before they have to take the fins off them to release them from the nets—'

'What happens to them – if they're live – once they've had their fins taken off?' Sheila interrupts.

There's a disbelieving outletting of breath at the question.

'OK, you lot,' Greg defends. 'Sheila deals with human health and safety, not cetacean—'

'The same thing that would happen to you if someone cut your arms and legs off and threw you back into the water,' one of the observers calls out.

'Ah – thank you, Richard,' Greg counters. 'No doubt your diplomatic skills are packed away ready to take on board with you. And the process *wouldn't* be the same, in fact. Unlike us, dolphins don't have an impulse to intake air below water. Without tail fluke and fins, they lose all power and steerage, Sheila. And, not being able to reach the surface, they suffocate unless they exsanguinate – bleed to death – first.'

Greg gives an ironic laugh, raising his eyebrows at Graham.

'Right! Now we've cleared that one up, I'd like to say finally, I know some of you have experience with fishing boats. For those of you who haven't, you'll find that the fishermen work really hard – out at sea for, say, six days at a stretch and keeping the fishing going twenty-four hours a day. This means they'll be hauling catches on board day and night and in all sorts of weather conditions and – within the realms of personal safety that Sheila has so comprehensively itemized for us – you need to be there every time they do, bearing in mind that some of the fishermen will resent you being there at all.'

'Oh, come on, Greg,' Peta interjects. 'Tell it like it is, why don't you?'

There's a little release of laughter and Greg grins at her, lets his eyes rove over the students, seeking contact with them all; these guys soon to be gone.

'Any questions?'

Canada

Herschel is sulking when Sophie gets home. Feigning indifference to her return, he gets up from the window ledge, stretches, circles once and lies down again, slow-blinking green eyes; watching her, but out of focus. Sophie scoops him up and carries him round the apartment as she accesses e-mail and checks the answerphone and – only then – does he condescend to purr.

Cassie has phoned about going to the movies. Ali's phoned about going for a run. There's a message from Jacob – could one of his students swap some of the telescope time she's got booked at the Plaskett? There's some information from Hawaii about her next observing run; a message from the postgrad student from biochemistry, asking her out again; a request from one of her students for an extension to a deadline. Nothing at all from Tom. Well, of course there isn't, she thinks, putting Herschel back down on the window sill. It's been months now. And that's fine.

There's sunlight on the glimpse of ocean she can see

between the buildings and, as she lifts her face to its rays, remembrance leaps, replaying the way Tom used to gentle her face, used to be tender with her on lazy Sunday mornings, here, in this room, together. Frowning, she turns the memory away, as others crowd in: skaters bursting onto the hockey rink; Tom among the tumult of red-kitted players; catching her eye at the usual barrier among the crowd, her gloved hands holding the rail today; his fleeting face set, his glance towards her brief then turned to the players – searing by; her sudden comprehension of him moving from her in more ways than the immediate; drawing something out between them to breaking point across the ice; wrenching from her in his frozen wake, the deadening guilt of déjà vu.

Reinholdt had introduced the idea to her gently, talking in general terms about the continued playing out of roles with a partner which we played as children with our parents; allowing her to reach the specific for herself.

'You mean I do this deflection strategy thing with men, too.'

'From the pattern you've described . . . it's certainly possible.'

She turns her attention again to her mail; smiles as her hands land on a particular letter: confirmation of the vacation she's just booked. At least that's one unhelpful pattern broken. Sophie's response to Reinholdt's question about vacations had been an outlining of how difficult it is for Richie to go away; the facilities he needs not always available; the extra worry it creates for her parents. Reinholdt had smiled gently and reasked the question, making it clear he was asking about her *own* vacations, not Richie's, so that she'd blustered something about tacking on a weekend here and there on her visits to telescopes and then she goes home a couple of times a year.

'Hard to send a postcard home otherwise, I suppose,' Reinholdt had suggested, dropping his gaze to the floor. 'Having a great time. Wish you were here.'

She'd rather dismissed his notion. Went out and booked a vacation the next day just to prove a point to herself. She hadn't told her parents and Richie, though. Several times this weekend, she'd wanted to tell them. Started to broach it, even. Found herself changing her own subject.

The phone rings and it's Ali.

'You're back! How was it?'

'Oh – it was fine.'

'Is that fine, fine – or hell, fine?'

'Fine, fine, mostly. It was great to see my dad and Richie was on excellent form, so yeah, it was fine, fine. How are you?'

'Ready to run. You?'

'Are you going *now*?'

'I could leave it ten minutes.'

'Make it fifteen. I've got to change and it takes me ten minutes to get there. Harbour front in fifteen?'

'Excellent.'

And it's good to run, to pace with Ali, side by side along the sea road. They're good at that, gentle warm-up for the first ten minutes, checking how each other is doing before pushing ahead, challenging but staying abreast, just, nudging each other on, her body pleased to loosen out, to sweat out, to blot out, to jog steadily home and hot shower and stretch out and – oh, God! look at the time. Students to meet at the Plaskett at nightfall in forty minutes from now, a twenty-minute drive away, the cat to feed, herself to feed.

She smiles as she drives once she sees the curiously perfect curvature of the hill outside the little city and the perfect white curvature of the observatory at its height. She loves this place, she thinks, following the steep road that winds up round.

From the summit, there's the glimmer of city lights in the distance – not enough to illuminate the night sky; clear tonight, the Milky Way clearly visible. She loves this place: the panorama of dark hills; the distant water inlets disappearing into darkness; the lofty elegance of the eighty-year-old dome that seems almost luminous in the dusky light. Inside, the huge two-storey telescope mount that's a marvel to her still, its shape a curving lower-case 'h'. She loves the sense of history, its unlikelihood: the telescope's huge mirror hauled up the hill by a team of horses.

Her feet ring on the metal stairs and, though she's not late, five of the six students are there before her. Dan, especially bright and communicative; Justin, intense – slightly unnerving since she's found out he's made the effort to read every single paper she's ever published. The other three students are also-rans, but perfectly competent and hardworking enough. There's a deferential murmur of greeting as she arrives which she meets with a smile and a cheerful hi in the low pastel light of the dome. It's the students' first time at this telescope, so she'll work through with them tonight. Simple exercises, finding their way round the equipment and the sky. She'll set them that task later, taking images of mainsequence stars at varying distances, further and further out into space, letting them get to know the telescope's reach. She smiles as she takes them through to the control room.

South-west Wales

The teacher had handed them a label each; a sticky-back label with their names neatly printed. Seb could read his name, written out in full, though the 'b' was a bit funny. The labels were to go on the wall by the coat hooks they were allocated. Each hook already had a colour picture of an animal or flower or fruit. Seb saw the dolphin straight away and – waiting in line – willed it to be his, but no. It went instead to the boy standing in front of him; the sea horse to the girl behind, leaving him stuck in the middle with an animal he knew from his book to be a wallaby. A wallaby. Tears of humiliation welled.

'That's right, Sebastian,' the teacher said as she pressed near to read his label, so that Seb caught her scent, like marmalade. 'Just stick your name next to the picture.' As if he hadn't already known what she wanted him to do. Biting his bottom lip, he stuck his name on the wall.

*

'Wallabies are pretty cool, you know,' Greg says later, at home with Seb on his knee.

Seb looks directly at Greg with soulful, disbelieving eyes.

'We can't always have exactly what we want, Sebastian,' his mother says across a hiss of steam from the iron where the pile of pressed clothes neatly grows.

'Hey,' Greg says, his hand spanning the little shoulders. 'Shall we do some counting? That teacher will be dead impressed when she finds out how good you are at counting.'

Upstairs in Seb's underwater room where they won't get in the way, they make themselves an island of cushions and from it fling out a sea of shells. The large plastic sweet-shop jars are nearly full these days; the shells brought back by Greg in ones and twos or collected by Seb from the sea's edge: tokens of special times gathered in a jar, spreading out now in a shining sea. Sitting cross-ankled on the cushion island with Seb in the embrace of his knees as the boy dips his hand in a jar for more shells, Greg picks up the strange scent of school; his son's hair infused with it.

Seb learned to count with these shells, Greg placing them on the floor, one next to each finger and the thumb of Seb's splayed-out hand, then for both hands, then for his toes, too. And when the boy said – I wonder how many shells there are, Greg had shown him an easy way to count them, sitting with him on the island, banding the shells together in tens, counting up ten tens to make each hundred, so that at four, Seb had some concept of his ten times table.

Then there was the time colour came suddenly into it, Seb cross at the start of the game when his father placed ten shells together and that simply wouldn't do, so Greg had waited to see what the new tactic was; watched while the boy placed different colours together: the shades of pale lemon placed next to each other, the pale browns, the greys, the pinks, the pure whites, the stipple-patterned purples. Seb was so intent, Greg had left him to it that day; had gone through to his study to work; come back to check the boy was OK, found him sleeping, curled up on cushion island, surrounded by little hillocks of same-coloured shells.

Today it doesn't seem to be counting or colour. Greg waits; risks upending a jar for the rest of the shells to cascade out; an action which can get him into trouble if it doesn't fit the plan.

Seb sighs. 'We have to make waves today.'

'Right.'

'Not like *that*,' Seb chastises as Greg starts to pile the shells.

'You show me.'

The boy sorts through, picks out some white shells – perhaps colour does matter today, after all – lays them out in a shallow curve, then starts on another curve a little space behind and parallel to the first.

'Oh, I see,' Greg says. The shells click to his searching fingers. 'A bit like the mosaic you made at nursery.'

By bedtime, the waves roll in, white at the edge of cushion island, followed in by darker hues, so that Greg has to help Sebastian fly to bed across the sea.

'I'm the dragon! I'm the dragon!' the boy squeals, mid-air, then, once he's in bed, 'Do I *have* to go to school tomorrow?'

'You do,' Greg says, settling him in.

'And the next day?'

'And the next day. Just like your mum and I have to go to work. Do you like our sea?'

The boy nods.

'I've got to go across a sea to an island soon, Seb.'

'Have you?'

'Yes, well, not for a while yet. Not until a few weeks after Christmas.'

'Can I come?'

'No, Seb. It's work. And it's quite a long way and you have to go to school.' He stands to reach the globe down from the shelf, spins it so that Seb can see the place. 'It's one of these islands here, in a sea called the Caribbean, around about here,' he says pointing, 'although the island where I'm going is too tiny to be shown.'

'Is it a magic island?' Seb asks, measuring the Atlantic Ocean with the span of his hand.

'I don't know. I haven't been yet. I think it might be. Mag*ical* anyway. The weather will be lovely and hot and no one lives on the island except three men who look after the lighthouse and there will be lots of seabirds and dolphins, too, which is what I'm going to see.'

'Will there be a dragon?'

'I don't know, Seb. There might be.'

'Will you read me a story?'

Greg tousles his son's hair. 'You're a demanding boy today.'

'Will you, though?'

'Where did we get to – oh yes – the princess had just taken her leap onto the dragon's nose. "'Hold your fire!'" the king shouted to his sailors,' Greg begins, without their book in his hand to refer to, while Seb scrabbles to reach it from the bedside cabinet.

'Wait! Wait!' Seb squeals, thrusting the book at his father, but Greg continues, leaving Seb to locate the page – his drawing of the boat with burning sails.

'"'Come back here, you little horror!'" the King yelled to the princess.

'"Finding the dragon's nose a little hot for her feet, the princess scrabbled onto the top of the dragon's head, then slid down his long neck to his shoulder.

'"I do hope they didn't hurt you,' she said to the dragon, nestling into the crook of his wing as the dragon turned his head to look at her. 'They don't *mean* to be mean. They just don't *think* very carefully,' she said, stretching up to scratch the dragon behind his ear – a gesture the dragon appreciated very much – it being a particularly difficult spot to reach.

""'Oh, well, I can see why they might be cross,' the dragon said sadly. 'I did damage the sails.'

""'There is something you could do that would be *really* helpful, though,' the princess said and, standing on tiptoe she reached up to whisper in the dragon's ear.

""'Come back here at once!' the king called again.

""'It would be rather better if you came here,' the princess called back. 'This kindly dragon has agreed to fly us home.'

""'What!' the king said rather rudely, the dragon thought. 'Oh, well, I er, well, humph, well.'

""'We'll take that as a yes, shall we?' the princess said, budging up to make room for him."'

Part Two

East Caribbean

Another flying fish leaps from the water, rainbow-darting through the air. Greg lets his eyes follow its flight, at a tangent away from their bucking boat. One hundred metres, two, it flies before disappearing into swell that meets it head on. Heavy swell here; rough, sudden hillocks of water making the rigid hull shudder. Funny not to be skipper; to let someone else cope with this criss-cross chaos of angry water whipped white by counter-currents and the rising wind; to sit, a passenger, under the spray dodger, his back to unfamiliar Caribbean seas. The man who is skipper steers skilfully, needing his split-second responses. He's been running the gauntlet of this crossing for years. Still the boat is tossed – clean out of the water sometimes, the propeller clean out so that the engine screams to be suddenly churning air until the boat slams back into water and the prop gets its grip, edging them forward to be thrown again; the high-speed plummet into each jarring trough leaving them all quieter. Speech, in any case, would be impossibly lost under the engine's din, the rush of air, the pounding thumps into water.

Jan grips the awning post, her knuckles white. The entomologist on the team of scientists gathering to work on the little island, she's getting soaked. I don't care about getting wet in these temperatures, she had said, but I'll be sick for sure if I sit with my back to the motion, so she stands to face their way of travel, clinging on. At each descent her feet are forced from the floor, jarred down again as the boat crash-lands. From the tautness of muscle at the side of her face, Greg can tell she's gritting her teeth – defence against the smell of dead fish and diesel. Greg has seen her face turn from sun-rosed to white. Now green begins to make its mark. He looks at his watch. They had said the crossing would be about two hours – another forty minutes to go. Catching her eye, Greg gives what he hopes is a reassuring nod – not long now. She nods grimly, raises her eyes briefly to the heavens.

Greg's eyes follow their custom of searching waves for fins, but really it's too rough for that, the crests and troughs and the boat's own motion blotting out any reliable sightings. He hopes he will get better seas beyond the island, where the water is deeper.

Across the boat, Tim catches Greg's eye, looks out to the starboard sky, mouths 'frigate bird' with an ornithologist's authority. David, the conservation biologist, looks too green round the gills to care.

People stir as the motion eases. Over the bow, pale rock rises from the sea: the island of Sombrero, undercut into over-arching curves. As the boat nears they can see how the swell pushes up into and sucks out of cavernous hollows easily big enough to swallow their boat. No harbour. No beaches. No landing stage. Just this tiny inlet narrowly in the lee of the island and even then the skipper must fend off the sharpness of overhanging rock – letting off his five passengers to the ladder lowered down by figures on the bulbous rock face – before swinging the boat out to safer distance. Ropes too have been lowered from a gantry, to haul up boxes – the boat on its fortnightly supply run and the only one which calls.

The passengers climb the ladder: the lighthouse keeper, arriving to start his six-week watch and the team of scientists come to do their conservation assessment of this isolated place. A fortnight is all the scientists have. Barely time for a snapshot in environmental terms – but crucial evidence to balance out commercial bias; to bring to a court already in session.

After the ladder, they climb steep steps hewn from rock. Greg's hand traces fossilized shell and skeleton polyps of coral: this island thrust up from undersea by some long-ago movement of the seabed. Seb would be beside himself.

Emerging above the rock, they are met by the kindling smiles of the island's only inhabitants: three lighthouse keepers, Caribbeans about their business, now, of bringing supplies ashore. Their handshakes too are warm, quietly welcoming these strangers to their island isolation.

The sea to the north does appear calmer and, looking out from greater height now, the plume of spray caused by a whale's exhalation is easily seen, blowing a few feet into the air. Greg sees the animal thrust its body from the water, pushing nearly clear to flip on its side, triggering a line of fountains as it impacts down in a breach, the long white pectoral fin clearly visible, so that within moments of arrival Greg has his first certain identification: humpback whale.

Sitting on coral, Greg waits for the ringing tone. There it is and almost immediately answered.

'Daddy!'

'Hello!' Greg says, standing. 'How did you know it was me?'

'I'm in bed. Mummy said if I went to bed you would phone.'

'Did she? What have you been doing today?'

'Nothing. Where are you?'

'*Nothing*? I'm sure you did *some*thing. How was school?'

'It was OK. Where are you?'

'I'm on the island I told you about.'

'*Are* you?'

'I haven't seen any dragons yet, but I *have* just been sharing my lunch with some lizards.'

'Is it *lunchtime*?'

'It is here. They're rather beautiful lizards, Seb, deep black all over and – the one looking up at me now with *very* bright eyes is about . . . well, including the tail, it's about the same length as my foot.' He walks on and three more lizards dart from rocks near his feet. 'There are *loads* of them.'

'Are there *hundreds*?'

'I don't know how many. One of the scientists here will know that soon, but there are lots. You have to be careful where you tread. The lizards are endemic, Seb, which means,' he says as more lizards scuttle, 'even if you looked everywhere else in the world, you wouldn't find this type of lizard anywhere, only here on this tiny island.'

'Not even in Africa?'

'Not in Africa, or Asia, or America, or anywhere.'

Nearby a seabird screeches at him, a brown booby, indignant at his nearness to her nest. Setting his back to the buffeting wind, Greg sits again, trying to appease the bird. There are so many nests here, it's impossible not to be near.

'So someone will start counting the lizards tomorrow—'

'Why?'

'And study what they eat.'

'Why?'

Greg laughs, hesitating before getting into all that. 'Because of the space rockets.'

'*Space* rockets! On the *island*?'

'Rockets which put satellites in space that go round the earth.'

'*Real* space rockets? Have you *seen* any?'

'No. The rockets aren't here yet, Seb. I rather hope they never will be. There are lots of birds here. Even more birds than lizards. Some rare ones. I'll show you in the book when I get home. If the rockets are launched from here, the birds would be killed and the lizards and perhaps the dolphins, too. That's why I'm here. To see if there are any sea creatures that might be harmed.'

'And then the rockets wouldn't come.'

'Well, no. The men might still bring the rockets. They are men who think the rockets are more important. Or money, anyway. They can make a lot of money if they bring the rockets here.'

Down the phone comes the rustle of the duvet. The connection is so clear it's as if Seb is next to him. Low overhead birds wheel through the brightness of Caribbean sunshine, their shadows skim the rock, flicking across Greg's body.

'Are you snuggled down, Seb?'

'Yes.'

'How's your mum today?'

'She's OK. Have you seen any dolphins?'

'No dolphins yet, but I did see a humpback whale earlier.'

The rustle of bedding again, quick this time.

'A hump-whack whale is the one in the middle, isn't it, Daddy?'

'Sorry?'

'In the *middle*,' Seb says. 'The one in the middle.'

'In the middle? Oh yes! The one in the middle of your chart on the wall. Have you got out of bed again?'

'Yes. Only to see the hump-whack.'

'Well, that's OK, but hop back into bed now,' Greg says from across the Atlantic. He hears the give of bedsprings down the phone. 'Where is your mum?'

'She's downstairs. Do you want me to get her?'

'It doesn't matter. I can phone her later,' Greg says, toe-ing aside loose coral. 'Are you cosy now?'

'Yes. Where are *you* going to sleep, Daddy?'

'In a tent. There's only the lighthouse here – a tall metal tower – and the building where the lighthouse keepers stay and that's more or less it, so the skipper from the boat I'll be using and the scientists, including me, are staying in tents.'

'Like your tent we stayed in?'

'No. More like Grandpa's tent – the A-frame one. Listen, monster. I must go and get some work done now. Are you snuggled down?'

No answer – just the raucous call of seabirds at his shoulder.

'Seb?'

'Yes?'

'I'll phone you tomorrow, OK?'

'OK.'

'Don't forget to push the button on the phone, will you?'

'OK.'

'Sleep well, monster. Push the button now.'

The phone line clicks to dial tone.

Greg begins to pick his way back across coral. The rock – left broken by last century's mining – is loose and difficult and tips underfoot, and then there are the birds. Out-numbering the lizards, they nest on the ground in rocky dips. Every few metres there's a solitary chick, large and decked in fluffy down, the white of the rock it is among, or perhaps an egg rests in its harsh nest of splintered rock and three long feathers pushed against lichened stone, no parent, for a time, to shade its helplessness from this hot sun.

Corkscrewed-squawks puncture the air from close by and middle-distance and to the edge of this rocky place. Near by, sleek-brown, sharp-billed, beady-eyed defensiveness; the way between birds so narrow it's hard not to make the adults fly. Elsewhere, the grace of their gliding flight or the groundedness of community, of territory mapped just so. *Their* territory, a fearsome mother at his feet scolds.

'Hey. Be pleased I'm not a space rocket,' Greg soothes, moving quietly away.

Having fished and returned to Anguilla with the catch and the lighthouse keeper going off watch, the little boat is back again and ready to go out with Greg on survey. Greg has spoken with the keepers, using their local knowledge to confirm the transect he'll be following, plotting the course on the laptop, feeding it into the GPS. All set. The ladder is lowered for him and he is going down to the vibrant blue when he sees the dark shape in the water near the rock face. Swinging his gear and himself on board, he grins to the skipper and shakes his hand again; while digging out the mask from the kit bag.

'We have a turtle here,' Greg says, indicating along the overhangs and taking off his shirt.

'Ah, yes. Often there are turtles.'

'Ten minutes all right – before we go out?'

'Sure. Be careful.' The skipper's hand mimes the suck of water under ceilinged caverns; the banging of heads on rock.

'Sure,' Greg says, mask on and sliding over the side of the boat, slipping his feet into fins, pushing off to see for certain.

There's the water, warm about him; the rhythm of his steady finning; steady breath to draw down through the snorkel; his body, gliding through shafts of sunlight in the water's clearness; the sense of depth dropping below him; a silver-blue glitter of fish and there – the turtle, turning her head in quick alarm, so that he slows and stays his distance. Green turtle? No! Hawksbill! As she loses her fear, dismissing him as uninteresting and returning to her foraging, he sees for sure her distinctive profile. Hawksbill. He rests in the water, watching; his body lifted and moved by eddies that lift and move the turtle too, so that they drift in parallel, a flip of fin or foot correcting a move too near to the rock face.

She turns and takes herself to the surface, raising her face just enough to break the water's skin, letting her nostrils through. Taking delicate sips of air, she stays a while, then swims down again, her back to him, busy with things of much more import, snuffling along the rock face, an old woman suddenly window-shopping and watchful for coins on the ground, the pattern of her rounded shell the scarf round old shoulders.

He sighs out long breath. Not anthropomorphism now. The heat must be getting to him. *Hawksbill*, he reminds himself as he floats in warm water. *Eretmochelys imbricata*. His second marine mammal here and this one on the endangered list globally. Run-off of rocket fuel just what she needs.

He fins back to the boat: observation to note down, then off and out. New seas to explore.

'Say that again,' Greg says, slicing zucchini in the lighthouse kitchen.

Tim finds his place and reads again, "'At a minimum, there is likely to be a 70 to 80 per cent loss of masked booby nesting habitat.'"

'They recognize that and *still* they're going ahead?'

'Obviously you didn't hear Rocket-launch Man on the BBC news.'

'No?'

'"You don't mean to say I should put aside multi-million dollars' worth of business for the sake of a few seabirds?" was the gist of it.

'No matter,' Tim continues, his head in the environmental-impact assessment still. 'It seems the "effects of the rocket-launch site project on the endemic lizard, *Ameiva corvina*, are expected to be of a *positive* nature".'

'How *ever* do they work *that* out?'

'Something about a revegetation programme.'

'But the lizards aren't herbivores.'

'Maybe they're thinking of food chains.'

'Doubt it,' David snorts. 'I've been through that document with a fine-tooth comb. The limited number of species it *does* consider are regarded in complete isolation from one another.'

Jan nods her agreement. 'At best it's a quick count of the most obvious animals and plants and even then the methods they've used are wonderfully flawed.'

'Still, it's good for us the document *is* so appalling,' Tim says. 'All the more for us to get our teeth into. I especially liked their assessment of rocket-launch noise.'

'Oh yes – the likely noise level at a distance of thirty-five miles. No mention of anything nearer.'

'What about at thirty-five metres?'

'Deaf lizard.'

'Singed lizard, too, I should think,' Greg says, swooshing vegetables into a boiling pot. 'How wide is this island? A quarter of a mile, isn't it?'

'At its widest.'

'I can't see much of the island fauna surviving a single rocket launch.'

'Me neither. What about the marine mammals, Greg?'

'In relation to noise? Hard to say. As you know, noise doesn't transfer easily from air to water, so the submerged mammals may well be all right. Anything surfacing for air coincident with the launch might be a different matter.'

He thinks of the pod of spinner dolphins he saw this afternoon, 300 strong, their turbulent leaping from the water to spin and dive and swim and leap, and spin and dive and leap.

'Could be devastating for those above water if they are caught in the sonic-boom footprint. Damaged hearing, so their echolocation is shot to pieces, so they can't feed or orientate themselves. Those that don't become prey themselves, or strand and die, would die of starvation.'

'The odds against that timing, though: surfacing mammals and a once monthly launch?'

'Impossible to put a figure on it, but it may be more likely than you imply. There are a lot of cetaceans out there.'

'They might just dive for cover and the launch would be over before they would need to surface again,' Jan suggests.

'That's possible, although, as you know, trying to predict an animal's response without any empirical evidence is guess-work at best.'

'So – what then? A theoretical model?'

Greg nods. 'I've already started a couple of PhD students working on models, yes. One dealing with how the rocket-launch sounds would transfer from air to water, another on the effect of sound within a given object – the way it would resonate around and affect cranial cavities of a given species.'

'We haven't got much time.'

'Nor much data at present,' Greg agrees. 'I think, if I ask NASA nicely, they should be able to provide some statistics about rocket-launch noise.'

'Might be pleased to oblige, in fact,' David comments. 'I wonder if those guys at Cape Canaveral know how close a competitor is getting to cornering a commercial side of the market they could accommodate themselves.'

'Might just mention it in passing when I ask for some stats. I think the potential damage to feeding ground for the hawksbill turtle might carry more weight as an argument against development, though. I've seen hawksbills every day since we arrived. Green turtles, too. And I think what you guys are coming up with is going to be more tangible still. We've been here – what? – six days and already the picture emerging—'

'Yeah, yeah,' David interrupts. 'The place is dripping with rare or endangered or endemic species. And all the major trophic levels in the animal component of the eco-system are here. Species interdependence clearly indicated. You know, it's a miniature Galapagos. Really, it is. I just don't see anybody listening to the environmental story whatever we come up with. The thing's gotten so much backing. Local government approval – those socioeconomic promises made: jobs, education.'

They are silent a moment, knowing the truth of what he says, and the door opens on their silence as the lighthouse keepers arrive.

'Hey! You got that meal ready yet?' Desmond calls as he saunters in, grinning now he is freed – on alternate days – from cooking while the scientists are here.

'Oh, God – the food,' Tim says, turning to rescue the fish dish from the oven.

'We've been talking rockets, Desmond,' Greg says, pass-ing him a bottle of ice-cold beer. 'What do *you* think about this island being used as a launch site?'

Desmond nods at what looks like a tide mark high on the

wall, a few inches below the ceiling. 'How good are rockets in seawater?'

It takes them a moment to grasp his meaning.

'Is *that* where the water rose to?'

He nods. 'In the hurricane.'

'Sure hope you guys were somewhere else.'

'They take us off by helicopter when the hurricane's coming. I showed him this when he came here.'

'Rocket-launch Man?'

'Yeah, but he say it's no matter. He's gonna build a b-i-g harbour wall.'

'*Is* he? It's not on the plans here. Just a barge docking point for bringing over the rocket parts.'

'That was before he came here and heard how the island is awash in the hurricane, so he thinks now he must build a harbour wall the length of the island. Wind was just forty miles an hour the day he came,' Desmond says. 'Water was coming up then. Washed some of the nests away.'

David shakes his head. 'The conditions here must push the wildlife through some pretty tight genetic bottlenecks.'

But Greg is thinking rocket plans still.

'A harbour wall to hold back a hurricane.'

'Seems that's the idea,' Desmond says, nodding solemnly. Greg catches his eye and Desmond breaks into a huge grin. 'Now, don't start me laughing.'

David snorts a hard guffaw. 'King bloody Canute.'

Greg shakes his head. A harbour wall to hold back a hurricane from this dot of land in this expanse of sea. Hilarious if it were just some scatterbrained idea; if this unique ecosystem wasn't going to be obliterated in the attempt; if the project wasn't steaming ahead. Bloody hilarious.

East Caribbean

Rachel, Rachel, he feels himself gather, Rachel, blood racing, God, that's so good, he'd forgotten, he'd forgotten the tautness of her body, how deeply she can take him, how completely he covers her body with his, her buttocks tightening to the lift of his tight grasp and – oh, God – the pain again! There at his hip. He wakes on the very verge of coming, tips his weight away from the sharp rock goading him through the groundsheet, onto the hardness of the sleeping mat, onto his own hardness, stifling his breath, not another bloody wet dream, don't wake David again, his body too far gone to stop; the dream holding him: the soft press of her breasts as he yields his seed to the unyielding ground.

He throws off the sleeping bag's hotness, throws himself onto his back. What the *hell* is this? It's almost every night since he's been here. It's like being a bloody teenager all over again. And wasn't that Rachel he was dreaming of? Rachel! Why Rachel? It's been years. Steadying his breathing, he listens for David's, but his own is still too loud. Thank God there are just the two of them in this three-man tent. Embarrassing enough, this proximity – David teasing him at breakfast in front of the others – what was he on and could he have some – before Jan came in and they'd changed the subject. It's like being back at school.

Darkness lightens then dims again as the beam from the lighthouse sweeps high over the tent – a glow stained green by the colour of canvas. In the running light he sees David's stillness, listens again for his breathing and hears it this time: long and slow.

Greg moves to the mouth of the tent as shadows swing to the next beam sweep. Unzipping insect netting, he crawls out into darkness, the moon behind cloud cover tonight, only the light's steady arc cutting through darkness high overhead. The rock is sharp beneath his feet as he takes off his boxers, mopping the rest of his wetness with them; chucking them over a guy rope, next to the pale shape of towels drying. He stands tall to stretch away the camp's confines; stretching the small of his back, arching out the crick in his neck. At least his libido is pacified for now – wretched maniac to whom he is shackled.

He stretches again, the night air warm on his body; the day's wind dropped to nearly nothing and, nearer to him than the generator's smothered thrub, the sea is a whisper, still; a rounding sigh. He draws deep breath, lets out his own unbidden sigh; his body cooler. He wonders if this cloud will amount to much. They've been lucky so far – a kindness of weather he suspects is rare. Yesterday was just stunning, out on the water on night survey; in darkness two miles off this scrap of land, rocked by a benevolent sea silvered by moonlight, listening – faint console lights on their faces – to whatever the hydrophone might pick up. He'd got some close recordings of dolphins, he couldn't be certain what species; Atlantic spotted, he thinks. He'll match the tapes with others once he gets home. And God, those manta rays were something, coming up to his torchlight held under the water, wing span much wider than he is tall. Twice as wide? Three times? He had used it as an excuse to slip into the water; suspending himself in darkness by the boat, marvelling at the beauty of their slow-motion swimming flight, the push of water on him from the movement of their winged fins as they circled his pillared beam of light.

He hears the scrape of an opening door, sees the chink of falling light, hears the footsteps of one of the keepers crossing to the tower. Going on duty to check the light. Didn't Desmond say it was his turn tonight? Taking the day's swimming shorts from the guy rope, he steps into them and softly calls a greeting, groping into the tent at the foot of his bag for a T-shirt to put on. 'Hey, Desmond! What do you think of this cloud cover?' And it is Desmond, sleepy and pleased to say hello before he has to climb the tower stairs.

'Well, he's nothin' much. Barograph not doin' much.'

'No? More wind in the morning, though?'

'A little bit. Nothin' much. You done with running up the tower today?'

In the afterglow of the lighthouse beam, Greg catches Desmond's grin, teasing him still from this evening, the lighthouse keepers and scientists alike laughing at his madness: Greg running up the tower a few times in his need for the type of exercise not possible among the loose rocky terrain and the ubiquity of wildlife. Greg laughs, 'Why? Do you think I should sprint up a few more times?'

'*Def*initely. Or perhaps you don't have to run this time, but you should come up. The tower is a diff'rent experience at night.'

So Greg follows him, barefoot over the harsh ground, taking support from Desmond's shoulder till they reach the smoother concrete near the tower. Inside, their feet are on metal stairs, the sound of Desmond's boots echoing up the metal column; shadows from dim lights running ahead of them round the spiral stairway; red lights here, better for night vision from lookout points on the way up. Getting higher, they see the lights of shipping out to sea and, at another window, the dim glow from a distance of the island of Anguilla.

'Lots of shipping,' Greg says, pausing on that side of the narrowing tower.

'Always busy,' Desmond calls back.

Where the spiral staircase narrows to an end, metal ladders begin. At the end of the second, a hatchway leads out to the gallery platform encircling the outside of the tower and Greg goes through it, leaving Desmond to go about his routine checks.

The light beam is on the opposite side of the tower as he closes the hatch behind him, so that the darkness seems complete at first and, sitting, all he senses is the drop below the metal grating and the breeze, stronger at this height and warm on his skin. Slowly his eyes adjust, picking out the pinprick lights of shipping and the gloomy luminance of cloud-muffled moon. He rests against the tower, shuffles to one side a little as his back contacts the big, rounded rivets holding together the curved metal plates. He feels the tower shudder faintly to the trundle of the turntable, a little height above his head. Can't be long now 'til the light comes round again. There! Straight overhead now, the light streams, piercing out, an overhang leaving him strangely shadowed, so that he stands to look down the length of the beam, but it's gone, sweeping past him, a certain dizziness in it, little now to gauge his place by so that he laughs – wondering if it could send a man to madness, waiting for this light, like some visual version of water torture – and he sits again, his back to the relative steadiness of the tower, away from the teasing, dark giddiness of breeze.

Slowly the lights of shipping re-emerge and he wonders about their journeys from and to; what nationalities are on board these little capsules of culture set adrift, crossing and re-crossing hazardous seas. Little pockets of human purpose, passing one another, unknown.

Again the light swings round. He stays sitting this time, letting the light swoop past, seeing the frantic flight of insects in its shaft. He wonders how far the beam reaches out to sea; whether it's overwhelmed first by darkness or by the curving surface of the earth and who worked it out – the men with pencil and paper and geometry – the tower to be built just so high.

The handle on the hatch door turns and Desmond ducks through to come and sit beside him, the tower in darkness again, so that Greg is reminded of a moment with Seb at an old-fashioned fair; their dark climb to the top of a helter-skelter, waiting for their kaleidoscope ride into light.

'Everything as it should be in there?'

'He's fine. Smoke?'

'Thanks, but no.'

The match flares in the darkness.

'How long till you can go home again, Desmond?'

'Four weeks.' He growls a laugh, 'Hey! I miss mi wife.'

'You married?' Greg asks, surprised.

'Yeah. Started young, hey? We got a little girl.' The cigarette end glows more brightly as he draws on it. 'Every time I go home she's just growed up so much more,' so that Greg thinks again of Seb – across an ocean where the sun will already have risen round the Earth's racing turn.

Shadows race over him as the light sweeps round.

In Flight

Sleeping, Sophie speeds towards the rising sun. She wakes with her face against the fuselage wall, opens her eyes to a sunlit tracery: ice crystals at the edge of the cabin window; white cloud cover below. She straightens her horribly stiffened neck and – sleepy-eyed – smiles. Glancing at her watch, she finds darkness has passed in hastened time.

Well, of course it has, Sophie, sleepyhead.

On the screen in the back of the seat ahead there's an icon of an airplane heading east still, then the stats get overlaid: 39,000 feet; 700 miles an hour; outside temperature minus 65. She quite wants to pee, but the fat lady in the aisle seat is dozing still, head back, mouth open, legs protruding out into the gangway; so instead Sophie resettles the meagre pillow; cosies the red blanket back around; closes again her drowsy eyes.

Fly me away, then, Airline Pilot. Hey there, Scotty, beam me up.

East Caribbean

There's a gigantic, cutout, painted full moon, behind palm trees which ripple to a warm sea breeze, fluttering in golden artificial light over the guys on stage, who send their stuff chanting out into the night: reggae-proud and reggae-beautiful and reggae-fine and laid-back-tight. How can they do that, Greg wonders, as his body moves and sand slips in between his toes – how can they be so utterly relaxed and yet be note perfect: solid, unfaltering, each musician engaging perfectly one with the others: music magicians spellbinding the crowd. God, it's so *good* to be out of Britain and the sense he has these days of the country crashing about his ears – so good to be here, with this warmer weather and the glimpses he keeps getting of a warmer ideology.

He feels the second nudge at his elbow, Tim easing through the crowd to bring him more beer. Greg takes the bottle as Tim leans across to yell something in his ear that gets engulfed by reggae, so that Tim raises his eyebrows, nods across to where David and Jan dance, looking rather earnestly into each other's eyes, and Greg gets the message – *What did I tell you?* Greg grins and, tipping back his head to laugh, catches the eye of that *beaut*iful black girl again; sees her slender, cat-like grace. She's been catching his eye all evening, nodding once, smiling, mouthing hello, dancing in the crowd. He sees that gradually she's getting nearer, isn't she? He looks round; finds the palm trees still in their place, only the girl getting nearer through the crowd. My God, he's being hunted! And he laughs as he dances, sobers himself with the thought – only another day here, when really he'd like to stay much longer, for years even, if only he could be black, to be really part of this, not just a white outsider; to be black and merge with this moving crowd and glancing round in the heady warm darkness diffused with the stage's golden light, he finds nearly all the faces are black, so that – seeing them – he can – for a moment at least – forget his own skin. And it isn't just the music and beer talking, nor the outside air that's done it, heavy with the scent of marijuana. Walking through the town today, so many people had stopped to say hello and three separate vehicles stopped – strangers offering him a lift and the young man sitting on the wall waiting for his girlfriend simply wouldn't let Greg go without conversation; grinning and kindly and inquisitive conversation. And see now, on stage, the singer brings on a younger man; stepping aside to nurture new blood. All this – the kind of community Greg would want for Seb, he thinks, as the warmth and the crowd and the push of the reggae wrap round him in the darkness like the beat of some great heart.

The crowd swells with the action of applause, then more applause to the new band coming on, straight on, rolling the momentum as the singer appears, grey streaking the black of his dreads. That's something else they do here, Greg thinks, reminded of the deference shown today by two boys in the street to the word of an elderly passer-by: this culture presumes and honours the sagacity of age.

There's a lift in the crowd as they greet the main man, this singer of years, pushing out the reggae and – moving to the music – Greg brushes or is brushed by someone and turning – hey – he sees it is her, the beautiful woman, young thing, not seeming to mind that he's an outsider, close by him now, dancing with her back turned to him, half-turned, her shoulder turned, the curve of her hip so very closely turned; so closely in his body space. In the press of the crowd, her shoulder touches him, his fingers brush against her arm; a fingertip touch brought into being by the rhythm of the music; their bodies moving to the rhythm of the music. Gently he draws her to him. See! How sweetly she slides into his hands; leaning her weight towards him as their bodies sway to the reggae tune in the dark cocoon of the warming crowd.

*

'Thought for a moment you were going to try and bring her back to the hotel,' Tim says the next and final day as they stride to the big debriefing meeting. He pulls a face at Greg to register the protest of a nearly usurped hotel room-mate. 'Thought I was going to end up sleeping in the corridor. Not that I could have blamed you, I suppose,' he says, pulling another face: lusty appreciation this time.

'Hey!' Greg counters, grabbing the scruff of Tim's neck as they walk. 'Listen, upstart. We danced, OK?'

'Yeah, yeah,' Tim goads, countering Greg's grasp.

'Married man, mate,' Greg says wryly.

'Take that into account, do you?'

'Always have done. So far.'

'Tamila!' a woman's voice calls from behind a house set back from the road.

'Tamila,' another woman picks up the call from the line where she hangs out washing in the garden. 'Tamila,' she calls to the child she can see playing with others across the street. 'You muddah callin' you.'

The early-morning heat is enough already to cause the men to pace from tree to tree, making the most of available shade. Still Greg feels sweat start at the back of his knees.

'Now here's a *truly* remarkable woman,' Greg says as they turn into the office entranceway and see the director of the charitable trust who has taken the initiative to summon the scientists here from overseas. Just opening the office door, the sun glows on the black of her skin and the deep golden yellow of her full-length dress.

'Good morning!' the richness of her voice sings out.

West Caribbean

The white house is close to the beach. Very close. The garden fronting onto the sand with scarcely a boundary marked, the sandy soil soon giving way to sand entirely. The white bunkroom is lofty, with sloping ceilings, and – jutting out towards the beach – it has large windows in three walls so that, when you turn the handle to open the louvred glass, the sea breeze comes right through the room: gently, filtered and diffused by insect mesh.

From the top bunk she chooses, Sophie overlooks the sea, through palm-tree fronds, past classic, white Caribbean sand. She sneaks up to her bunk, that first early evening – taking time away from the others – to watch the sun setting with nearer-the-equator speed, no lights on in the room, just a gentle wind whispering through, so she feels more as if she is outside than in, as if in a hammock slung between the trees; only in some ways better than outside, away from where fierce sand flies bite.

Newly met Maddie comes, hunting Sophie out, bringing

bottles of icy beer; clambering up to share the sunset so that the women loaf about together on the bunk, swapping stories of lovers and futures and schooldays in the fading crimson light; like moments Sophie might have let herself have as a teenager, if only Richie had been whole.

In Flight

Watching the world pass by below: seas and countries he has never seen. Jewelled islands in brilliant sunshine: tree-covered emeralds set in shorelines of white gold scattered, glistening against an aquamarine that deepens its tone with the deepening water. And just as he thinks – Seb would feel it's like being on board the beautiful dragon – the alarm on Greg's watch triggers. Time to phone home.

'You know how the dragon sees all the countries sliding by?'

'When he's flying with the king and the princess on his back?'

'That's right – well, that's what it's like here, Seb, on the plane on the way to another island in the west Caribbean this time.'

'Are you on a *pla-ne*?'

'I *am*, with lots of sea below me of a very beautiful blue and little boats leaving white trails in the water and we could see some islands, too, but we're leaving them behind now. How are you?'

'I'm OK.'

'Did you have a good day at school?'

'It was OK. Have you seen any dolphins today?'

'Not since a couple of days ago. Are you in bed?'

'I'm putting the shells back in the jar.'

'Have you been making a sea with them?'

'No. Pyramids.'

'Pyramids!'

'Yes. Richard says pyramids are cool because there's always a dead body in the middle.'

'Oh, well, building pyramids must be fun.'

'Richard says he's going to build a pyramid in his garden and—' His voice trails off and Greg hears Ella's voice in the background, urging Seb to bed and then muffled sounds as she takes the phone from the boy.

'Into bed now. You can speak to Daddy once you're in bed. Have you cleaned your teeth? Into bed, then. How are you, Greg?'

'Good, thanks. How are things with you?'

'OK.'

'Who's Richard?'

'Anyone would think he's a demigod the way a certain person reveres him. In fact he's a little tyke two years older than Seb. They met in the playground last week and it was hero-worship at first sight.'

'Into pyramids, I hear.'

'Yes. At least it might get Sebastian off the shells for a change. Where are you?'

'On the plane on the way to Miami.'

'On the plane? Must be costing a fortune.'

'It's where I am at his bedtime, Ella. I promised to call at bedtime.'

'Here he is, then,' Ella says and Greg senses the phone passed back.

'Is it getting cold?' Seb asks.

'What do you mean, Seb?'

'When the dragon flies with the king and the princess on his back it gets colder each day.'

'Oh, I see. It will be cooler than it was in Anguilla and Sombrero, but no, it will still be quite hot. Are you snuggled down?'

'Yes. Will you tell me a story? The bit about the dragon flying.'

'Just that bit then,' Greg says, glad he brought a printout of the text; shoving it into his hand luggage at the last minute, Seb offering to do the drawings for him, not thinking the thing could be complete without them. Greg smiles now at the thought, leafing through to find the right page. 'The three of them flew for several days,' Greg begins from memory, 'the dragon growing rather fond of his passengers. Even if the king was rude, the princess was lovely and would help the dragon scrub his scales every evening after a long day's flight.'

Finding the page, he reads on: "'And it was wonderful to watch the world pass by below them: seas and countries the dragon had never seen. Not that the king saw very much of it, as he seemed to spend most of the journey asleep, snoring in a rather unkingly way. Every day, the weather became cooler, so that the princess, and even the king, were pleased to curl up close to the dragon at night; the warmth of the dragon's body keeping them warm too.

"'Cooler and cooler the weather became as the three journeyed on, until one day all the world below was white and the air around them, too, was white with a dusting of something in the sky.'"

The flight attendant walks by, offering guava juice. Ice? she questions with her eyes and a gesture towards the container. Yes, please, Greg answers with a nod and a brief smile as he reads.

"'Are these feathers?' the dragon asked as they flew.

"'No,' the princess said, in between her father's snores. 'It's snowing.'

"'Oh,' said the dragon, not quite sure what snowing was, but liking the way the white bits landed on his scales and magically changed to water in a cooling sort of way. 'Very refreshing.'

"'We're nearly home now,' the princess said.

"'Are we?' the dragon asked, rather disappointed to think that the journey would have to come to an end.

"'Yes, look,' the princess said, leaning forward and pointing to where, in the distance, tall towers climbed.

"'What's *that*?' the dragon exclaimed.

"'Home,' the princess said. 'The palace where we live.'

"'As they got nearer, the dragon could see the palace was made of huge slabs of blue ice and, on the top of the mighty walls, round ice turrets towered. The dragon did feel rather proud then, bringing the king and the princess home and, holding his head high, he flew in a circle around the palace three times. Soon people below were hurrying and scurrying, getting ready to greet the king. Trumpets blew and carpets were unfurled and the page boy ran to tell the queen." Are you snuggled down still, Seb?'

'Yes.'

'I'm going to have to go now.'

'Why are you?'

'It's very expensive to phone from the plane. I'll read you some more tomorrow, though. OK?'

'When will you go to sleep?'

'Not for several hours yet. It's the afternoon here.'

'Why is it?'

'I'll show you on the globe when I get home Seb. It's only a couple of days now till I'm back again, so I'll see you soon. Press the button on the phone and sleep well, monster.'

There's a press of bodies at the evening market; beautiful bodies on display: tight-breasted women and tightly toned men promenading between stalls of silks and silver; beautiful bronzed flesh tautly revealed, pausing where waves of music collide, to touch ceramic masks of weeping clowns; to finger trinkets. The chic Italian café wafts out an aroma of coffee to mingle with the thick sizzle of hamburgers at the stall on the street and there, a little clearing in the crowd where men protest their machismo and women squeal to have the live snakes draped round their necks, scales slinking over skin; one snake greeny-grey, the other pale blond: two three-metre pythons. Snake tongues flickering, their thwarted heads constantly weave: vainly seeking an altogether different jungle. Greg takes side streets down to the beach, finds it straight and long and lined with buildings and goes back to the little hotel, past women on roller blades and men out jogging. Each one so very beautiful.

Early-morning pastries on the hotel balcony overlooking where the market was, the stalls gone; only street sweepers now, sweeping and wheeling their carts and calling out to one another under an intermittent canopy of trees. It occurs to

Greg it may be just because time feels pressing that he feels so keen to be gone.

The taxi drops him back at the airport, by the glassless booth under the concrete flyover, where the girl who served him yesterday already sits in the captured pall of traffic fumes and the captured thundering of traffic noise and the captured, steadily building heat. He races up the escalator, finds himself in easy time for his flight, by a long way first at the desk to check in his baggage, yet still the hour feels pressing and he chastises himself for the self-indulgence that has necessitated this stopover when he should probably have gone straight home. He glances at the departure board then out of the window at the waiting planes, pacing till his flight is called.

The little aircraft banks steeply and he sees, revealed, the long straight of Miami Beach, built to the very edge of the sea, then – as the plane levels – the stretching acres and acres of suburb reaching to the horizon's curve. Sighing, Greg sinks back into his seat, letting the plane's turning bring sky to his eyes.

West Caribbean

From the boat as it comes to shore, Sophie sees two figures on the beach. Nearing, she recognizes Paul – the project coordinator come to meet them – but not the man with him and just as she's wondering who he is, Anna says as she helms the boat towards the beach, 'Looks like the Brit arrived OK,' so that Ned asks, 'Who is he?'

'Marine mammalogist,' Maddie tells him. 'He and Paul were students together.'

From the shore as the boat comes in, Greg smiles at something Paul is saying, or rather at the face he is pulling; a till-then-forgotten expression seen during PhD days out in the field, gathering their shared data. Paul would pull that face when something significant came to hand: some con- cluding information, some hard-won success. He pulls it now at Greg's compliment on the great set-up here; the obviously well-run field centre Paul has just shown him round. Greg grins across at him; breathes in sea breeze; breathes a little tension out. Of course it's reasonable to stop by here for a couple of days. How could he be so near and not look up this dear friend?

The bow nudges its way into sand and – between the other, standing people – Sophie sees the Brit's even smile, the warmth of it, as he says hi to Maddie and reaches easily up to take the metal case of cameras from her grasp, turning to carry the thing safely away from the sea.

Maddie must be the MSc student Paul told him about, Greg supposes, going back to the boat, and that must be Paul's co-scientist, Anna, at the helm. She looks a good sort: confident, relaxed. The others must all be the current volunteer team – and as he counts them – four, five, six – his eye lingers on the last, the woman towards the stern of the boat. Narrowing his eyes against the glare of sun on sea, he glimpses a litheness as she gathers up belongings; glimpses the pale, soft colouring of her hair.

'Greg!' Maddie laughs, trying to pass more gear down to him.

'Sorry, Maddie.'

Over the mêlée of moving people and passed-forward baggage – rucksacks and cameras and the cooler boxes – Greg and Sophie's eyes meet – one, warm, long second of contact held across activity and banter and the boat's rise and fall as the little waves make difficult the disembarkation. Only glimpses of each other after that, now caught between – now blocked by – others: Maddie and Ned and Jacques and Ian and Joanna and Elizabeth, whom Paul and Greg help down from the boat – Sophie the last of them to come ashore. Oh, *here* she is, then, some inner voice firmly asserts, as Greg reaches out a hand to her, *here* she is: a first touch of skin on transatlantic skin as he catches her arm to ease her leap to land. There's the lightness of her in his lifting; the splash of her feet in the slushy sand; the warm ease of eyes on eyes and her first words to him, 'Thank you.'

'You're welcome.'

Formal greeting in this informal place. Eyes smile at the incongruity: pale eyes, blue, resting steadily on his.

'See anything exciting out there?' he asks, as they turn and walk together up the beach – a shocking sense of rightful place as he asks her about her day, now that she's come home.

'Oh – we saw so much!' And she tells him of the whales and dolphins they have seen and the shark and the eagle ray; her hands in elated animation, her lit face turning to the calmness of his countenance. All the while his stunned sense of certainty; the absolute conviction pumping through with his blood; the complex simplicity of it: here-she-is.

'Couldn't really miss this guy,' Paul says later among laughter at dinner; ten of them round the candlelit table; student antics being retold. 'Sure we were looking for dolphins.

Didn't really wanna see 'em *that* close. Jumped clean out of the water, landed *bang!* in the middle of the boat.'

Greg shares a little glancing laugh with Sophie, a raise of his eyebrows at these secrets of PhD days revealed.

'Greg here saying, *Good time to get some skin and blubber samples* and I'm saying, *Let's just get this bugger out of here. Don't wanna share my boat with a thrashing, eight-foot bottle-nose.*'

'However did y'get him outta there?' Ned, a Californian journalist, drawls.

'Oh – we shifted him. Still got the scars, but we shifted him. Easier than shifting that nurse shark that snuck up on us.'

'*Nurse shark?*'

'Greg and me, minding our own business on the seabed, busy with a grid we'd put down a month or two before, taking our notes twenty metres underwater. Next thing I know, I look up and there's this nurse shark peering over Greg's shoulder, like he wants to read what it is we're writing. Didn't quite know how to tell him – they don't teach you sign language for, *Don't look now, buddy, but there's a shark on your shoulder.*'

Greg glances again at Sophie through the laughter, gives another wry grin. Sophie widens her eyes in reply, gives a little smile, looks away. The irony of it. Just when she wants to put into practice some different way of being. Just when she's at last met someone with whom the electricity positively crackles. It's so very rare, that. The sense of something worthwhile, of something special. So very rare. Another reason why she's in the habit of deflection. She glances across at Greg. No good. For all the electricity, it's no good. She'd seen it as they walked into the house this evening, their arms full of kit from the boat: the glint on his left hand of wedded gold. She'd pursed her lips against the slap of disappointment. No good.

Greg laughs again at Paul holding court. It's excellent he can talk like this after all his recent sadness. Some of it is the beer talking, of course, but no harm in that, Greg thinks, as Paul launches into the one about the two of them at sea with engine failure and a tropical storm brewing.

'Don't you miss it all?' Elizabeth asks once Paul has done.

'Oh, me?' Greg asks. 'Pembrokeshire has its moments. Miss the climate. Miss the phosphorescence. Those night dives we used to do, Paul.'

'Oh, yeah.'

'Phosphorescence?'

'Tiny plankton,' Paul supplies. 'They give off light when you stir them up.'

'You can sit on the seabed at night,' Greg says, 'and turn off your dive light, so you're in pitch-black darkness and then if you start waving your arms about you generate phosphorescent showers through the water – myriad tiny spots of

light.' He grins at the memory. 'It's like having stars streaming from your fingers. You can sit on the seabed and make
whole galaxies with the turn of your hand.'

'Then, if one of you does that,' Paul picks up, 'fills a quick
universe –' he laughs, flailing his arms around to demonstrate
the needed motion – 'the other can turn somersaults and be
a spaceman, floating through the stars.'

There's a burst of laughter at the image. 'Sure would like
to know what you guys were imbibing,' Ned intones.

'No,' Sophie's gentle, unneeded defence comes, 'They
do train astronauts underwater. They do. The weightless-
ness.'

'*Oceans,*' Ian *Star Trek*-mimics, '*the final frontier.*'

'Must have been some pretty shit-hot stuff,' Ned continues as Greg's eyes warm across the table to Sophie's: to her
warm, direct eyes and her almost imperceptible smile.

In the meal's aftermath, Paul's scruffy, long-haired, lop-eared
dog scrounges leftover chicken bits in the kitchen.

'OK, Juno.' Maddie soothes. 'You can have your dinner in
a minute.'

'*Juno?*' Greg queries, bringing the last of the used crock-
ery and grinning at the ludicrous doggy-aggrandizement.
'Wasn't Juno a Greek goddess?'

'Roman, in fact, and I hope you're not suggesting she's
not worthy of the name. It's an asteroid, too, apparently, one

of the brightest and best Sophie tells me and she should know, being an astronomer.'

Greg stops in his stacking of dried dishes. 'Sophie's an astronomer?'

'Not just a pretty face, hey?' Maddie says, tossing Juno chicken skin.

Greg opens the cupboard to put the dishes in. Sophie – an astronomer.

'We were just talking about you,' Maddie says and Greg turns to see Sophie coming in carrying empty bottles she has gathered.

'Hope it was good.'

'I hear you're an astronomer,' Greg says.

'Oh that,' Sophie says, putting empties back into the crate.

'Do I get to hear about it?' he asks, watching her.

Sophie straightens and looks at him. 'Sure.'

'Excellent,' Greg says, taking a couple more beers from the fridge; taking her by the elbow to steer her out of the kitchen; ignoring her protests that her chores aren't done.

'Yes, they are,' Maddie contradicts. 'Just finishing up here. Go talk astronomy.'

In the sitting room, Ned croons Neil Young songs to a guitar ever so slightly out of tune. They sidestep back to the dining room, where Jacques pores over papers with Paul, their heads together round lamplight, leaving Greg and

Sophie to sit at the table again with its still-burning candles. She brings her knees up to hug, watching him flip the beer-bottle lids.

Passing her beer, he sits himself with his back to the room, letting his eyes adjust to this dim corner and her quickening presence in it, the candle flames' reflection in the night window, the pale light in her pale hair, catching her cheekbone. Eyes meet, linger a moment until Sophie looks down at the bottle in her hand.

'So what marine mammalogy are you involved with when you're not on the seabed making enough stars to fill a universe?' she asks, looking back up at him.

He smiles. 'I suspect your astronomy is a tad more sophisticated,' he deflects. 'What is it you're working on?'

'Well – several projects.'

'For example.'

'Ah – the next observation run I'm booked onto is as part of a team gathering data to find out if there's a black hole at the centre of our galaxy.'

'Of *our* galaxy?'

'Yeah. At the centre of the Milky Way. It's not my project, I'm merely one of the minions gathering data. Feel fortunate being involved with it, though.'

He raises his eyebrows. 'Hadn't realized a black hole at the centre of our galaxy was a possibility.'

'We're not entirely sure it is.'

'So – is the earth about to be consumed?'

'Not by the black hole, if there is one, no. It's too far away. It will be the sun in a few billion years' time, when it expands into a red giant, which will almost certainly consume the earth.'

'Ah, well – I should think we will have run our course as a species well before that.'

'Really?'

'Should have thought so. So, how does the black-hole study operate?'

'Simple in a way. I mean – gathering and reducing the data requires extremely sophisticated instrumentation, but the theory behind the study is simple. Do you want me to—?' She makes a gesture of ongoing explanation.

'Yeah, yeah,' he insists.

'OK. Well, although it's not possible to *see* a black hole, you can see the effect it has on things – things on the event horizon: that's the – the lip if you like – around the edge of the black hole,' she says, running her little finger round the lip of her beer bottle. 'So, you have to measure the speed at which the stars are orbiting. We know the speed at which stars of a given mass orbit round the galaxy, but the study has revealed that stars of the same mass close into the centre are travelling *much* faster than we would expect – more than a thousand kilometres a second, which would suggest that they are being drawn towards something we can't see which is of immense gravity. Since the masses of the stars are negligible compared to the central dark mass, each orbit is basically a measure of the dark mass and they confine it to within the radius of the orbit. So if you have a large enough mass in a small enough volume, you've made the case for—'

'A black hole.'

She nods. 'Told you it was simple.'

'I'm sure that's the least of it.'

She sweeps her hair back from her face.

'There can certainly be plenty of problems getting and analysing the images. We have to superimpose thousands of images so the data-reduction system can compensate for the distortion caused by the atmosphere, for example. The project's in its fifth year now. The data so far has confirmed the high velocity at which the stars are orbiting. With luck this year should clinch the result. Other than that I spend a lot of my time studying galaxies and then there's the undergrad tuition.'

'And your galaxy work is?'

'I'm particularly interested in what happens when galaxies collide.'

He raises his eyebrows. 'I had no idea they *do* collide.'

She smiles. 'Well, they do.'

'So if the sun expanding to a red giant doesn't get us . . .'

He laughs.

'Oh, no. No galaxies around likely to come into contact with ours for some while.'

'Well, that's a relief.'

She laughs at him.

'I'm serious!' he laughingly protests. 'The destruction colliding galaxies must precipitate.'

She nods. 'Lots of *construction*, too, though. The collisions trigger giant bursts of star formation.'

'Ah – so that life can begin all over again in a few billion years' time. I suppose that might be some consolation to the highly evolved being on a planet circling a star in a galaxy that's about to be annihilated.'

'If, indeed, such a being exists.' Her smile reflects his. Warm eyes.

He shifts a little in his chair, brings an ankle up onto his knee.

'So, where do you do all this work?'

'I teach at the University of Victoria on Vancouver Island.'

'Not full-time?'

'No, no. Three mornings a week. I can use the instruments we have in Victoria almost any time. We've got two optical telescopes, but I also need others. The observation work for the black-hole project has to be done from Hawaii. I can do more of the galaxy study from there, too. And then there's work on dust discs I'm due to start in the next few months.'

'Dust discs?'

'Rings of dust round stars where planets are thought to form.'

Minutely, he raises his eyebrows.

'Isn't it difficult, getting telescope time for your work?'

'At the big telescopes, yes, it is. Really difficult. You have to make an application which a selection committee assesses for suitability and scientific merit. Whole process usually takes about six months.'

'Pretty devastating if they say no, I should think.'

'Oh, it is. The chances of success increase a bit once you get known; once you've published a bit; once you're involved in some highly regarded research. But you're right – it can be tough. Careers have foundered on the failure to secure telescope time.'

'Funding easy to come by?'

'No! Is it for you?'

He shakes his head.

'Constant worry about where the next contract's coming from.'

She nods her understanding.

'I'm two years through a five-year fellowship now, so I'm let off that hook for a while at least, but after that—' She shrugs. 'To an extent, it's a case of putting out proposals and seeing which ones attract funding and being ready to shelve the others even if they are your passion. To an extent, funding tends to follow fashion, too. Does it happen that way for you?'

'Perhaps not so much. Some funding is attached to numbers of students.'

'Well, for me, too.'

'So the courses have to appeal to the students, otherwise no students, no funding from that source. There are other sources. Conservation bodies will fund certain projects. Industry—'

'Industry?'

'Environmental-impact assessments.'

'Ah.'

'And there is some governmental funding – meeting legal requirements relating to environmental awareness and conservation. Nice when the work takes me abroad, as it sometimes does. The travel must be a bonus for you, too.'

'Yeah, I do enjoy it, although – as an astronomer – wherever you go, you end up spending much of your time at an observatory in front of computer screens. There is a move towards remote-observing, so that a telescope operator controls the instrument in line with the astronomer's requirements and the astronomer—'

'Stays at home?'

'Yes.'

'Makes a certain amount of sense, doesn't it?'

'Mmm. Not the same, though. I always like to be there to see for myself what the conditions are like. And then it's good to be around if there's some troubleshooting to do.'

'And the camaraderie?'

'Yes. You don't get to meet with other astronomers if you observe remotely. Although –' she laughs – 'because it's a fairly small fraternity, it often happens that you can trek halfway round the world only to meet up with the same crowd anyway all equally sleep-deprived and pale.'

'Did I leave my camera in here?' Elizabeth asks, busying in. 'Oh, yes, look, there it is. Could you reach it for me? Thank you, honey. You guys *have* to come listen to Ned. He's doing Bob Dylan now.'

'Oh, sure,' Sophie says.

'We will in a little while,' Greg adds.

'Well – don't be long now,' she adds, bundling off as Paul calls from across the room, 'How's it going, Elizabeth?' so that she stops to speak to him.

Sophie looks back to Greg to find his eyes already on her. She drops her gaze, looks back up again, hugs her knees more closely, feeling the fringed edge of her sarong skirt brush the bareness of her feet.

Elegant feet, he sees, before letting his eye follow the slender sweep of her arm, bare-skinned from wrist to shoulder, to the soft fabric of her sleeveless chemise, the long line of her neck where her hair is swept away.

Searching her face, he finds her eyes already on him; holds her gaze, softly.

In peripheral vision the window reflects the split image of the Frenchman, standing to stretch before stooping to gather papers.

'So,' Sophie says quietly, 'what science *are* you involved with?'

He smiles across at her. Shifts his weight in the chair.

'Like you – several projects.'

'For example.'

'I manage a photo ID database, documenting dolphin populations – very much along the lines Paul does here – just I do it in a lousy climate.

'I also teach undergrads from a field centre in south Wales, plus I supervise some postgrad work. And, like you, I spend a lot of time in front of a screen – I'm working on software which can identify cetacean species by analysing their call signatures. Plus management stuff – I'm coordinating a team of observers on fishing boats who are there to monitor the number of dolphins getting entangled and suffocating in fishing nets – which, we're pretty sure, is a lot. Then I'm helping to field-test a device which goes on fishing nets in an attempt to reduce the number of dolphins caught.'

'A kind of bird scarer for dolphins?'

'Alerter, rather than scarer. Trouble with scarers is they only seem scary for a while before the dolphins begin to regard them as a dinner gong and go charging towards them instead of away.'

'Ooops.'

'Quite. And then other bio-acoustic stuff – whatever comes along. I did some work recently attempting to assess the impact seismic testing has on dolphin activity and well-being.'

'Seismic testing – that's using compressed air, isn't it?'

'Yep. Firing it down to the seabed and monitoring what returns to the vessel in an attempt to identify oil fields. And then I've just been to an island in the east Caribbean – which is how come I've washed up here. Again, that project was environmental survey work with some bio-acoustic consider-ations.'

'And what does your wife do?'

'My wife?'

'Sorry, I . . . Your ring?'

He draws breath, 'Yes. Yes. Ella's a librarian. She works in the university library. We have a son. Sebastian. He's five.'

'How lovely,' she says, looking away, so that Greg has a sense of her slipping from him.

'Do you?' he asks.

'Do I?'

'Have children.'

'Oh. No.'

She looks down at the bottle in her hands, tracing the lip with her little finger.

More downhill slide as Paul calls across, wanting comment on some cetacean dive depth detail, as Elizabeth comes back in again, so that Greg has to indicate it's of no consequence at all as Sophie gets up, links an arm through hers, to go with her and listen to Ned. Downhill slide – he feels her slip from him – and it's right, of course, he thinks later, joining the others; she's right to remind him of Ella. Dreadful the ease with which he's all but forgotten her in these days he's been away. She's right, he thinks, glancing at her, eyes meeting across the sitting room, he – purse-lipped – nodding his acknowledgement of her well-timed reminder, looking down, sliding open the glass door; releasing the insect mesh, slinking out into the night.

West Caribbean

Three up front in a rusty pickup, Paul and Greg with Sophie in between them, and though Paul drives slowly, potholes in the unmade track pitch the vehicle; swaying their bodies so that Greg grows tense at the proximity of this woman he is so very drawn to and cannot have: her arm now close to, now brushing his; her scent in his nostrils; peach sarong opening along her honey-coloured calves. Undergrowth meets across the track, so that the vehicle noses like a boat through water or perhaps like a submarine as vegetation submerges them, too; only it's noisier, branches scraping and whacking back, thumping hard against the truck. Juno, the second-row seats to herself, makes silent snaps at foliage that drags, like fingers of seaweed, along the glass. And, given that it's warm already, it's good, Sophie thinks, that the rusted-open windows won't close; until a banana spider, larger than the outstretched span of her hand, is catapulted in through the jammed-open space to land squarely and with a little thud in her lap.

'Shit!' she yells, leaping in the cab's confines, so that Greg jumps, too.

'Where'd he go?' Greg laughs, steadying her, the spider thrown to the floor as Sophie draws her legs up fast.

'Shit! Do they bite?'

'Oh, he's OK,' Paul reassures her, groping at his feet to find where the mighty spider landed. 'He's OK. He won't hurt you.'

There is a clearing still, of sorts, around the wooden cabin that used to be Paul's home. The forest has grown up to the veranda, though: branches like long arms reaching in.

'You know not to come into contact with this, don't you?' Paul asks Sophie as they get down from the truck. He points to the leaf of a particular tree, rounded with a prominent central vein.

'Poisonwood,' Sophie supplies.

'I told you already, didn't I?'

'You did, but it's good to be reminded.'

'It's just that it only takes the least contact with it and you'd be stuck with the mother of all itches and a rash which spreads like wildfire and inevitably gets infected.'

'You said.'

Paul laughs. 'I did, didn't I?'

'Just call him Captain Caring,' Greg says, grabbing the nape of Paul's neck as he passes, then calling after him,

'Need a hand in there?' as Paul disappears inside the building.

'Nah. They *must* be here somewheres.'

'Oh, look, Sophie,' Greg whispers as she comes up the wooden steps beside him.

'Where?' she says, trying to follow his gaze out into the forest.

Greg catches her elbow, brings his head next to hers, manoeuvres her gently. 'There.'

'Oh, yes!' Against the density of foliage where shafts of sunlight pierce through the canopy, the fast, darting flight catches her eye, that and the iridescent green of the plumage. Its body no longer than her middle finger and scarcely as broad, the bird hovers by blooms; flits from branch to branch. In hovering, she sees its long, thin bill.

'Hummingbird?' she queries, leaning to him as she lifts her mouth to whisper in his ear.

'Yes. Cuban emerald.'

He glances down at her face as she watches the tiny thing, her fair brow beneath the tangled hair; his hand beneath her elbow still, the weight of her arm resting in it.

'Precious thing,' she says, glancing at him, a full look a moment, a little smile, a move away at the sound of Paul's footsteps on the hollow wooden floor.

'Knew I'd left them here,' Paul says, re-emerging from the darkness of the hut, a canvas-wrapped bundle of outboard-motor parts in his arms. 'I'll move out of here properly one day.'

Greg glances into the building: undergrowth pushing at the little window in the far wall; dusty wooden floor; a mattress on a metal bed; tin oil lamp on the table.

'You guys want that dip before breakfast?' Paul asks, putting the bundle in the back of the truck.

Through a forest raucous with parrot call, they do a side-stepping dance, avoiding ubiquitous poisonwood over the short distance down to the sea. Moments to remember in following her: forest sun dappling her pale skin, gilding her hair; her litheness in avoiding poisonwood trees; her quick smile; her laughter; the glance of her eyes seeking his.

They emerge from vegetation a few metres above sea level, out into full sunlight to overlook the beach and the rich brilliance of aquamarine.

'Doesn't anyone live round here?' Sophie asks, finding densely treed coastline stretches from the beach in both directions.

'Two houses about four miles that way as the crow flies,' Paul says. 'You have to go back up to the road and down again to reach them, though, so more than twenty miles by truck.'

'Amazing place to have lived, Paul,' Sophie observes.

'Sure is,' he says, starting to jog down the dunes with Juno chasing his heels. 'Last one in has to—' but his words are lost: muffled by the shirt he pulls over his head.

'Paul lived here with his girlfriend,' Greg says as he and Sophie reach flatter terrain. 'Broke up about six months ago.'

'Ah,' Sophie says, watching Paul run into the water. 'Must be difficult for him to come back here, don't you think?'

'I think it probably is.'

He stoops to pick up a conch shell. Brought up the sand by a stormy sea, the opulent shells litter the beach, left in curved line upon curved line. Balancing the huge shell in both hands, Greg presents it to her, watches as she turns the thing over, the creamy-white outer shell rounding to pale then livid pink: shiny, glossy, inward-turning. She looks up into his eyes a long moment.

There's the touch of morning sun on her skin, the beautiful sun-freckled brown of Greg's shoulders as he wades into the sea ahead of her, his well-toned flesh and the beauty of the water, her sense of her own body slim and healthful as she peels off her shirt and follows him in.

'Is it a good moment to say I'm not the best of swimmers?' She laughs.

'*What*?' Greg says, turning in the water, his breath catching at the sight of her: the soft swell of bikinied breasts, the slender slight swell of her belly. 'Not a good swimmer?'

'Well, not as good as you, for sure. Never even *thought* about making underwater galaxies,' she says, smiling, wading her thighs through water towards him. 'I can swim well enough for this, though.'

Finding the seabed, he stands as she nears him, the water slick on his shoulders. 'I was going to say – as part of the volunteer team, I should think Paul has put you all to the test, hasn't he?' Greg says, eyes on eyes across the little distance.

'You bet.' She trails aside a strand of hair. 'Six lengths of the beach without stopping followed by fifteen minutes' flotation.'

'There you go, then. You'll do.'

He watches her as she glides away into a reasonable breaststroke – nicely timed – then pushes into the water to follow her.

There's the skin of his arms, browned from Sombrero, as he stretches out his body in the pale translucent blue. There's the sun's warmth and the water's warmth, the light's dance and the sea's salty buoyancy and – underwater – there's white, ribbed sand and the kick of her pale legs, sun-dappled through the water now. Surfacing, he sees her head bob before him, the froth of her pale hair floating on water like so much sea-spun spume.

They swim the length of the little beach till, too soon, Paul is calling them – a keen sense of childhood rekindled: the heaven that is summertime play; not wanting to be called in.

'Sorry, guys,' Paul says as they catch up with him on the dunes. 'Captain Caring feeling the need to get back to HQ.'

'It's fine, Paul,' Greg assures him, turning to take a last glance at the beach. 'In any case – good time to get out of the water,' he says, pointing back to movement beneath the surface of the sea: the fast-moving, cruising-dark stealth of a shark.

It's only the first few miles of track which are quite so overgrown. Once at the junction, although the dirt road is deeply rutted still, the undergrowth is tamer.

'Guys come through here quite a bit,' Paul says. 'There's a cove they use for fishing and then there are feral pigs they hunt. And – oh – here they *a-r-e*,' he drawls, bringing the truck to a halt at a corner where the track is blocked by another pickup. 'Or at least here's their vehicle.'

Deserted.

Greg peers to see any possible way round, but the tree trunks are dense here, close to the road. Paul switches the engine off, tries the horn.

'They might have left the keys in,' Sophie suggests.

A thump that sets the truck rocking. A thump from the side. Then frenzied, demented, angry barking, big dogs' faces at the jammed-open window. Greg whips his arm away, shrinks back from the long-toothed heads, two dogs, then three and – from the back seat – Juno, straining retaliation, teeth bared in hideous snarling, so that Paul reaches an arm back to restrain her.

'Jesus. Where the fuck are these guys?'

Through the forest they saunter. Two white men. One with a jerrycan. The other with a gun. The nearest nods brief recognition to Paul.

'Good attack dogs you got there!' Paul sings loudly.

The man with the jerrycan bashes it on the backs of the dogs, who yelp and cower. 'Get in the truck,' he snarls at them, squeezing past Paul's pickup.

It's Paul who backs, round the corner and a few hundred yards more to where the trucks can pass.

'Caught anything?' Paul asks as the windows draw level.

'Not yet anyways,' the driver says, his eyes on Sophie's breasts.

'Still. Good day for it,' Paul says, driving on past the dogs in the back of the other truck, who lean to strain out their furious barking.

Two miles more and the smoke begins; seeping out across the roadway.

'Our friends' handiwork,' Paul comments.

'They started this?'

Paul nods. 'Drives the piggies out so they can take a shot at them. Leaves them less cover once the fire's been through.'

'Drives everything out, I should think,' Greg comments. 'Are we still in the national park?'

'Yup.'

'I thought there are ground-nesting parrots here.'

'There are. Endangered species.'

Sophie thinks, too, of the hummingbirds.

'Will you report this?'

'No point. These guys know where I live and in any case the police wouldn't do anything. These guys know where the police live, too. Still – hey – it gives the poison-wood a boost. Grows back faster than anything else,' Paul says, driving aside from where flames dance at the edge of the track, licking up the trunks of trees, catching branches which overhang.

'Isn't there a danger those guys'll get cut off by this fire?' Sophie asks.

Paul laughs. 'We can but hope.'

'You OK?' Greg asks her.

'Sure.' She laughs, though she's glad to have Greg close beside her. 'You?'

'Yep. You OK, Paul?'

'Hell, yes,' Paul sings out. 'Always like meeting with the neighbours.'

""Welcome home!' the people sang.

""Welcome home!' the queen said as they landed.

""'Welcome home!' said a dragon, who was sitting at the queen's side.

""'Oh!' said the dragon. 'Isn't that a dragon?' He'd never seen another one of those before.

""'Of course it's a dragon,' the princess said. 'This is Bethsheba,' she continued, introducing the dragon to the other dragon first. 'And this is my mother, the queen.'""

Greg hunches the phone to his ear, freeing his hand to turn the page of the manuscript where it rests on the inflatable hull. He feels the rubberized fabric is scorching: mid-afternoon heat of the Caribbean sun.

""'Oh, yes,' the queen said later at tea, 'it's always an honour to have a dragon about the place.'

""'Absolutely,' said the king, who, the dragon thought, was an awful lot nicer now they'd arrived home. 'Useful little chaps to have around. Got a frozen pipe needs thawing, bit of a snowfall needs clearing away, want to get through the ice to do a spot of fishing, nothing can beat a dragon, don't you know. And as for building – perfect little wizards when it comes to cutting ice.'

"'Bethsheba tapped a claw upon the table. 'I think we might do a little sightseeing,' she said.'"

Someone clambers back on board from swimming, spraying a shower of cool droplets onto Greg's sun-warmed back.

""'Of *course* you will,' the queen sang jauntily, while

positively glaring at the king. 'We'll miss you when you return to Nadria.'

"'An awful lot of people seem to say that here, the dragon thought, as he and Bethsheba whizzed down sloping ice corridors so wonderfully cool to the feet.

"'"We'll miss you when you return to Nadria,' said the doorman, as he let the dragons out into ice gardens where gardeners worked to sculpt ice trees.

"'"We'll miss you when you return to Nadria,' said the soldier, opening the ice palace gate.

"'"We'll miss you when you return to Nadria,' whispered people on the city streets, pausing respectfully to watch the dragons pass.

"'"What's all this about Nadria?' the dragon asked.

"'Bethsheba looked at him in amazement. 'You really don't know, do you?'"

'I have to stop there, Seb.'

'O-o-h-h-h,' protest voices behind him, so that, turning, Greg grins to see a little semicircle of eavesdroppers listening in on the story, Sophie among them: beautiful, dropping her gaze away.

'*Just a little bit more*,' Elizabeth stage-whispers.

'Sorry, Seb?' Greg asks down the phone, turning away to regain concentration. 'Oh, yes. We've just stopped for a break, but we've seen about twelve bottlenose dolphins and a Blainville's beaked whale and three pilot whales. Yep,

Seb, they're all on your chart and I'm home the day after tomorrow. Yes, not tomorrow, the day after tomorrow, on Saturday, so I can show you then, OK?'

He hears the little splash and splatter of someone slipping back into the water.

'You bet, Seb. Sleep tight, now, monster,' he says, clicking off the phone and turning, he sees it is Sophie who has gone.

The sun does its setting as they near the home shore and find themselves among a pod of dolphins: bottlenose adults and juveniles and two or three recent calves. Maddie works to get the dorsal-fin pictures, but it's difficult: about twenty animals surrounding the boat, showing off, displaying and leaping and then the light fading, sending the westward sky and sea golden, while in the east, behind shoreline palm trees, a silver moon rises, huge and only two days past full, littering silver light onto the sea, so that it's impossible to know which way to look first – there where the dolphins' backs, silvered with moonlight, round against deepening blue or there, where their black silhouettes overlay rich ochres and reds. Science slides and – changing cameras – Maddie starts to take a different type of picture.

'It's ballet,' Sophie breathes to Greg as two nearby dolphins dive in perfect symmetry.

'They know how to celebrate, don't they?' Greg says at

her side, feeling her hand lightly touch his arm, feeling her weight shift towards him.

For minutes more they stay spellbound, then in an instant the dolphins are gone, as if the sea is suddenly empty of them. No sound. The gathering night is suddenly chill, the sun's colours quickly draining and Paul fires the engine up, pushing them on through darkening air. She must be cold, Greg thinks and reaches out his hand to where she sits beside and ahead of him, touching her shoulder; no words possible over the engine's drone. Her flesh feels cool through the thinness of its covering as he draws her body back towards him: a simple sliding move down the boat's raised angle as it planes.

There's the gentle bumping of the boat across the water's calm; his wide breast warm through his shirt against her back. She sighs as she leans her weight against him, her shivering subsiding as they share their bodies' warmth.

Nearing the beach, he must let her go; help with the gear off-loading as before. An offshore breeze brings an acrid scent: distant charring forest. And hey, Paul indicates as he jumps down at the edge of the water, isn't that smoke – not cloud – that drifts across the moon?

On shore, hot showers then more team work: the collating data team; the input onto the computer team; the cooking team; the equipment repair team. The never on the same team. He yearns to take her aside.

He yearns to take her aside and say what?
He settles badly in his bunk.
Home the day after tomorrow.

West Caribbean

A brown face at the breakfast back door; a child's face pressed against frosted glass.

'Hi there, Charlie,' Maddie sings. 'Come on in. Did you have breakfast already?'

The boy, seven or eight years old, slips into the room, bare feet; a leg of his brightly coloured shorts rucked up. His big brown eyes move from face to face, then to the buttered toast Maddie proffers.

'Hi, Charlie,' Paul says, coming in to refill the coffee jug.

Charlie takes the piece of toast; the butter greasy on his fingers. 'There's a whale on the beach,' he says before sinking his teeth in the toasted crust.

The little breakfast hubbub stops.

'On the beach here, Charlie?' Maddie asks.

Charlie nods, chewing.

Old sheets and towels and buckets and gel are the best they can do on the falling tide, the twelve-foot whale too well aground to move till the tide comes back to refloat her, so, meantime, not letting the skin dry is paramount and they scurry to soak linen, placing it over the whale they feared for a moment might be dead, but no, there again comes the sudden blow out of air, the swift sucking in, don't let the water into the blowhole and, yes, smear more gel there and round the rim of the weeping eyes, yes, more water, keep it coming, careful not to step on that pectoral fin, Ian. *Ian*, the pectoral fin.

What do you think? Greg and Paul's eyes ask each other's once their aid is in place.

'Leastways she's got the sense not to thrash around. No point thrashing.'

Greg nods agreement. 'Breathing rate's been constant since we got here.'

'So what is she?' Elizabeth asks, kneeling at the whale's head, where she's been all along.

'Minke. Juvenile – fortunately. We wouldn't stand much chance of refloating an adult. They grow to thirty feet or more.'

'Looks in very good nick.'

'Was before she rode up here.'

'You have to worry about their internal organs getting damaged by the pressure of their own weight when the animal's not supported by water,' Anna explains.

'So what brought her up ashore?'

'Couldn't say.'

'What time's high water, Paul?'

''Bout midday.'

Then Maddie's there, coming back from the house, where she's been for more towels, a sense of hurry on her face. 'There's another one,' she calls.

'*What?*'

'A phone message to say there's another stranding about a mile north of here. Sounds like a goose-beaked whale.'

'A different *species*?'

'Sounds like it.'

'You get many strand here?'

'No. One a year. In the whole Bahamian chain of islands. Tops.'

'And multiple strandings are nearly always the same species. One will follow others in. Don't usually get different species.'

Paul and Greg look at one another.

'Maybe the description's wrong. Maybe it's another minke.'

'They seemed pretty sure. Said it was a whale with a snout.'

'We'd better get up there. Can you keep this one going here, Anna, and I'll go take a look at the other one? Track runs by the sea there, so it shouldn't take long to reach it. What are we now? Ten o'clock. Should make it back easy by mid-day and we'll have a go at refloating this guy.'

And then Paul's mobile rings. News of another one. A dolphin this time, stranded on a nearby cay.

Paul and Greg look at one another. What the fuck is going on?

They split into three teams, Paul's to check out the beaked whale, Anna's to keep the minke stable while Greg's team takes the boat to the island Paul has pointed out, a twenty-minute zip across water to find the stranded dolphin.

They see it at the water's edge – a little crowd of locals gathered round the animal – a sleekly dappled Atlantic spotted dolphin, its tail fluke moving so that, at a distance still, Greg thinks there might be some chance, till he sees the tail is being lifted only by the water's rise and fall.

Landing, he gets no response to a touch round the blow-hole. No response to a touch of the eye. No breath, the locals say, for an hour or so.

A little girl with an empty margarine container scoops up water and splashes it down on the dead dolphin.

'She's been doing a great job,' Greg says as her mother lifts her out of the way.

Automatically he checks for signs of fishing-industry trauma. He finds none. The practice different on these islands. No gill nets. No mid-water trawlers. No by-catch. He finds no outward signs of injury. He takes the rope Sophie brings from the boat. Sophie on his team at last. Shame the brief has turned out to be grim.

'OK, all we can do now is take him home.'

'How do we do that?' Elizabeth asks.

'There might be enough of us to haul him across the bow of the boat,' he says, counting heads: Ned, Elizabeth, Sophie, four teenage lads on the beach keen to help and the woman with the little girl. Nine including him. It may not be enough for a few hundred pounds of dolphin. 'No heroics, OK?' he says, his hand on the shoulder of the tallest boy. 'This is quite a big animal we'll be trying to shift, so let's make sure we don't hurt ourselves in the process. If we can't bring him across the bow easily, we can always tow him along behind the boat.'

He ties a rope round the dolphin's tail stock; uses the boat to drag him backwards into the water; noses the boat onto the beach. At first it doesn't seem that it can happen; the rope snagging across the boat; the boat sliding away. They persevere: the boat driven a little further up the beach; Elizabeth in the water, keeping the body at right angles to the hull; Sophie and one of the boys on board, making sure the rope and the body can be pulled freely. On the boat's other side, the three black boys and two white men haul. Half on board, the tail fluke snags, catching beneath the inflated hull, so that they must stop hauling while Sophie and the boy lift the tail fluke free. Then suddenly it's done, the dolphin's body sliding across the hull, then slithering round so that its head slumps onto the floor of the boat, its tail fluke draped over the side. Not perfect, but good enough and they can travel at good speed now, Greg keen to get the boat back, in case it's needed for the other whales.

'What you got?' Paul's voice asks, coming over the radio's fuzz as Greg helms the boat home.

'Dead Atlantic spotted dolphin. Adult male.'

'Any visible damage?'

'Only where we've put the rope on him. What about you?'

'Juvenile Blainville's. Still with us. Anyways, we're coming up to high tide here and we could use some help to refloat these two. How near are you to setting off?'

'We're on our way already. Got the dolphin more or less across the boat, which means it's handling like a car with a flat, but we shouldn't be long. What plans do you have for this one?'

'Need to get it iced down as soon as we can, but I think it'll have to wait until we've got these two back out. Perhaps if you could slip him into the water near where the minke is and anchor him down and leave Ned and Elizabeth to help Anna, Jacques and Maddie out, and then come on here by boat. Just follow the coast up, you can't miss us.'

'Interesting to think about the big picture, Paul.'

'Isn't it? I'm gonna be on the phone once we've got these guys back in the water.'

A few minutes later the VHF crackles into life again. Paul. Another reported beaked whale stranding.

By midday the tally is seven, four different species; spread out over a few miles, so it's difficult to know which way to go first. The minke Anna's team was with refloats well and swims strongly out. The Blainville's beaked whale doesn't. Three times they float her off, three times she swims in a left-handed circle, coming back to strand again, cutting herself again on rock, so the water stains red and sharks – drawn to the smell of blood – have to be fended off with paddles from kayaks.

Once more they put the tarp around her, rocking her over first onto one side, sliding the tarpaulin under, then rocking her the other way till they have her in a sling: disorientated, distressed, damaged thing.

'I think we should try taking her much further out before we release her.'

So they wade into the water, chest deep, to hold her alongside the boat before motoring ever so slowly to where the pale blue water deepens, only then letting her go. She lies in the water a time, a shallow breath out and in; a single, feeble flap of the tail fluke, a few minutes stillness, then another.

*

The whale restrands and dies on the beach 200 metres from the house, metres from where the minke whale stranded in the early morning. Of the four now known dead, the dolphin could be shipped out for post-mortem, but the other three are much too large and so – at Paul's contact – the pathologist comes, catching the afternoon flight from the mainland, Maddie picking him up from the airport. Once on the beach, methodically he takes the head to pieces.

There's the digging-a-trench-in-the-white-sand team: a deep trench to bury the whale bits in that come, unwanted, from the pathologist's knife. Bits to save – eyes, teeth, skin – are placed by careful rubber-gloved hands into neatly labelled polythene, then into a cooler box with ice. Like sandwiches at a seaside picnic. Only the guest is being dismembered and it needs a saw to get through the skull.

Sophie – not sure how much she wants to witness – walks a little way to gather the sheets they used for the minke, rinsing the sand-encrusted things in the sea; letting the breeze and the talk drift over.

'It's a bit like CCTV in the parking lot,' she hears Paul's voice say. 'If you know there's been some incident, you want to make sure the tape doesn't get wiped, so I just asked guys in the navy department if they could be sure to hold on to the underwater sound recordings from their hydrophones for the last couple of days.'

There's another wet towel to pick up.

'Oh – all the time,' Paul's voice says. 'Part of their passive surveillance for submarines. It's their *active* surveillance that we suspect causes the problem.'

And there, another sodden sheet.

'Yeah – a *really* loud noise underwater. Not sure yet if it causes the whales physical damage, or if it just makes them panic and take off.'

Someone says something Sophie doesn't hear. Then Paul's laugh reaches her. 'Oh – they're not gonna give me *that* kind of information.'

The sheets are awkward in the water and Maddie comes. A hand lightly on her shoulder; some word of help offered so that the two of them work together to rinse out and wring out and place in the tarp, the sheets they fold at the water's edge.

The high, thin beep of a watch alarm sounds. Greg's. She heard it yesterday on the boat. She sees him switch the thing off, reach to his pocket for the mobile phone he's borrowed from Paul, leaving his work with the shovel for a time to phone his son at bedtime.

'I don't suppose astronomy ever gets this bloody,' Greg says, a few minutes later, arriving at her side as she stands to peer gingerly at the dissected head.

'No,' she says, glancing at him. 'Or only when we're fighting over data. Not very scientific of me,' she adds, knowing he's noticed her hanging back.

'Being affected by this? Why should you be immune? It's not your field, and even for those of us whose field it is –' he gives her the briefest of grim smiles – 'it's not exactly the state we relish seeing them in.'

'How was Sebastian?'

'Wanted to know – as he always does – if I'd seen any whales or dolphins.'

'Ah.'

She nods towards the exposed whale brain, the skull placed aside, upturned, like some monstrous empty nut shell. 'Anything exceptional here?'

'Yes. Some brain haemorrhage,' he says, indicating the area.

'And in the *ears*,' Gordon, the pathologist suddenly announces. 'Paul!' he calls, so that Paul hurries across. 'Let's get some more pictures in here, can we? Looks like there's been haemorrhaging in the ear canals.'

Greg and Paul look at one another.

'Let's get some *really* good photographs.'

By sundown the tally has reached eleven. Five they've dealt with and news of six more: two returned by locals to the sea, four more heard of that evening, stranded and almost certainly dead.

The Atlantic spotted dolphin's in the freezer, along with the head of a Cuvier's beaked whale. Gordon has postmortemed three others, so they're running out of places to put the samples: eyes, ears, organ tissue, teeth, skin, blubber, stomach contents.

Sophie takes it upon herself to cook.

'Mind which freezer you go to Sophie!'

'Thanks for that, Ned.'

A glass of wine in, she suddenly finds she's thinking of her mother. No! More – she's *behaving* like her mother: when things get grim, be busy in the kitchen; as if order could be restored through nourishment.

Again it's Maddie who comes to lend a hand.

'It's not your turn either, is it, Maddie?'

'No. It's Paul's by rights, but he needs to be on the phone right now and besides . . .'

Ah, well. Not the only one, then, wanting to dole out nourishment.

'Anything coming from Paul's phone calls?'

Maddie nods. 'He's just heard the navy were near here on exercise last night.'

'So is it conclusive, then, about the naval activity causing these whales to strand?' Elizabeth asks, breaking the silence at the dinner table: eleven weary people, eating late by candlelight.

Sophie looks up, waiting for the answer.

'No, no,' Gordon says, his round glasses catching the candlelight. 'We can't be certain of anything yet.'

Paul clears his throat. 'There does seem to be something of a history, though, of this kind of naval activity coinciding with atypical mass strandings. There's an underwater submarine detection device—'

'We don't know that they were using that here,' Gordon interrupts.

'Known as low-frequency active sonar,' Paul continues, calmly 'which sends out a very loud signal underwater and the vessel that sends it out measures the signal which returns, allowing it to detect any submarine in the signal's path.'

'It's worth remembering sound behaves very differently underwater from the way it behaves in air,' Greg adds. 'It travels much faster underwater, so that it's possible for them to detect subs at some distance.'

'There was a stranding in Greece—' Paul says.

'And in the Canaries before that,' Greg adds.

Paul nods. 'Where this kind of naval activity was taking place. In the Greek stranding twelve Cuvier's beaked whales died. How many was it in Fuerteventura?' he asks Greg.

'The total in 1989 was twenty-four. I forget the ones before that.'

'Was there the sort of brain and ear haemmorhage that we've seen today?' Sophie asks.

'There's no data on that. No one thought to look for it then. Why should they? It hadn't really been thought possible at that stage.'

'But it has since?'

Paul nods. 'Hence Gordon's here. He's the ear man. World expert.'

'But as I say,' Gordon continues, 'nothing conclusive yet.'

'Is there anything further you can do which might come up with a conclusive answer?' Sophie asks him.

'Yeah. We can put the whale head through the CAT scan back at the university and that should give us a clear idea of whether or not blood has been forced into places it wouldn't normally go, letting us know if it's a pressure trauma which has caused it.'

'Like a very loud sound,' Ned suggests.

'Yes. We can also decalcify the ear bones and make histological slides which will show us the same thing: where blood and brain fluid has been forced through – if it has. As I say, nothing conclusive yet.'

'But it's such a co*incidence*,' Elizabeth says.

'Yes, but, of itself, that's not conclusive,' Gordon says.

'Where do you get your funding from?' Sophie asks suddenly and from the corner of her eye sees Greg break into a grin.

'There are various sponsors of the project,' Gordon says.

'Sixty per cent US Navy, isn't it, Gordon?' Paul supplies.

'It is one of the ways the navy are meeting their environmental responsibilities, yes.'

There's a little silence.

'Well, doesn't that make it a bit difficult for you – being funded by the people who might be responsible for this?' Elizabeth asks.

Another pause in which Gordon strokes his moustache.

'No, no,' Paul supplies for him. 'Bit like that project Greg did for the oil company. When he identified the detrimental effect their testing was having on the dolphin population, you went right ahead and published your findings, isn't that right, Greg?'

'Absolutely. After all, science isn't science if you let a minor detail like who's funding you come into the equation.'

'And they didn't withdraw their funding, did they?' Paul grins, playing stooge.

'No, no. Just somehow forgot to renew my contract.'

'Inefficient admin, probably.'

'Oh – almost certainly. Can't get the staff.'

Soon before dawn, Sophie fights into wakening; dripping sweat, sobbing. Oh, God! Others in the room to hear! Sleep-drunk, she staggers down the bunk ladder, room dark, feet stumbling, arms sleep-weak – shit! Only this much – Richie fell. Holding her sobs, the press of nightmare still – her effort desperate to claw up weight, too much weight, inert weight: a dying dolphin, Richie in his chair, impotent flip of the dolphin tail, useless flop of Richie's arms, heave him up, his dolphin dead-weight. Sinews scream. She drops him and his head hits concrete, his skull cracking open neatly in two, fluid flooding out, her father peering at the bloodied brain. *That won't do, Sophie, that won't do.*

At the outer door, she gulps breath, the door latch not giving to her sleep-feeble fingers; not giving, then – sickening effort – the latch turns, sliding the glass door, stepping against forgotten insect mesh, her foot, her face against the metal-gauze grid, fingers fumbling to unlatch the screen, which gives, releasing her, outside, warm air, heart thumping, letting go of her sobbing, *it's all right, it's all right, it's a dream, that's all, just a dream, just a dream, calm yourself, calm.*

'Sophie?' Greg's voice behind her.

'It's all right,' she blurts out, wondering however she missed the sound of the door.

'Are you OK?' His voice, nearer.

'Yes,' she insists, her breath catching still.

'Bad dream?'

She nods in the darkness, new tears welling. 'I've woken you,' she pushes out.

'No. I wasn't sleeping.'

She feels the lightest touch on her shoulder. However did he find her in the dark?

'It's OK,' he soothes, bringing her to him, enfolding her. 'It's OK, now. It's OK.' He waits, holding her, feeling the stumbling rhythm of her breathing. 'We had such a day of it yesterday,' he murmurs, swaying his body to rock her a little, 'it's not surprising there have been some bad dreams.'

'Which my psyche utilizes to full bloody advantage,' she spits out, turning – her head against him still – rubbing her wrist across her eyes, 'to torment me in new and excruciating ways.'

He gives a soft grunt of laughter in her hair.

'That'll teach you to have such a resourceful psyche.'

He feels her deep shuddered breath intake; feels her body warm against his; feels the sharp bite of sand flies at his ankle, rubs them away with his foot.

'You OK?'

She nods her head against him. He feels it as a nuzzle at his neck; feels the spareness of her naked shoulders; feels the cadence of her breathing lengthen; the soft press of breasts through her shirt.

He releases her a little, only to find she leans her weight towards him, so that he holds her again; detail emerging as the grey dawn lightens: the white shoe-string strap of her nightdress lying askew across her shoulder. Turning his face, he rests his cheek lightly on the softness of her hair, closes his eyes, keeping his touch lightly round her, hearing his breath give voice to her name.

'What time is your flight?' she whispers against him.

He pauses, not wanting the moment broken.

'Greg?'

'Ten thirty.'

'A.m.?'

He nods his head against hers.

She can begin to make out his shirt's colouring now, blue with some darker block of colour. She closes her eyes; brings her face closer against the fabric, breathing in the smell of him.

'Well, Greg – that's pretty lousy timing.'

They walk, barefoot in the sand, stars disappearing with the rosing glow of dawn. The whale carcass is at their backs. Greg glances over his shoulder. In the half-light, the headless gutted hulk could be some beached and half-buried hull. Let that illusion lie for now. Far better things to think of. He stops to hold her face with his hand, running his thumb beneath her eye.

'I thought of changing my flight.'

'Did you?'

'I did, Sophie,' he says, letting his eyes explore her face.

He drops his hand and they stroll slowly on.

'I thought – in the circumstances – Paul could use having me around. Thought Seb could last out a day or two more without his father. Thought the students could do without their tutor for the first couple of days. Thought perhaps the problem lurking with the observer programme could go on hold for a time.'

'Is there a problem?'

He waves a hand dismissively. 'So it seems from my e-mails. One of the observers not wanting to go out again until they've spoken with me.'

'Doesn't that mess the whole programme up?'

'It doesn't help.'

'But you didn't – change your flight?'

He shakes his head. Stops to touch her face again, stroking hair from her forehead and eye. 'Didn't think my judgement could be trusted, Sophie. Wasn't sure I wanted to stay for professional reasons.'

He shouldn't touch her like that, then, she thinks, as her face mutinies nonetheless, nudging against his palm. She turns away, wanting him, walks on a pace, so that he walks, too, beside her. All the while the light comes up, revealing more of them both to one another – the white filigree fabric of her nightdress blown about her ankles, the blue of his shirt that's faded lilac after all. She turns her eyes to scan the sea, locates the little fishing boat whose engine she can hear a long way out across calm water.

'What about your family, Greg?'

'Ella, do you mean?'

'Ella, then.'

Greg shakes his head. 'Ella wouldn't miss me. Oh, well, for childcare perhaps. I'm useful to her for that.'

'Nothing else?'

He shrugs. 'She has a part-time salary, plus she has income from her grandfather's trust, so she certainly doesn't need me for my money and she makes it fairly clear these days she finds my body pretty distasteful.'

'*Does* she?' Sophie asks, then blushes and laughs at her revealing emphasis. 'Well, there's simply no accounting for taste,' she says, laughing with him at his broadening grin. She looks down. Walks slowly on.

'Weren't you going to gather more shells for Sebastian?'

Thrown by her changing of the subject, he says nothing.

'Weren't you?'

'I'd like to add a couple more at some stage this morning.'

'Well, then,' she says, 'sun's up.'

He accepts her distancing and they pace the beach a while, a few feet from one another, searching, eyes downcast, till something white catches the corner of his eye. Some garment left on the beach. Somehow familiar. It's not her nightdress, is it?

Looking up, he sees her wading out into the sea, stripped to the nothing she was wearing underneath, pale-skinned buttocks high and tight, arms akimbo at the water's rising. He worries about seepage into the sea from the whale carcass further down the beach. Perhaps recent enough for it not to be a problem yet, plus the thing is currently high and dry, but he must warn her nonetheless.

He watches the rise and fall and rise and fall of her head and shoulders in the water and he aches to join her, but – feeling uninvited – instead resumes his search for shells. He watches, though, when she comes from the sea bearing something she stoops to pick up from the surf; walking – taut, leggy thing – to where her clothing lies, wet hair straggling on her shoulder, the shine of droplets on wet-skinned breasts. She slips the nightdress over her head, rubbing her wet face once against her arm as she walks towards him.

'How's this for Sebastian?' she asks, placing something in his hands – the light, fragile brittleness of a fan-shaped shell.

He has a three-hour wait at Miami airport for his connecting flight back to London. He doesn't pace this time, just sits, staring into nothingness, a knot of sickness in the pit of his stomach; leaving his seat at some stage to eat, thinking that will mask it, which it does, a bit.

He thinks of the Cuvier's beaked whale they stopped off to leave the pathologist with. Reported to them this morning, it was on their way to the island's airport for Greg's flight out and the charter plane Paul had hired to scour the coastline in a search for more corpses. The beached Cuvier's had been attacked by sharks – it's dorsal fin, pectoral fins and tail fluke all gone; bitten off while the animal was alive so that blood had pumped out and very little was left in its body.

'Tissues should be in fresh condition for you, then, Gordon, seeing as this one is totally bled out,' Paul said as they left the pathologist to it.

He feels a traitor. That's it, Greg reasons. His sense of sickness. He feels a traitor – leaving Paul to it.

'Hey, but you've been great,' Paul had said at the island airport, distracted, flushed, hurrying to meet his own rendezvous.

Greg takes out his laptop. Might as well use the time – the Sombrero report he'll be pushed to get to once he's home. He boots the computer up and opens files, but only sits staring at a darkened screen, thinking instead of Sophie on the beach: their conversation as they walked back before breakfast – or monologue more like – *his* monologue warning her against swimming now that the whale carcass is here and even after the council have been to bury the remains in the sand, it's most likely that oils will seep to the surface, he'd told her, bringing God knows what contaminants with them. And from there he'd got onto toxins passing up through the food chain, being stored in the blubber of top predators like this whale on the beach; how stranded animals that wash up from the North Sea have to be treated as toxic waste: their bodies burdened with heavy metals and organochlorides –

did he wax lyrical or what? – DDT, PCBs – toxins off-loading in the milk of the mother – her life's accumulation unwittingly dumped as she suckles her firstborn; mother's milk the opposite of safe, he'd said, the resulting compromised immune system leaving the youngster little defence against disease; repeated to a lesser extent with the next born, but to some extent with all of them.

Christ, Greg!

He snaps the lid of the computer closed.

Of all the things he could have said.

Nearing the house, they could see the flap and fight of turkey vultures round the carcass. He *had* tried then, a last-ditch attempt – 'Sophie, I—' – only she had stopped him, literally, a finger to his lips. And what was it she said?

The ding-dong over the airport Tannoy. His flight to London called.

What was is she said?

'What happened here?'

No – not that bit –

He moves to ease the stiffness of his neck; half opens his eyes as the man from the central seat clambers over him.

Not that bit. What was it she said later – when she put her finger on my mouth.

Sleep-sliding, memory flounders, meanders through its own thoughts.

'What happened here?' she had asked, tracing a finger along the jagged scar on his forearm.

He had puffed himself up: mock machismo. 'Oh, you know. Close encounter with a great white.'

'*Really*? That's shark bite?'

He had laughed at her. 'No.' And she had thumped him on the shoulder, so that he laughed again and feigned great injury. 'Owww!'

'*What*, then?'

He held his hands up in surrender. 'Scrap metal. A farmer had thrown some into a hedge and I was stupid enough to fall onto it. I was ten or something. My father had to stitch my arm back together.'

'Your father's a doctor?'

'Yep.'

'So's mine.'

No – not that bit.

He moves again, resettles the pillow.

It was later. What did she say when I tried to tell her – when she stopped me?

'Why don't you take one for him?'

Not then –

'Why don't you take one for him?'

He had shaken his head, looking with regret at the queen conch shell, *Strombus gigas*, knowing Seb would simply love it. It was the only one Greg had seen on this beach, not like the other day, the day before yesterday, when the beach on the opposite side of the island had been simply littered with them.

'Endangered species. They're on the CITES list now.

'CITES?'

'Convention on International Trade in Endangered Species. You have to apply for an export permit to ship one out.'

'We saw so many yesterday.'

'Seems daft, doesn't it? After all, the creature is dead, it's just a shell lying around that will get ground down to nothing. It's about creating markets, though, or rather not creating them. If someone were to scoop up that lot we saw and sell them, a demand would be re-established and, before you know it, people would be fishing for live ones to meet the export trade. Paul says they're pretty hot on it round here now, thank heavens. Actually locked some tourists up for a time who were found with one of these in their bags.'

'I could do it for you,' she said, as they strolled back. 'Apply for an export licence. Paul said he's going to have to do that before he can ship the samples from the Blainville's whales over to the mainland for analysis.'

'He will have to, yes, for the same reason.'

'So I could go with him and—'

'You'd do that?'

'Sure.'

Greg's turn then to stop her talking, turning her to him, cupping her head in his hand, tipping his head to kiss her briefly on the mouth, once, twice, before wrapping her round with his arms and hauling her in; holding her against him.

'You wonderful woman.'

'Well, only if you think he'd like one,' she had said of the *Strombus gigas*, laughing.

The jangle of the trolley wakes him. The air steward bringing food.

And – sitting up – it comes to him, clearly and in one, the thing she said to him that morning as they stopped near the house. She'd looked down, moved the sand with her toes as he'd started to stutter something inept, unequal to the sense he had of the enormity of this moment in his life; his sense of connection to her; his sense of loss at having to go, till she'd looked up, her finger stilling his lips.

'You've unlocked me, Greg, these last few days.' Her blue eyes on his as she turned to leave, her fingers touching his arm, then gone. 'That's such a gift.'

South-west Wales

It's like riding with a stranger: the car strangely small; her scent strange; her hair dyed a different colour. He knows it must be his doing – this disjointed perspective brought about by jet lag's distancing: as if his life is taking place at the further end of a corridor; his world viewed through the wrong end of a telescope. He tries to bring himself a little nearer; concentrates on the immediate. His clothes feel gritty on him; the back car seat strangely empty of Seb; windscreen wipers smear away rain. She's asking him something – *did he sleep on the plane?* Did he, he wonders. *An hour or two*, he hears his voice say.

Ella hadn't been there at the station to meet him, so he'd bought coffee at the station café, stirring in the sugar he doesn't usually take; craving the cigarette he last craved seven years ago; wondering what the twenty-odd hours since he left have brought for Paul; remembering Sophie's finger on his lips; remembering her body as she walked into the water; so that Ella eventually arrived unnoticed.

'No Seb?' he questioned, brought back to now and the café and his wife before him, suddenly aware he is unshaven and brings with him the smell of travel; seeing the way her mouth puckers at his stubble as she stoops towards him and half-kisses his cheek.

'He's playing with Richard for the day.'

'The whole day?'

'He's due back after lunch.'

'I don't even know Richard.'

'Does that matter?'

Bad start, Greg. Back off. Back down. Go home. Get some sleep.

Half-opening eyes. The curtains closed on the overcast after-noon. Seb in the low light doorway with a gun. The boy creeps forward to see if his father's eyes flicker. They do! He points his gun and fires and fires, making the gun noises in his throat.

'You're dead! You're dead!'

'Hey, monster!'

'You're dead!' Seb shouts and runs from the room, thud-ding down the corridor, thumping down the stairs.

'Hey!' Greg says, throwing back the duvet. 'Come here, ratbag!'

He catches him in the sitting room, scoops up the little body, which fights him, only *really* fights and struggles and kicks and won't give up: head back; back braced; legs and arms flailing.

'Put me down!' he yells, almost screaming. 'Put me down!' his face red, tears in shining, distraught eyes, and Greg must put him down or drop him, watching in amazement as the little ball of fury runs from the room, runs outside, slamming the back door.

'Oh, Sebastian!' Ella's voice calls from the kitchen. 'I do wish you wouldn't *slam* the door.'

Greg leaves it a few minutes, going back upstairs for more clothes, then, by the back door, he shrugs on a waterproof, picking up Seb's jacket to take out with him.

He finds Seb squatting on the big stones at the edge of the shell pit in the light spit of rain, dragging a stick across the soggy sand. The skin round his eyes looks red; his nose a little snotty.

Greg locates the second stick, there – where they leave them – slightly hidden under a bush: their drawing sticks; their building sticks; their sticks for learning letters in the sand. Seb is hitting his stick against the ground. The boy's arms are goose-pimpled with cold. Greg judges – nonetheless – it's not the moment to offer him the jacket he has brought. He goes to sit beside him, but Seb shifts, shouldering him out, forcing his father to sit further away. Marking a big circle in the sand, Greg draws two eyes in it with tears and a big, sad, downturned mouth. Seb whacks it away with his stick, scuffs his feet across it.

'Hey, monster. That was my masterpiece.' Greg smooths a new area. 'Do I wreck your drawings?' he asks, drawing a shallow semicircle, a pointed little head emerging at one edge, two elbowed front leg-flippers, two little back flipper-legs. '*Do* I?'

Seb says nothing; shakes his head once.

'OK. Well, don't wreck mine, please.' He draws the serrated edge of the turtle shell, drifts a little nearer to Sebastian. 'This is the hawksbill turtle I saw swimming off the rocks at Sombrero who gave me a very startled look until she realized I wasn't going to eat her. Oh – and these are the pilot whales,' he says, smoothing more sand, starting to draw three rounding backs, the trailing edge of their dorsal fins notably concave; emerging in unison from the water. 'Did I tell you about those? They were moving through the water together in perfect timing with one another, moving as if they were joined in some way, rounding and diving and rounding and diving, like horses on a carousel at the fairground. Do you remember going on one of those?'

Seb nods. 'No – not like *that*,' he says of the wave Greg is drawing, getting up, scrambling over his father's foot, a hand for balance on his father's knee.

'Oh. OK. How should it go?'

Using his stick, Seb makes an adjustment to the wave.

'Oh – quite right, Seb. That's *much* better.'

Seb pokes his stick into the ground. 'What about the hump-whack?'

'*Oh*, yes. The humpback whale. Well, if you could look down from the sky onto our little boat, it might look something like this,' Greg says as he draws. 'And then the humpback whale came up out of the water right in front of our little boat, and do you know what?'

Seb shakes his head.

'The whale's back was *much* wider than our boat.'

Seb thinks about it, looks at his father's drawing. 'Even wider?'

'Even wider. And when the whale dived and swam on ahead of us, the movement of its tail underwater left a calm patch on the surface. You know how you leave footprints in the sand?'

Seb nods.

'Well, it's a bit like that, only instead of pressing down, like your foot does from the top of the sand, the whale moves its tail below the surface of the water and leaves a sort of tail-print up above it.' Greg scuffles up a busy sea surrounding his plan of the little boat, then smooths some circular areas, spaced out in a line.

'So you can see which way the whale is going,' Seb says, sidling nearer to sit between Greg's knees.

'Exactly,' Greg says, bringing the boy into the warmth and the shelter of his own big jacket. 'Exactly, Sebastian.'

They walk in the rain up the valley where Greg usually runs, exploring the little gullies between tree roots in the stream. Ella comes with them for once, so that Greg strolls beside her. He sees Seb slide a sideways glance at them.

'So how was your time away?'

'Productive. Well worth going to Sombrero. There's an important ecosystem there to protect if we can. I'll have to get the report written up in double-quick time.'

'And how was Paul?'

'We had a mass stranding to deal with.'

'I meant how was *he*? Didn't he split up with his girlfriend not so long ago?'

'Yes. Seems to be coping.'

Seb scrambles out of the stream to hide behind a tree and ambush them, leaping into their path and firing his gun at them both.

'Let's have a look at that, Seb,' Greg says, holding out his hand for the gun, which the boy brings: a detailed plastic replica.

'Wherever did you get it?' he asks.

'Richard gave it to me.'

'Did he? Richard your friend from school?'

'Yes. Can I have it now?'

Greg purses his mouth and gives the gun back to the boy.

'Richard sounds like a charmer,' Greg comments as Seb runs off.

'He's not the most subtle child I've ever met, but I don't suppose we can choose Seb's friends for him.'

'I thought we said no guns.'

'We did.'

Greg puts a couple of hours in on the Sombrero report, phones Peta and John, arranging to see them at the field centre the next day, then gets round to unpacking. His clothes bring the scent of the house in the Caribbean and a mind's-eye image of Sophie, sitting by the lamp – legs tucked up – in the big wicker armchair.

The shell she gave him from the water's edge is all packed up; padded out with cottonwool in a box that Maddie found. He takes the lid off, removes some cushioning, revealing the delicate, translucent, peachy thing: a tall slim triangle of corrugated shell, like a half-folded satin fan, only hinged at one long edge, a little longer than the length of his hand from watch strap to just beyond the ends of his fingers. Holding the shell between fingertips, he lifts the thing to the lamp, seeing light scatter through its pearled opalescence, skimming across its peachy sheen. Peachy. He can scarcely feel the weight of it in his fingers; its translucence like the finest fabric, only brittle. And it's reasonable to keep it as his own, he thinks, knowing that – with Seb – it could get broken in moments. He tries to remember what it's called, *Pinna* something, he thinks. He reaches the book down from the shelf, remembering the moment she put the shell in his hands, how he'd seen its peachiness was the colour of the skin at her throat. He finds the reference in the index. *Pinna nobilis.* Ah – that's it. Noble Pen shell. '*Twenty species of pen shell world-wide in tropical and sub-tropical seas. As recently as the nineteenth century, the animals were harvested to obtain the golden-brown byssal threads, which were used to make stockings.*' Its translucence is like the finest fabric, or like a white shirt when it clings to moist, peachy skin.

He places the shell on a shelf at eye height, beneath where it catches concealed light from above and – sensing he's watched – turns to see Sebastian peeking in.

'Hi, monster.'

Seb comes in, pointing at the shell. 'What's *that*?'

Greg laughs. 'Come and have a look.' He picks the boy up so he can see. 'It's very fragile, Seb, which means it will break easily.' He shifts the boy onto one hip, reaches the shell down with his other hand. 'Be *really* careful,' he says as he passes the shell to the boy who takes it with both hands ever so gently. 'Isn't it lovely?'

The boy nods, holding his breath, giving it solemnly back, clapping his hands twice once they are empty.

'You can see why it has to stay up there?'

The boy nods, squirming round to push his face against his father's chest, hugging into him, so that Greg brings an embracing arm round, notices again the little body is stockier, grown more solid while he's been away.

'These are for you,' Greg says, turning back to his unpacking, handing Seb the T-shirt-bundled more robust shells he's brought.

And here is stuff to tidy away: ticket stubs to file for expenses; boarding passes; salt-stiff clothes to put out to wash; the newspaper Ella might like to see; the box to throw out which the shell came in; the scrap of paper that falls from it, fluttering to the floor. Pick it up – so much ephemera – as Sebastian is asking some question – *What did you say, Seb?* – only just noticing as his fingers start to scrumple that something is written on the little piece of paper and, pausing, he sees it is her name, written in a slanted hand: sophie.douglas@aol.com.

As Ella slides into bed she undresses, slipping the nightdress off. Her signal. He had wondered why she had turned the lamp out already, leaving just the TV's flickering at the end of their bed as he watches the news.

'I don't think Seb's asleep,' he says as she comes to lie just a little distance from him.

'It doesn't matter.'

He wonders what she means: *It doesn't matter*. It always

has mattered up till now. Ever since Seb was born it has mattered. *Not now, Greg. We'll wake the baby. Not now, Greg. Seb will hear.*

He gives his attention back to the television – more Palestinian and Israeli posturing.

'You've been away,' she says from her little distance. 'I thought you might—'

'Well, Ella, that's – that's really considerate.'

He feels her hand on his forearm as his mind plays Sophie, walking – naked – into the sea.

He thinks of getting out of bed and moves his hand to flip back the duvet as Ella moves her leg against the length of his – her gesture – and he sighs as his body abandons escape plans; turns instead to her and – knowing foreplay is out of the question – draws the width of his shoulders over her, draws his body over her, penis butting up against her; waiting to see if she really will.

'Is that what you want, Ella?' he says, brushing hair from the face she turns from him, eyes closed. Pushing on, he feels her flesh give as his face seeks Sophie's face in the pillow.

In a matter of moments, Ella goes to the bathroom. Lying back, scarcely sweated, Greg hears the shower start, hears the metallic tick of water pipes; wonders what it is to have sex with one woman while thinking of another. He runs a hand back through his hair as Paul's voice on the TV says, '*In nature, whales simply do not strand in this fashion.*'

What!

'*A total of fifteen now –*' it *is* Paul's voice, over images of stranded whales – '*with only a few of those surviving to be returned to the water.*' Footage of Paul, then, on the beach outside his home; his voice calmly insistent. '*Early post-mortem results reveal haemorrhaging in or around the ears and in some instances there has also been brain haemorrhaging.*' The shot changes to an aerial view of a naval ship under way, the interviewer voice-over saying, '*. . . the possibility of damaging sonar emissions. A statement has yet to be issued by the US Navy, although these shots were taken yesterday of naval vessels under way a few miles from where the strandings occurred.*' Greg leaps from the bed – '*so far dealt with by a team of scientists and conservation volunteers*' – wondering if there's time to get downstairs to the VCR – '*clearly not expecting anything on this scale*' – but no, there she is, Sophie in his bedroom, volunteer-team vox pops – '*Well, of course, no, not at all what we expected*' – the picture crystal clear – '*We've just done what we can to help with the situation we found ourselves in. The important thing now seems to be to identify the cause.*' Cut to Gordon, glasses reflecting light, stuff about nothing being conclusive yet, cut to interviewer on the beach, summing up, cut to studio. Sports news.

Greg drops back onto the bed, lets out the rush of breath he's been holding, gropes in the TV light for the remote, fails to find it, flings himself onto his belly to reach the socket in the wall, flicking the switch to turn the TV off, wanting silence and darkness to hold her image in, the five-second footage of her: the clarity of her measured words; her measured gaze at the interviewer; blueness: sky, eyes, shirt; tangled blonde hair shot through with sunlight; the familiar chain around her neck he hadn't even known he'd noticed.

He lies in darkness, his chest feeling somehow tight, hearing the hurried beat of his heart, hearing the sound of the shower running.

South-west Wales

'There were two in that haul,' Peta says, referring to the notes on her knee, as the video shows the fishermen bending over to cut the harbour porpoise carcass from the net.

'You've been able to bring most of the by-catch back to shore?'

She nods. 'Don't know how the pathologist is managing to keep up with us. Oh, this bit is good.' She laughs as the shot changes: lumpy hand-held footage of a fishing boat at sea alongside the vessel Peta was filming from.

'Oh, *what!*' Peta's recorded voice squeals.

An out-of-shot male voice laughs and says something the camera doesn't catch as Peta's take zooms in to men on top of the second fishing boat's cabin roof: three fishermen, dancing in a line, stark naked apart from the one on the left, who wears his wellies still, as they try to coordinate their hand-on-hips dance, proud-flopping their manhood for Peta's benefit, for the woman they've heard is on the boat alongside.

'Oh, nice one, Peta.' Greg laughs. 'No sexual harassment, then?'

'What are they *like*?' Peta's recorded voice laughs as the camera sweeps, jerkily, along their line-up.

'Oh – they were just larking around,' she says in reply to Greg. 'They're a bunch of good guys. Both these crews. Big softies – no pun intended.'

John says nothing. Folds his arms. Unfolds them. Gets up.

'More coffee anyone?'

'So your skipper wanted payment for landing dolphin carcasses, John?' Greg asks as John brings the coffee.

'Fifty quid a time,' he says.

'Ah,' Peta says, 'they break the law catching them and then want to be paid for the privilege of landing them for us.'

'Didn't think the budget could quite stretch to it,' John adds.

'You're damn right it can't.'

'Hope it can stretch to some new gear for me, though.'

'New gear?'

'Wellies, for example.'

'What happened to the other ones?'

John makes a hand gesture: the chucking of something aside.

'They threw them overboard?' Peta exclaims.

John nods.

'*Bastards!*' Peta hisses. 'How are you supposed to get round the boat without them?'

'Or at least,' John qualifies, 'my wellies were in the wet locker when I went to sleep, gone when I woke up and not to be found, although I searched the boat for a couple of hours – to the great amusement of the crew. I could use some new oilskins too.'

'They didn't throw *those* over?'

John shakes his head, reaches to the carrier bag under the table. The orange dungarees he pulls out have been slit up the outside of both legs. A mockery of an evening dress, Greg realizes, as he sees that fishnet stockings have been drawn on the trouser legs in heavy indelible felt-tip pen. The stockings are topped by a suspender belt and – duplicated on both the dungarees and jacket – pubic hair has been scrawled in great curly swathes and a pierced bellybutton beneath huge tits, fitted with elaborate rotating tassels, drawn in mid-spin.

'Oh, they *have* got a sense of humour. Anything else?'

'Oh, you know – fish in my sleeping bag, wet sleeping bag, not letting me eat—'

'*What?*'

'Dry bread and water for three days.'

'Jesus. Listen, John, I'm sorry you've been subjected to this. I'd never have sent you if I thought they would do this to you.' Greg chucks his pen down on the table. 'Why the *hell* do people agree to have observers on board in the first place if this is the way they're going to treat them?'

'The skipper wasn't too bad. It was just the crew.'

'And this?' Greg queries, touching his own eyebrow to indicate John's, where half an inch of one end is missing.

'Ah, yes,' he says, running a finger across the lighter patch. 'They thought I could use a hand shaving.'

'They shaved your *eyebrow*?' Peta asks.

'Big guy sitting on my chest at the time.'

Peta exhales sharp breath. 'This is *appalling*.'

Greg pinches the bridge of his nose. 'OK. I have to ask – before I go and tackle the skipper on this one – do you think you did anything which might have provoked this response?'

'Oh, yes, I did,' John says straight away. 'I was there. All the provocation they needed.'

Moonlight slants into the room; the window pattern elongated across the foot of the narrow bed, reaching another across the four-bed dorm. Greg lies, wide awake; silence; stillness.

I need to work late, he had said to Ella, *so I may stay over – the students due in tomorrow – so much to get through before they arrive.* They had looked at one another – the briefest of glances through this transparent veneer of perfect common sense.

'I'll pop back in time for Seb's bedtime again tomorrow.

186

We said you'd do the school run this week, didn't we? Assuming that's still all right with you . . .'

Common sense and perfect politeness.

'Will you want supper tomorrow?'

'No, thanks. Not while the students are here. I'll be at the field centre till late.'

He wishes he'd thought to bring the whisky with him. A shot to help him sleep. He'd only had half a pint in the pub, unlike John's skipper, who'd had quite a lot, who'd thrust his face into Greg's and said, 'Listen, I've got a bloody living to make. If nancy boy can't hack it, tell him to piss off.'

'Come on, Matthew. You said you'd help me out.'

'He has,' one of the crew with him said. 'Nancy boy's still got his bollocks, hasn't he?'

That's the trouble with the whole scheme, Greg thinks, running his eye along the edge of moonlight. It depends entirely on the fishermen's goodwill. With Peta's skipper, Mick, it's great. He knows there's a problem with dolphin kill, is bothered by it and wants to help sort it. As for the others. Greg pushes out breath. How *else* is he supposed to get this thing done? There's bugger all in the way of government backing. A dribble of funding. No clout. He turns over in bed. There's no way John can go back out on the same boat again. Unless he can find a different boat for him, there'll be another week of data lost. No takers in the pub tonight. He wonders if there's any chance tomorrow. Perhaps if he goes begging early morning in the harbour.

Getting up, he pads barefoot into the office, grabbing his fleecy jacket, booting the computer up to search by its light through the database of Milford-based boats to see if there's anyone he hasn't tried yet. He scrolls quickly down past the gill-netters. Peta's out with gill-netters and resources are too tight to justify sending John out on another. And anyway, it's almost certainly the pair-trawlers where the worst of the problem is. That's why there's the hostility to observers, of course: knowing there is something considerable to hide. He runs down the list of trawlers – so many Spanish-owned and crewed now: quota buy-outs, flag of convenience, only docking in Wales to off-load their catch onto Spanish lorries to transport back to Spain; keeping the Spanish processors busy. Absolutely no chance of getting observers on Spanish-owned boats. He makes a mental list of the few boats which might do, perhaps if he gets down to the harbour early with John, they might be in with some slight chance. The *Mary Jane* – she's always seemed like a tightly run ship, and the skipper, what's he called? – so the thought which pushes foremost really shouldn't be Hawaii.

What?

He pauses in his scrolling.

Hawaii.

What about Hawaii?

She said she'd be going to Hawaii soon to use a telescope.

Still not understanding, he sits, waiting for the point to emerge. The computer image changes to a screen saver. Slowly swimming cartoon fish. The blup of cartoon bubbles from their mouths. There's the starfish Seb likes best. He shifts the mouse to bring the data back and it's only as he starts to scroll through again that realization suddenly arrives.

'Oh, *yes*!' he stage-whispers, alone, out loud.

Pushing back the chair, he clicks the light switch on and stands, barefoot in his boxers, hauling the filing cabinet open. This year's international marine mammal conference – not that drawer – he slams it closed – not that drawer, the middle one – is due to be held in Hawaii this time – month after next, isn't it?

But you've already said you're not going, Greg. Too much to do here, you said, remember? The submission deadline has probably passed; not that you've anything ready to submit *and* the funding's probably all been allocated; to say nothing of the unlikelihood of the dates coinciding with Sophie's dates for using the telescope.

Worth checking, though.

His hand lands on the piece of paper. Twenty-fourth international . . . to be held on Maui . . . April 18 through 23. He hunts for the registration date. He can make it by a whisker. And it may be that the timing is bad for most of his work – too soon to present the findings of the observer programme; the net aversion device not yet sufficiently tested; and it will take months to devise and run a model for rocket-launch sound propagation through water – but now that the mass stranding has happened. God knows that needs to be really carefully documented, but *really* carefully. Paul and he had discussed it on the way to the airport, how they and Anna should produce a paper together. Again an atypical stranding. Again coincident with naval activity. And now they've gathered evidence of physiological damage. Not gonna let the bastards walk away from it this time, Paul had said. A presentation at an international conference would be the perfect place to start – sounding the alarm for all those in whose seas the sonar technology is used. And Paul is due to go to Maui anyway, isn't he? He glances at the clock – one thirty-five a.m. – working out what time that makes it in the Caribbean.

He can find out about funding in the morning, he thinks, as he dials Paul's number. There was that workshop at the conference they wanted him to run. That should do it. Just Sophie's dates, then.

Worth checking.

South-west Wales

There are good days – working days – the weather uncommonly kind, letting work it has halted before go ahead. The bunch of students come: third-year undergrads working with the net alerter device; four ashore with the theodolite and plotting software on a laptop; four at sea, setting the net, alternate days with and without the device, using the hydrophone and binoculars to confirm sightings of porpoises. Greg guides the students to where he knows the harbour porpoises feed, a routine he has already documented well. He dives with one student to watch the porpoises before the net is put in place: the animals nose down, bodies vertical as they dig in the seabed, leaving little humps behind them: crater-feeding, so intent on locating prey beneath the sand that – at such times – they can drift into set gill nets, the all but invisible filigree of micro mesh going unregarded until too fatally late. There was a time on the first net day when he'd had to dive in earnest, going in again with one of the students, David – competent, level-headed guy – to cut loose the porpoise who – they could tell from the jerking of the floats on the surface – had become entangled in their unannounced net. Greg had taken a skimming blow in the belly from the tail fluke, cursing himself underwater – such an elementary error, lucky near miss – silly bugger – recovering himself to approach again, the two of them in unison this time. Hold still. Hold still. You bet I want you out of here – the knife, running slickly through the netting – the kick, again, of the tail fluke, freed; seeing the beauty of her flight to the surface to gulp down air. They are long days, dictated by wild porpoise feeding times, early morning and late night, when the land crew are disabled by darkness, so they take it turn and turn about, sharing the tasks out. Then there's the POD that arrives – the porpoise detector – an underwater device which specifically picks up porpoise clicks: analysing direction and number and proximity.

'Well, that's a damn sight easier than hanging around freezing half the night with a hydrophone.'

'Isn't it?' Greg says, grinning at the student's sleepy face: pretty girl, Sally, who reminds him of Peta.

And Ella brings Seb up one evening, the students making a fuss of him, Sally doing drawings, Andi and Dan playing piggy-in-the-middle, David giving shoulder rides so that Seb giggles till the tears run down and never mind that the dragon story has been booted into touch because Richard says it's silly, because Richard says it's only for little kids, because Richard says that bit at the beginning, that bit when the dragon goes huff and puff, has been taken from another story. Oh, yes, Sally says, I'll huff and I'll puff and I'll blow your house down, it comes from the three little pigs. And Bethsheba, Sally queries, as Greg outlines more, shouldn't that be Bathsheba? Never mind, then, that the dragon story has been quite kicked out: Dad is solidly in favour again, back and bringing Seb among these people and giving him this love and time and fun. And never mind, either, that Ella doesn't stay, goes, instead, home; or out again with the women from work; best leave it at that. Greg drives home each night before Seb's bedtime; back to the field centre again mid-evening for porpoise monitoring with the students and for sleep.

And all the time e-mails come and go. From John on the trawler Greg managed to place him on – the skipper of the *Mary Jane* doing him proud, if only to dissociate himself from his brother-in-law who can't keep proper control of his crew, and of course they'll land the by-catch free of charge, if Matthew said he'd help out, then he bloody well should of and it's not the first time John's new skipper has had to bail his brother-in-law out. Greg feels a weight lifted. John all right. Another week of data saved. Worth getting up at four thirty the other morning and going down early to the harbour to beg.

There are e-mails about Sombrero, too – the report to

send through in time for the public meeting in Anguilla. And e-mails about the conference in Hawaii: funding slowly coming together and a presentation slot secured; the workshop agreed and, then, Paul's e-mails: could Greg scan the stranding images he's got and send them through plus thoughts on presentation structure – a discussion of detail and, no, there's been no comment from the navy still. No more comment from Sophie, either, but then – he's had confirmation from her long before he'd made the conference arrangements.

'Will you be in Hawaii when Paul, Anna and I are?' he'd written in an e-mail to her.

A reply had come that day: 'Your conference finishes a day before my observation run ends.'

'On Maui?'

'No – the scopes are on Big Island – next one along from Maui.'

'Shall we meet, Sophie?' he had written, beginning to wonder if she was being evasive.

'Hey! Can you stay on after the conference, then?'

'I could – if you'd like to meet up.'

'Yes, Greg. I'd like to meet up.'

He'd imported an image across from Clip-Art, sending it through to her as an attachment: a bright yellow, great big, grinning sun.

Part Three

Hawaii

'Are you going to bed now?'

'No, Seb. I've only been up for a couple of hours.'

'*Have* you? What time is it?'

'Nine thirty in the morning.'

'*Is* it? I'm just going to bed.'

'I *know*, Sebastian.' Greg laughs. 'That's why I'm phoning
you.'

'To tell me a story—'

'To see how you are—'

'The dragon story.'

'I didn't think you *liked* the dragon story any more.'

A little silence down the phone.

'I didn't think you wanted me to read that one to you.'

More silence as Sebastian waits.

'Seb, I haven't really got time for a story this morning
because I'm at the big conference I told you about and I have
to go and be there to answer questions with Paul and Anna –
those friends from the Caribbean.'

'Are you in the Cabi-rrean?'

Paul walks past the pay phone, making signs to Greg that he should hurry.

'No, Seb. I'm in Hawaii. Don't you remember we looked on your globe and saw those little islands in the Pacific Ocean? Remember?'

'*Moree* has been to Hawaii.'

Not Moree again. 'Has he?' Recalcitrant, wily, imaginary boy who has been absent for a long time now until his recent, sudden re-emergence.

'*Moree* said it was quite hot and there were lots of hump-whack whales.'

Paul walks past again, eyes wide in mock-manic insistence, tapping a finger against his wristwatch, Anna nervously pale-faced beside him.

'Well, perhaps I'll bump into Moree while I'm here.'

'No, you *won't*,' Seb says quickly. '*Moree's* here with me. *Moree's* going to school with me tomorrow.'

'Oh, *really*!' Oh, God. How ever will they cope with Moree at school? Will a real place have to be made for him as it has to now at the table at home? Will real books have to be given out and extra real lunch provided?

'I didn't know Moree goes to school.'

'He's just started.'

Paul grabs Greg by the shoulders; starts to remove him from the phone.

'Listen, Sebastian,' Greg says at the end of the stretched-out wire, 'sleep well. I have to go now.'

Paul takes Greg by the neck, pantomimes strangulation.

'Why do you?' Sebastian asks.

'I have to go and talk to some people. Goodnight, now.'

'Wait! Wait!' Sebastian calls.

'What *is* it, Seb?'

'Say goodnight to Moree.'

'Oh. OK. Goodnight, Moree.'

The international conference – held in a different venue every year – has grown so large that three lecture rooms run simultaneously. It divides the audience, of course, but still the numbers are high, most seats filled as Paul begins.

Greg listens to the script he helped write; trying to bring objectivity to it still. The context helps: familiar words less familiar in the vast space of the air-conditioned hall. Where are the weaknesses? he asks himself again as he listens, looking out over listening faces. The laptop shows him the pictures the audience sees projected onto the screen behind him: the stranded Blainville's, the dissected skull, the bloodied internal ear; the haemorrhaged brain; the other strandings Greg didn't see, found after he had left them to it.

His ear listens. His eye wanders.

It could be anywhere, this high-ceilinged conference

room: exposed blond brickwork next to creamy plastered areas, no daylight; concealed lighting and spot-lighting, the pale wooden railed gallery, high-quality audiovisual gear. Good facilities. Faceless. It could be anywhere. Only the framed photos in the foyer – large, soft, grainy black and whites of a stunning Hawaiian girl caught in an athletic swirl of hula on a beach – link this anonymous place to a culturally specific place 2,000 miles from substantial landmass. In here it could otherwise be forgotten.

The intentness of a man watching Paul from the front row draws Greg's attention again. Greg sees his cheek flex with the gritting hard of teeth; his mouth pursed tightly as Paul winds up the talk.

The first questioner to gain the mike points out the major weakness.

'You don't seem to have made direct reference to a pathologist's report.'

'Ah – that's not available yet,' Paul answers. 'The ears and in some cases whole skulls were flown out to the mainland to be CAT-scanned and for histological slides to be made, but the results of that have yet to be published. The pathologist did say during post-mortem that the straightforward visual evidence left him in little doubt that some pressure trauma had occurred.'

'But that's not published yet either.'

'No. This only happened a couple of months back and I

had hoped that a gross post-mortem report would be available at least. Ah – that hasn't been the case, but you can see for yourselves from the slides here that these animals stranded atypically and with damaged ears and in some cases brain haemorrhage. We know that much happened.'

There are questions, too, about naval activity and questions Greg fields on underwater topography in the area where the strandings took place and its possible effect on sound propagation.

The man from the front row leaves during the applause, hurrying away, and only then does Greg recognize him: he's the scientist who blew the whistle on the mass stranding in Greece a few years ago which happened concurrently with the NATO naval exercise. Watching him go, keeping himself to himself, Greg can guess his purpose: vindication.

'There was a sense in which he was ostracized,' Paul explains to Anna as they drink coffee in the mid-morning break.

'Who by?'

'The university he worked for and by some of his colleagues.'

'You'd think they'd be pleased – wouldn't you – bringing the thing out into the open – or did professional jealousy creep in?'

Paul shrugs. 'Whatever it was, people were critical about his representation of the idea – too speculative, not represented in sufficiently classic scientific style to be taken seriously.'

'Even though he'd been published by a major peer-reviewed journal,' Greg adds.

'Isn't that rather like saying, sorry, I'm not coming to tackle your fire because I don't like the way you structure your sentences?'

'As you yell from the third storey of a burning building,' Paul agrees with her.

'Admirable, isn't it?' Greg says. 'Of course, we *do* have to know what type of fire it is before we can tackle it effectively.'

'Yes – but not much help going into denial there's a fire at all.'

'I'm afraid that's more or less what happened – with fairly devastating results professionally and personally for the scientist involved.'

Anna's face opens with dawning horror. 'So this is what you guys meant when you said we must present this stuff especially carefully.'

'Yeah – well – there's the evidence now,' Paul says.

'Nearly,' Anna corrects him. 'There's *nearly* evidence – in a pathologist's report that has yet to be written by a navy-funded pathologist.'

'Part-funded.'

'Large-part-funded.' She half-laughs. 'Hey guys – thanks.

This sounds like just the sort of move I needed to make at the start of my career. Following in the footsteps of an ostracized and debunked colleague.'

Paul wrinkles his nose. Bad smell.

'It's just a case of recording – objectively – what we witnessed that day, Anna – or those days, in your case,' Greg says, 'and then presenting the collated information. That's what we've done here today. Nothing more, nothing less. A presentation of fact. I didn't make any of it up. Did you?'

All week the waves are massive, breaking hard onto the beach, hardly letting swimmers in, so the conference centre pool is useful, empty early morning when he comes, and – in the evening – underwater lit as soon as the sun dips. It's small, though, so he builds the habit of a couple of dozen warm-up lengths before running down to the beach; running along the beach and back: good time to spend with himself away from the conference's busy intensity; good time to think of Sophie – a little stretch of sea away. He casts his eyes offshore as he runs, as if he might see Big Island, though he knows it lies away to the south-east and the beach here faces west. Nothing to see but sky and sea, of course, Greg. Idiot.

As the conference ends and people pack and students take down piece by piece the forest of poster presentations and the crowd thins out to prepare for partying, he feels it all the more keenly: the strictures of this little distance. Sophie on the next island. At dusk he jogs back along the beach, the lights from the centre twinkling behind blown palms. He ought to be sociable, he ought to go and shower and change and get ready for the party. And he will. He will. Be good to have some time with Paul and Anna. He knows how it will be, though – those casual glances of newly met colleagues will reveal themselves tonight. That Spanish MSc student, for starters. She's been dogging him since they got here. *Great tits*, Paul had whispered on her third sortie in Greg's direction. And they are – she is – simply stunning: ripe fruit fairly begging to be plucked and God only knows the extent of his hunger. Just not for her.

Sand gives way to concrete and – barefoot – he slows. Yes, he'll shower and change and go to the party and, much more to the point, he'll fly on tomorrow to Big Island and to Sophie. Not long now.

Hawaii

The mountain top emerges from the unbroken white cloud round it like an island thrusting up through a foaming sea. The plane tilts on its rounding course as if to give him a better view and he makes out dark patches of mountain scree streaked with the white of snow and – as he wonders if this is the mountain she mentioned in her e-mail – the plane moves to where the sun reflects light off something shiny at the summit. He pushes his face towards the window, scrunches his eyes, but it's no good – still too far away to tell. He supposes it must be, though. At around – what was it she said? – 14,000 feet, wasn't it? At around that, it would have to be the highest mountain on the island, wouldn't it?

A few minutes later, it's obvious. The plane, continuing its long, banked curve, comes nearer to and rounds the mountain peak and there – picked out by brilliant sunlight – he sees several observatory domes: white, surreal, minimalistic things spaced out on the mountain top. He grins at the white and sky-blue beauty of it, at his sense of the closing distance from her. She could be there, now, on the mountain peak.

He leans back in his seat.

Don't be ridiculous, Greg.

She'll be sleeping now and he knows for sure they don't sleep at the summit. There's the fourteen-hour rule she'd mentioned in her e-mail – no one allowed to stay at the summit any longer – so they have to go back down to the astronomers' centre at 9,000 feet to sleep and ward off altitude sickness, before going back up for the next night's observations. Nonetheless – he grins again, remembering the pleasure he'd heard in her voice when he'd phoned her from the conference centre yesterday and she'd invited him up to the telescope – her last night's run.

'You'll have to leave your hire car at 9,000 feet,' Sophie had said. 'The insurance cover won't let you go any further and anyway it needs a four-wheel-drive vehicle to get to the summit. I should be at the astronomers' centre, but in any case I'll fix you a lift up from there. It's really important to hang around at the centre for an hour or so, to let your body adapt to the altitude and, Greg, drink loads of water, won't you? It's common sense really.'

'Sure.'

'And no diving within the previous twenty-four hours.'

'I wouldn't anyway – the flight.'

'And you shouldn't be coming up the mountain at all

if you've any medical problems – high blood pressure, respiratory problems, that sort of thing.'

'Sophie, it'll be fine.'

'Am I fussing?'

He had laughed gently. 'No. It's an extreme environment and you're right to warn me of that.'

'Well, it *is* extreme. I mean, most people are fine, but it has to be taken seriously.' She had laughed then. 'My turn to play Captain Caring. Sorry. I know you're used to looking after yourself.'

'And is it OK if I come?'

'Yeah, yeah. I've cleared it with the guys here.'

Which wasn't quite what he had meant.

He comes out of the airport into a pelting, warm, tropical downpour that lasts an hour or more then stops abruptly to leave steaming roads and mugginess as he picks up the hire car and checks into the hotel he doesn't expect to use until early the next morning; but seeing as he *has* got a room, he may as well try to sleep, knowing she will be sleeping now and wanting his wits about him later and then he was so late last night – the end of conference party. He fails to sleep, though – instead only making a wreck of the bed. The humidity, he tells himself.

He had heard that – of the earth's twenty-three climatic zones – all but a few exist on Hawaii. He'd been reminded of this on the plane, sitting next to someone who'd told him of wind-surfing a half-mile out to sea in seventy-degree waters while looking across to snow-capped Mauna Kea. And everything in between, each microcosm butting up tightly one against the other, Greg thinks, as his drive takes him through a stretch of rainforest then up to a more temperate region where land has been adapted to grassland and cattle ranching. At times mist swirls over sparse undergrowth on volcanic rock, the road obviously reclaimed, cut back again through black, broken, solidified lava.

She isn't there at 9,000 feet.

'Already gone up to the JCMT,' someone informs him, before disappearing – white rabbit like – down the hushed hallway. 'There'll be a lift up in an hour or two,' the man adds before he quite disappears. 'Help yourself to tea. And water – lots of it.'

Greg pushes out breath; paces across the empty lounge to the window, turns away again.

Thinking he may as well use the time, his pencil makes heavy lines: drawn and overdrawn; marks which start out as ordered bullet-point markers of field centre, postgrad, organized business and end up a dark brood of doodles.

Talk about sticking your neck out, Greg, he thinks, sensing the extent of his limbo, placing himself here, ridiculously, most of the way up a mountain, reminding himself at this last of the little he has on which to base his assumption that some good may come of re-meeting Sophie: a certain frisson of attraction. Two months ago. On a Caribbean beach. Probably just as much to do with being in the sun. Really, Greg. It's the stuff of teenage daydreams. Or worse. He shoves the pencil back in his pocket, wondering if he's just making the same mistake he made—

He rips the ruined paper from the pad.

The same mistake he made with Rachel—

He scrunches the paper into a tight ball, chucks it at the bin and misses.

The mistake of letting the want of one particular woman overrule everything else. Very clever, Greg. Very clever.

The final stretch of road is welcome grit. Door-slamming thoughts out, grinding them beneath the tyres of the four-wheel drive as the back end slews on the unmade track: zigzagging-steep and difficult to keep a grip, the conversation unfaltering though – a telescope technician, Seth, accustomed expert at the wheel; an Aussie astronomer up next to him; a Japanese astronomer with Greg in the back; the two visiting scientists going to the scope for a look round before their observing run begins tomorrow. He hears his own voice join in, usefully as far as he can tell, his thoughts once again ahead up the mountain.

The vehicle works its careful way up through cloud

cover, the undergrowth entirely gone now, the light and air and scree a uniform – just differently textured – impenetrable, dingy grey.

Giving himself to gravity, Greg leans back in the seat the gradient tilts. What the hell – it's a visit to an observatory. Well. He's never been to one of those.

Twenty minutes more and they burst into sunlight, into sudden, beautiful blue and white and gold and shadows beginning to lengthen now. The snow is much less than it looked from the plane. Cloud recedes beneath them.

Minutes more and there's the ice white of the observatory building; the air's bite: bitter cold as they open up the vehicle doors. There's the camaraderie of the men, the technician talking still of the moon buggy tested on this mountain – of all the earth, the terrain here found to be most like the surface of the moon. One small step for man, the technician teases as Greg gets out of the vehicle, his first foot contacting down. There's the zipping up of jackets, the bodily strangeness at altitude, the quickening of breath, the flurry of a heartbeat having to work harder here; the saliva somehow different in the mouth.

There's the name in bronze on the wall to pass – James Clerk Maxwell Telescope – as the men jostle in. There's the control room, run round with big computer screens, warmth, low light, the surprise of music – jazz! It's like bundling into a jazz café, a cyber café, with a bunch of mates, except the screens are huge and the only people here are a dark-haired man and the blonde-haired woman Greg last saw in the Caribbean. There's his face, with a mind quite of its own, broadening to a grin at the sight of her, as their eyes meet and hold over the boisterous arrival. There's the gentle nodding of his head; a much deeper breath to draw as her eyes hold his. Good. Good. Very good.

They linger in the dimness of the telescope housing, dwarfed beneath the huge latticed curve of the dish, letting the others go on ahead, feet disappearing up open metalwork stairs.

'How was your journey?' Sophie asks, smiling more than the question warrants.

'Worth it,' he states, grinning, so that her smile tips over into laughter.

'Well, it is a *wonderful* telescope.'

He laughs. 'Wonderful setting, too.'

'*And* I've got some really promising data.'

'Yes? As I said on the phone, you mustn't let my being here distract you.'

'Oh,' she says, her eyes indicating the telescope, 'this guy pretty much demands my full attention.'

'Good. Weather looks clear for you.'

'Not bad. That's one of the advantages of coming here.

It's a world-class site for that and – for the optical scopes – the lack of light pollution is excellent here.'

There's a clunk and the smooth whir of machinery as the giant observatory doors start to slowly separate, sliding apart; letting a widening chink of sunlight through that runs the whole four-storey-height of the building. Light is let in over-head, too, where part of the roof is sliding back.

'Does this screen stay in place all the time?' Greg asks, indicating the taut white fabric which also runs the height of the building; stretched from side to side and curving back over the top of the dish, so that the telescope is quite encap-sulated.

'Yes. It's Gore-tex – lets the submillimetre rays through while keeping the dust and the weather out.'

Shadows roll with the building's slow opening; the rich yellow of diffused sunlight widening across the screen.

'So how's your time here been?' Greg asks as they climb the metal stairs.

'Excellent. I was working from another telescope – the Keck – for the first four nights.'

'That was the black hole study, wasn't it?'

'Speed of stars on the event horizon, yes.'

'And?'

'Won't know the outcome until we take the data away and process it. Got some high-quality images, though.'

'And here?'

'Excellent, too. Some excellent images of galaxies last night. More tonight, I hope. I'm going to take an image for Richie first, though.'

'Richie?'

'My brother. He's into astronomy big-time. As an amateur, I mean. I've had to clear it with the telescope director here, because it's outside what I'd applied for this time, but they've said no problem.'

'Anything in particular?'

'The dust disc around a main-sequence star. It's something I'm due to work with from here soon in any case. Some IRAS images—'

'IRAS?'

'Sorry – the Infrared Astronomical Satellite. It was operating in the eighties and we're still utilizing IRAS images today – following up interesting findings with ground-based scopes. I mentioned it to my brother, so he's looked up the IRAS images on the web and he's been trying to get optical images of the same stars. He wanted me to take some in the submillimetre and even though I've managed to secure some time here for that in a few months from now—'

'Richie couldn't wait till then.'

She laughs. 'Patience is *not* his strongest point. I've told him – at best it can only be a snapshot. These images will take at least a couple of nights each to complete, so I'm not going to be able to get much in an hour or two.'

'I get the feeling you quite want to see, too, though.'

She grins. 'Well – perhaps.'

At a turn of the stair, they stand and lean side by side on the rail to peer into the telescope's dish.

'What size is this?'

'Fifteen metres diameter – the biggest in the world for this radio-wavelength range.'

The setting sun is performing alchemy, its deepening colours diffusing through the screen to turn the aluminium dish into gold; to burnish the white housing golden; to gild a roseate glow to her face. There seems some inner glow too, animating her speech.

'All these sections,' she continues, pointing to the dish's divided inner curve, 'can be adjusted individually to maintain the optimum surface.'

'How many sections are there?'

'Nearly 300.'

'No wonder they want to keep the dust out.'

She nods. 'It's precision stuff.'

He smiles warmly as she turns to look at him. 'Anyone would think you've found your *métier*.'

'Oh, I love it.'

'Not even a little daunting?' he asks, indicating the scale of it all.

'Using all this gear?'

He nods, his eyes searching hers through the honeyed air.

'It was, the first time I was a visiting solo observer, but not now, no.' She turns her gaze back to the dish. 'It just feels – exciting – a wonderful opportunity, a huge privilege, having access to all of this.' She laughs. 'At least, that's how it feels at the start of the night. Three a.m. can be a bit of a killer.'

He pulls himself back from the rail and from her. 'Time to start work soon?'

'Soon. Time to go on outside first, though, if you want to.'

'Love to.'

They climb the rest of the stairs, the exercise in this thinner atmosphere making his lungs work hard to gather oxygen, his heart pound hard to transport it, as if he is suddenly much less fit.

There's a door to go through which takes them out onto the building's flat roof. Cold within the telescope housing, it's even more cold without; the light wind-keen, but the so very beautiful deepening colours mean the temperature simply has to be borne. In a wide panorama, deep reds begin to streak through gold. They walk along the building's outer edge, the white cladding turned salmon pink beneath their feet; stopping to stand above the telescope hidden from them now; above the rounding of the screen; a sense, even, of looking down on the sun as it dips behind the cloud cover lower down the mountain. It's unbroken, the cloud cover – looking

215

for all the world like a perfectly feasible sea spread out far and wide below them: gilded by the setting sun; a gently rippled surface; occasional heaped clouds rising like islands.

'My addled brain has just started searching for fins,' Greg says as they look out from the building's end. 'We even have a sailing ship,' he adds, looking down onto the Gore-tex screen below, taut and bellied out – like some huge square rigger's sail viewed from the masthead.

Sophie laughs. 'Well, we do call them fishing trips, sometimes. Those observing runs when we don't really know what the hell it is we're after and just go trawling to see what we can catch.'

'There you go,' he says.

They stand, close now in the cold, the sun nearly gone.

'Presumably a spectacular sunset isn't all that good news for your astronomy.'

'That's right. There's more high cloud than I thought. It means there's more water vapour around – not good when you're trying to observe at submillimetre wavelengths.'

They are silent a moment, watching the darkening colour, feeling the nearness of one another. He brings a hand to rest on her shoulder.

'It's good to see you, Sophie.'

She brushes her face against his fingers, turns to regard him.

'Greg – could we have a talk about Ella?'

'Of course. Of course we can.'

'Only –' she sweeps hair back from her face – 'it's good to see you, too, so –' she shrugs – 'so I need to understand about Ella.'

'Of course. Tomorrow. When you've finished here.' He lifts his eyes to the darkening heavens. 'Don't look now.'

'Hey! Here they come,' she says, smiling to see the stars re-emerge.

'Come and say hi to SCUBA,' the technician invites as they catch the others on the way back down a second staircase.

'Oh, you should,' Sophie says to Greg. 'I must go get started,' she mouths, backing away as the technician talks.

Jazz still plays, melodious, laid-back, as Greg goes, a little later, into the control room; Sophie and Harry, the telescope operator, at work, so Greg leans against the door unnoticed awhile, loving the warm, dimly lit peace of the place, her gentle sense of calm concentration. She soon turns, though, from the screens to smile up at him.

'Don't want to disturb you,' he says.

'Oh – you're fine.' She pats the chair next to hers. 'We're just running some checks here. How was SCUBA?'

'I'd be pretty pleased if I'd designed it,' he says, coming to sit by her.

She nods. 'It's an impressive bit of kit.'

217

'Nah. Just think of it as a camera,' Harry calls across the room.

'Kodak disposable?'

'Yeah. That kind of thing.'

'Just that it takes images of minute amounts of heat emitted by dust particles goodness knows *how* many light years away,' Greg marvels.

'We aim to please,' Harry drawls.

'And the – pixels – what did he call them?'

'Bolometric detectors,' Sophie supplies.

'Bolometric detectors – cooled to absolute zero.'

Greg shakes his head. Minus 273 degrees Celsius. Contained in SCUBA in the telescope housing a few metres from where they sit. Must be the coldest place on the planet.

'We're running a noise check on them now,' Sophie tells him, 'so that we can exclude any pixel which isn't performing at its best.'

'So that you get the best signal to noise ratio?'

'Precisely.'

'Sophie,' Harry says, busy at his screens still, 'I just need to go check the reserve helium.'

'Oh – Seth did it – part of the tour,' Greg says.

'Did he?'

'Thing like an oil dipstick only much longer and he used a huge glove.'

'That's the one.'

'Said to tell you it was fine.'

'OK, Harry. Can we eliminate these cells now?'

'Yeah. There you go,' Harry says, keying commands into the computer.

'Time to run with these coordinates, then?'

'Sure.'

'Is this the image for Richie?'

She nods. 'Quick snapshot before getting down to the real business. You OK?' she asks, seeing Greg put pressure on the bridge of his nose.

'Nothing coffee won't cure. Is there somewhere I can make us some?'

'Yeah. Drink some water while you're there,' Harry says, indicating the way, 'Down the stairs – room with the couch.'

'Great. A kettle's one piece of technology I can cope with round here.'

'Wouldn't bank on it,' Harry teases. 'Damn thing always boils before it gets real hot.'

Greg laughs. Well, it would, of course, here at 14,000 feet.

She puts a printout of the image there before him, blue, red and yellow false colour thing – a dust disc, she tells him, round a star which doesn't register in the submillimetre but is here, she points, as he puts the coffee down, wanting not to slop it, his arm suddenly somehow not his own, having to scrunch his eyes up to focus, his head really hurting now, sounds beginning to blur, the new ORAC data reduction system, she is saying as if down a corridor, amazing resolution, she is saying, the surprising thing, she is saying, is what appears to be the disc's asymmetry, the non-uniformity of the ring, and what may be a bright spot here – and it *is* asymmetrical, he can see it is as her finger traces the image on the page; his heart working very hard; his head thumping – Sophie, I'm afraid I need some help here, he hears his voice-down-the-end-of-the-corridor say.

The chair rushes up to catch him as he sinks. Sorry, he wants to say, but can't for the oxygen mask quickly there and anyway he needs to breathe – Harry moving in peripheral vision, Seth's name called. Greg manages a self-derogatory raise of the eyebrows, his eyes locked on Sophie's now, her fingers against the pulse in his carotid, the voice of the TO talking on the telephone – *to get him back down to Hilo*, Harry is saying – *Hard to say, I've seen worse, but he's gone down pretty quick, safest to send him all the way*. Her eyes are anchorage, holding him steady as the tide sweeps, her hand on his shoulder. *No – luckily Seth's still here*, Harry is saying, *so we're still in business*. *Sorry, you guys*, Greg manages, his slow arm doing his bidding after all, moving the mask minutely away enough to let him speak. *Could be any one of us at any time*, Sophie is saying, fitting the mask snugly back, only not too snugly, he wants to indicate, as his stomach grips round sudden nausea and he wonders if he's going to vomit. Deep breath. Deep breath. Deep breath. Her eyes strong, her eyes steady. Harry on the phone again, *Expect the Brit back down, Greg Jamieson with a touch of altitude sickness*. Seth in the room – *Done what you needed to?* Harry's voice is saying – *Yeah*, Seth's voice, *good timing. Can you get yourself to the door, Greg? Sure*, his voice says, though he isn't. His head pounds as he stands. *Just slowly, now*. Seth and Harry, one at each side. Someone puts his jacket round his shoulders as he walks, Harry taking the cylinder and mask out for him, Sophie ahead opening doors. Outside air chill makes him gasp the more, but the vehicle is very near. *Mind the step, here. Take it easy*. Sophie there in the vehicle beside him, saying *I'll come down with you. No!* he says with all the vehemence he can muster. *No, Sophie – get your astronomy done. I'll be fine*.

And he is, little more than two hours later, resting back down at the hospital in Hilo. Head not quite cleared and feeling an idiot, but fine.

'And for my next trick,' he says to Sophie, who has phoned to see if he's OK.

'Hey! You mean you did it on purpose?'

He laughs. 'OK – circumstances beyond my control. Sorry for the distraction, though.'

'Don't think of it, Greg. We weren't distracted for long.'

'Getting some good images?'

'Pretty good and the satellite weather prediction shows this little bit of high cloud clearing away later in the night. You sure you're OK?'

'Fine. Seth was brilliant – hung around here until he could see I was OK.'

'Are they going to let you out of there?'

'In another few hours, I think. So. Can I buy you lunch tomorrow – or is that breakfast?'

'Oh – some time off! Yes, you can – be great.'

Hawaii

He takes out the photographs and passes them to her while they wait for their food to arrive.

'Oh!' Sophie says in surprise, as soon as she's glimpsed the dog-eared photo's subject matter: Greg and a woman who must be his wife and a boy between them who has to be Seb.

'We said we'd have a talk about Ella. Seemed as good a place as any to start.'

He watches while she looks back down at the pictures, wondering how they'll seem to her – the people he knows best whom she's never even met: his wife, his son, his parents, pictures from half the globe away; the setting an English country pub, in sunshine in the garden, the debris of an eaten meal and half-full glasses on a rough-hewn table; the splash of colour of high-summer roses.

'This must be your dad,' she says, turning one of the photos to him.

'It is.'

'You look so like him.'

She flicks slowly through three or four pictures, then stops to scrutinize one more closely, and he wonders which it is that holds her so much longer than the others. He watches her beautiful, studying face, worries about the judgement which may be about to come; but whatever it is, it feels right to do this – he wants his cards completely on the table. She looks so long, there's time to notice that the rain still beats down, dripping through the dense, lush wall of foliage outside the open window by their table, its hard rush onto the pathway loud; like the pummelling of a waterfall. He thinks of sliding the casement closed but the fresh air is good, so he leaves it.

There's a fall of her hair he wants to move from her brow so he may see her face more clearly. Reaching across, he finds the strand is damp to his fingers, wet still after running inside from her lift down the mountain. She looks up at his touch. He thinks her eyes seem troubled. Perhaps the photos weren't such a good idea.

'Which is that?' he asks of the photo she's spending time with. She turns the image round to face him. 'Ah.' The picture of Seb on his father's knee, one hand out for balance, the other on his father's breast as he reaches up to whisper earnestly in his father's ear; a three-year-old totally engrossed by his dad, who listens to his son with head tilted to hear, a face of concentration on what the child is saying, the broad hand of support on the child's back. 'These pictures are quite old. He's five now.'

'Loves his dad.'

'We have our moments.'

Perhaps he shouldn't have raised it after all, the spectre of Ella, his family life. Perhaps they would have been best left half a world away; neatly compartmentalized. He'd spent the morning making plans of places to go with Sophie away from this rain. Perhaps he's just blown it.

'Be nice to get out from under this rain cloud,' he says once the food has arrived and the photographs are put away.

'Hilo's on the wettest part of the island.'

'Shall we go and find somewhere drier after this?' He waits. A little moment of truth.

'I'd like that.'

They drive west across the island, slipping through microclimates, a new one every few miles. Greg stops the car on a ridge – for the view ahead, where lower vegetation thins and to buy pineapple at a roadside stall and because he wants to look at her.

'I should have warned you I'm lousy company after a long observing run,' she says from where she curls sideways in her seat, raising her head sleepily to meet his gaze when he gets back in the driver's side. He tilts his seat back to give him space in which to mirror her body language, reaching out to trace the line of her cheekbone with his finger.

'You're fine.'

She smiles. 'I rest my case,' she says, catching hold of his hand to lightly kiss it, resting their hands on the car seat together.

'What case?'

'From the photographs.'

He frowns and pushes out air in a little sigh.

'I shouldn't have shown those to you, should I?'

'Oh. I'm glad you did, Greg.'

'Yes? What case, then?'

'You like to touch. In all the photos with your dad and mom and Seb you're in physical contact.'

'Am I?'

'You are – even with the guys working on the field centre.'

'And? But?'

'But not with Ella.'

He thinks back over the images to see if she is right, then gives up.

'I've never thought of it in terms of the photos before, but it sounds right. I don't suppose Ella and I do touch often and when we do –' he shrugs – 'let's just say it's not what we do best.'

Her eyes look very sleepy and he smiles, running a finger round her fingers where they rest.

'What *do* you do best?'

'Ella and me? We provide a family unit for Seb.' He gives an ironic laugh. 'Which means we largely keep out of each other's way. Keep things between us on a superficial level. We've learned to be distant and polite. We don't ask difficult questions.'

'And if it weren't for Seb?'

'Oh, I'd have been long gone.'

She does sleep, once he drives on again. He sees her fingers slowly uncurling as changing landscape slipstreams by.

The water is warm as he swims beside her, keeping her a little ahead of him until they near the edge of where the sea is calm and stop to tread water while slow rounding waves raise them up and slow dipping troughs sway them down. They look back the 200 metres to the shore – white sands on the palm-treed beach, a sheltered cove on the island's sunny, dry western coast.

'Should be OK here,' he says, 'assuming my sources are correct.'

'What is it you're—' she begins, but already he is lying back in the water, stilling himself. Then he brings himself upright again and is grinning.

'*Beauty!*' he says.

'*What*, Greg?'

'Dip your head in and listen.'

He smiles to see her face change as she lies in the water, her eyes on his at first uncomprehending, then suddenly widening, her lips parting in wonder now, her gaze shifting away from his; eyes unfocusing as she listens with all her being to hear the plaintive-sweet, haunting song of the whale.

Her eyes flick back to his, her hand coming from the water to catch his arm, to bring him beside her in the water, to lie alongside her in the water and listen, floating, lifted by waves, to the distant, faint, alien sound.

His eyes gaze out into cloudless blue arching above his body drifting, weightless, in the warm sea as he notes the patterning of the whale song's phrasing: one line repeated to make a couplet; faint couplet followed by another faint couplet; the pitch in one couplet high then descending; the pitch in the next couplet high and spaced with silences, then one long, low phrase drawn out slowly on its own. All the while in the water, he keeps his fingers linked with hers: a closeness thing, a safety thing, making sure they drift together.

She sleeps again once they've returned to the beach, lying in the shade they seek out beneath the trees. She's so soon asleep, the water on her skin has had no time to dry; not even on this balmy day, in this warm and balmy breeze. He marvels at it, the speed and completeness of her retreat while her body is so very present still: her face more elfin where wet hair sticks; droplets there on her shoulder; breasts nestling on the thrown down towel; a balancing arm and knee slanting out into the sand; smooth body lines his eye won't relinquish: the rise of her thigh to a hip pushed high, the rounding-down slide to her waist, another slide to her tender belly. His penis quickens and it feels like stealing and he sits up suddenly, busies himself in digging out a book from the bag they have brought, then looks around him at the others on the beach: her guardian suddenly there on guard.

At dinner the spectre of Ella again – a request from Sophie to see more of the photographs.

'I've left them in the car.'

'No matter.'

A raised wooden building with the sides raised open to let in the sunset and the breeze from the sea; the restaurant busy and the food good and still he's not content.

She had only slept for twenty minutes on the beach, had come to as quickly as she had fallen and they had swum together and walked the beach and swum together again, only letting hunger drag them away. There are little silences between them now, though. A sense of awkwardness coming from her that he's finding it difficult to navigate round.

'How long will it take us to drive back to Hilo?' she asks, her eyes on his.

His fingers stop in their breaking of bread.

'Do you have to be back there tonight?'

'I'm kind of expected – one of the women from the astronomy centre.'

On the table, at the stem of her glass, end-on his finger-tips contact hers.

'I was rather hoping we could stay over this side of the island tonight.' He tilts his head to one side, lets a smile emerge. 'And tomorrow. And tomorrow night. And the next day.'

She does loosen up then, her smile widening to mirror his, leaning across the corner of the table to whisper in his ear, 'Are you trying to get me into bed?'

Though they can't have heard, people at the next table glance across.

Greg nods gently. 'Mmm. Definitely. Yes, I am.'

She half laughs, shakes her head. 'Ask a straight question.'

'Thought we could stay in a little place to the north of here. About an hour's drive, I should think.'

'You've booked somewhere already – haven't you?'

He drops his gaze, then smiles across at her.

'A man may live in hope.'

She widens her eyes by way of reply.

'I know it's very soon and – in other circumstances—'

'Small town, girl next door—' she fills for him.

He nods. 'We haven't got that sort of time.'

'Which might be a good reason not to bother at all.'

'It might,' he says, steady eyes on hers, the trace of a smile again. 'After all, you didn't ask me to come halfway round the world to see you and—'

'Oh – and the *con*ference?' she interrupts.

He shrugs. 'Perfectly justifiable from a work point of view and not at *all* the reason why I'm here.'

She looks down as if she might not believe him and he touches his fingers again on hers, insistent this time, demanding her attention and only when he has it saying, 'Sophie. I came to see *you*.'

Glances come again from the next table.

'Could we have this conversation somewhere else?'

It could be Britain they're driving through on this high road, the headlights picking out grassland verges; seemingly familiar field gates; tunnels of overarching trees. They drive in silence so that he wonders if she's sleeping, but glancing across he can see she's wide awake, her body-clock on daytime now.

'I'm still struggling to understand where Ella fits into the equation,' she had said as they strolled the dark beach parallel to the road – the negotiating ground between restaurant and car.

'I know you are,' he said, shoving his hands into his pockets. 'She doesn't is the simple answer.'

'That's kind of my point, Greg,' Sophie had said, stopping in the darkness. Car headlights had swept round on her as she reached down to release the buckle at her ankle. He had waited, left in darkness again, the day's stored heat coming up from the sand; the seawater shoosh of unseen waves; the swoosh of another car on the road.

'You're going to have to trust me on this,' he had said into darkness as he sensed her straighten up. 'Ella has long since forfeited her right to a place in the closeness equation.'

More car lights had caught her face a moment; burning a freeze-frame image in the darkness; her eyes' gaze down-turned.

'Is that what Ella would say?'

'I don't suppose it's how she sees it, no.' He had given a wry laugh as he gathered himself up to say, 'The point is, it's not an equation she would *want* to be included in. In fact, Sophie, she would be only too pleased to be completely left out of it.'

He had gritted his teeth, feeling the rising flush of humiliation.

'Sorry, Greg,' Sophie had said in the darkness.

'It's OK.'

'Sorry.' She had turned to find him, misjudging, her

shoulder bumping against his breast; touching her hand on his upper arm as he pulled his hands from his pockets. 'I'm just trying to understand.'

'I know.' Her hand on his breast then; his longing welling up to meet it; bearing his arms up to enfold her; sweeping his hand to the nape of her neck; drawing her close; feeling the fast, hard thump of his heart.

Car lights had swept over them then, reason to gather her even closer, only she'd pulled away a little, brought her mouth to his ear to whisper, 'There's another thing.'

'Yes?'

'It feels like for ever since . . . Almost for certain, I've forgotten how.'

He had leaned his forehead against her hair, breathed out a little grunt of irony. 'Oh, me too, Sophie. Me too.'

There's the descent from the high road into valleys, into a microclimate much more lush and tropical, the car lights catching yellow globes of grapefruit as they turn into the smallholding's driveway. There's the owner to greet, the annexe to be shown to, built in beneath the main house on the hillside and surrounded by greenery, one wall big-windowed with sliding glass doors opening onto an under-house veranda.

There's a shower to take – him first at her insistence when he'd hoped they'd simply share – a little nervousness between them now, a little nervous distance so that he sluices the day's salt from his hair while she insists on exploring the garden in the dark.

There's low lamplight in the empty bedroom, a few of her things scattered. He wanders into the unlit sitting room, his reflection in the window as he towels dry his hair. There she is, sitting out on the veranda: the richness of outdoor greenery round her lit by outdoor electric light. She has one knee hauled up to hug in front of some astronomy document she isn't paying attention to. There are eyes she turns to him which travel up his body set in different context now: nearer to the bedroom than the beach. There are slender shoulders to gather her by as she stands to face him; an *All right?* to whisper in her hair; the warmth of her *Mmmm* nuzzled against him.

'Shower's good,' he says as he gently sways her.

'I'd better go, then,' she says at his breast, staying exactly where she is.

There's the tenderness of her breath on his skin; the ridiculous tenting of the towel round his waist pushed out by the keenness of his penis so that Greg has to laugh. 'Just ignore him, he has no manners,' he says, manoeuvring himself to one side of her body, only she won't let him, brings herself back into contact with him, the words *Don't go* murmured against his neck and straight away there's the floodgate thing: forcing him to swift-air inhalation; his head flung back as if above water; its pressure inexorable, buoying him along to bear her swiftly indoors before him.

He's building a dolphin in the garden at home, life-sized papier-mâché on a twisted wire frame. Sebastian is giggling, his hands and knees covered with gooey glue. It's hot and yet the rain starts, tapping a little rhythm on the dolphin's paper sides. Seb looks worried, puts out his hand to feel the rain, looks anxiously up at his father's face, but the papier-mâché seems to be holding. 'A little rain won't make any difference, Seb,' he says as the rain stops and Sophie slips back into bed.

'What won't what?' she asks, pulling the hot covers off.

'Sorry?' Greg murmurs through his waking, feeling her body slide beside his, her damp skin fresh and cool from the shower; tasting the salt of her earlier skin still on his lips. 'Was I talking in my sleep?' he mumbles. His sleepy hands find themselves on her hips, sliding to her waist as she moves down next to him. Her hair is damp on his hot face as she kisses him gently on the mouth.

'You were. What were you dreaming?'

He tries to recall and fails, gives a little grunt which says, *No idea*. 'Can't have been as good as waking and finding you in my bed.'

'Got me where you want me, Jamieson?'

He brings a hand up to gentle round her head: lightly, her

head beneath his hand, lifting his own head from the pillow to look at her, then propping himself up on one elbow.

'Yes.'

He moves damp hair from her forehead, kissing her, running a hand along the length of her, feeling her body rise to his touch and she lets him make love to her slowly this time.

Hawaii

His watch alarm sounds at nine thirty the next morning and he leaps from the bed before he's quite awake.

'What's the hurry?' Sophie asks from among dishevelled bedding, watching bemused as he struggles into boxers.

'Seb's bedtime. Don't suppose for a minute there's a public phone here—'

'Use my mobile.'

'And the village is a mile or two away.'

'Use my mobile.'

He hears her this time. 'You got it with you?'

'In the bag,' she says, pointing.

'Do you mind?'

'No, no.'

He passes the bag to her, sinks back on the bed while she finds the phone. 'Thanks, Sophie. Sorry for the hurry. It's just that he waits for my call.'

'Sure.'

'How are you, Seb?' he's soon able to ask, sneaking a foot back under the covers to twine round her ankle.

'I'm OK.'

'How was school today?'

'It was OK. Moree had a accident, though.'

'Oh dear, is he all right?'

'Well, I *think* he will be all right. Miss Seymour said he shouldn't come to school any more, though.'

Nice move, Miss Seymour.

'What happened, Seb?'

'He went out to the sweet shop—'

'When he was supposed to be in school?'

'Mmm. He went out to the sweet shop and got runned over.'

'Oh no! Was he badly hurt?'

'I don't think he was *very* badly hurt. I gived him some medicine and—'

'Gave, Seb. You gave him some medicine.'

'I gi-gave him some medicine and he's better now. Have you seen any dolphins today?'

Sophie snuggles against his side.

'No, but we heard a whale singing—'

She hugs him at the memory and he brings an arm across to stroke down her hair.

'A humpback whale singing quite a long way off.'

'A very long way?'

'Probably. We had to listen very carefully and their song travels a long way underwater.'

'A very long way?'

'It can do, Seb. It can travel for hundreds of miles. Are you snuggled down in bed?'

'Yes, but Moree's not very tired though.'

'Isn't he?'

'Could you tell him the dragon story?'

'We've already done the dragon story this week. Shall we start another one?'

'Which one?'

'I don't know. A new one.' He strokes his hand along Sophie's hair. 'One about a princess in a tower with only the stars for company – and a knight who travels over oceans to find her.'

Sophie pulls away to look at him.

Greg gives a little shrug.

'But why did he?' Seb is asking.

'Why did he travel so far? Perhaps he thought she might be someone to love – or perhaps she needed rescuing.'

Sophie raises an eyebrow before moving to mime dizziness and to clasp her stomach and he thinks she's deriding the sentimentality and perhaps she is, but she's also, he realizes, role-playing a knight with altitude sickness. He laughs silently, pulls a face.

'Why did she need rescuing, though?'

'I don't know, Seb. Perhaps the goblins had shut her in the tower and wouldn't let her out.'

Really? Sophie's eyes, raised to the ceiling, say. There's the joggle of the bed as she leaves it, the swing of the towel past her buttocks as she whisks the thing over her shoulder, on her way to the shower.

'I don't believe in goblins,' Sebastian is saying, so that Greg feels like putting the two of them in touch – Sophie and Sebastian – so that they can sort the wretched story out between them.

'Don't you, Seb? I'm not so sure I do. Perhaps we'll think about it, shall we? Try again tomorrow, hey?'

They dress to gather grapefruit as the owner said they could, making it their breakfast on the veranda, where morning sunlight slants and a lime-green lizard-like thing comes to visit, moving fast along the wooden hand-rail, stopping halfway to turn and regard them. Greg and Sophie and the creature pause. The creature tilts its head.

'Whatever is it?' Sophie says.

Greg shrugs, shakes his head. 'No idea.'

Sophie takes a sip of coffee.

The lime-green creature puffs up a scarlet table-tennis-ball throat, retracts it again; scampers on.

*

They mean to go to buy more breakfast, but the day's schedule slides as more love needs making and more sleep needs sleeping, so that the boat nearly leaves without them, mooring ropes half-untied as they arrive. Other passengers smile at their breathless arrival. Setting off, Sophie sits to brace her body as the catamaran bobs through the rough slop of sea at the harbour mouth.

'Wouldn't be princess-like of me to vomit.'

'Understandable, though. All that time up in the tower.' He looks at the sea state and the weather. 'Be steady as a rock once they get the sails set.'

And it is – an easy two-hour sail to where they can pick up the mooring buoy. There are the DON'T TOUCH warnings he's glad they give about how easy it is to damage living coral; then masks and snorkels to dole out; the safety stuff to listen to. On the diving platform, she watches others.

'I've never done this before.'

'Didn't get round to it in the Caribbean?'

'No.'

'You'll be fine.'

His fingers run round the edge of her mask, checking her hair is clear of the seal, making eye-to-eye contact through the masks as soon as they are in the water, giving the hand sign he's shown her, the rounded 'o' of OK? which she returns, OK, and he moves his snorkel to say, 'Just lie in the water and test the mask out, Sophie.'

Her next OK is more convincingly given and – finger-linked – they fin towards coral to float on the surface and look down onto its pink and creamy richness and a teeming fecundity of brightly coloured fish and when he knows she's feeling at ease, he releases her to dive down and be among them, somersaulting to look back up at her there on the surface; his heart full, not knowing which he feels is the more miraculous – the rare and fragile realm below him, or that of Sophie, his lover, above.

Sailing the way home, they go forward to lie face-down in warm, breezy sunshine on the trampoline stretched between the catamaran hulls. Spray splashes up through the taut webbing, which gives a view down to the rapid run of sea beneath: blue, bright and breaking white rills tumbling gold – like the quick leap of fire – where the sun streaks through to play catch with the water. Their shadows are ripple-edged silhouettes of their supine bodies cast down upon the froth and foam. He sees the shadow of her arm move – her shadow hand reaching out to contact his shadow shoulder; merging with it moments before he feels her real fingers touch down on his skin.

He begins to take mental snapshots of her; wanting to secrete them away like treasure; knowing time is horribly short: Sophie making way for a little girl to join them on the trampoline, her full smiling focus on the child, the small hand held in hers; Sophie next to him in the car, her honey-skinned thigh to touch; Sophie barefoot in the annexe garden, her delight like a child's as she picks up fallen avocado pears; Sophie on the verandah at dusk, intent again on a printout of the image she took for Richie.

'Know what you've got there yet?'

She shakes her head. 'No. But I just *wonder*—'

'Mmm?' he says from behind her, his hands on her shoulders as he peers over at the paper on the table.

'I just wonder if it's a solar system.'

'Like *ours*, you mean?'

'Well – it would seem to be re*markably* like ours, Greg. Knew before I took the picture the star is the same mass as our sun. What I hadn't quite expected is that the dust disc –' she traces her finger round the doughnut shape – 'the dust disc is about the same distance from its star as the Kuiper Belt is from our sun.'

'You've lost me in the Kuiper Belt.'

'Oh, OK. Dust orbiting a star begins to get friendly and gather into clumps or planetesimals and then *they* get friendly and – hey presto – a couple of hundred million years later there are a few planets *plus* there's a bunch of remaining planetesimals – a disc of leftovers from the party.'

'The Kuiper Belt.'

'Yes and the remaining debris disc here—' She indicates the image again.

'Is like our Kuiper Belt.'

'At a much earlier stage, but, yes, and what's even more interesting is *this*.' She taps a finger on a bright peak in the ring image, then sighs out a laugh and pushes the paper aside. 'I really shouldn't *do* this.'

'Do what?'

'Take one snapshot and torment myself with the possibilities of what it might be when I'm not going to be able to get back to the telescope for a few months to investigate the thing any further. I don't even know if this *is* a bright peak and even if it is, it could be *any*thing, including some anomaly in the earth's atmosphere at the time the image was taken. I'd have to take at least a dozen more images over a period of time to make sure the peak is really there before I could—' She brings the paper back to her view and Greg sits beside her.

'Before you could?'

'Before being able to put forward the idea that it might be a planet or planets inside the dust disc that are causing this peak.'

'Ah – like making phosphorescent plankton shimmer.'

She leans back against him and laughs. 'Slightly different scale, but it's the same sort of idea. A planet ploughing its way through the dust disc would excite the dust, trapping some in orbit round itself and leaving a wake through the rest. And then the *other* thing is the significance of *this*,' she says, tracing the disc's asymmetry. 'This area which looks like a gap in the inside of the disc could be where a planet has passed through and cleared out the material that was there. Jupiter and Saturn do that with the inner edge of our Kuiper Belt.'

'More similarities with our solar system, then.'

'Yes.'

'Wait a minute – are you saying there might be an *earth*-like planet in there?'

She turns to fix her gaze on his eyes. 'The holy grail.' She laughs.

'Well, it *is*, isn't it? Aren't all the planets that have been identified so far – aren't they all—'

'Gas giants,' she fills in for him. 'Like Jupiter – no solid surface, no water, no breathable atmosphere.'

'But if this system really resembles ours?'

She shrugs. 'I really *mustn't* speculate,' she says, then immediately laughs. 'It would be something though, wouldn't it?'

'I'm already celebrating,' he says, getting up and heading for the kitchen. 'Glass of wine?'

There's the chilled bottle to bring to the veranda; the clink of glasses as he sets them on the table. There's Sophie, standing now, near the veranda wall.

'Geckos are back.'

And they are – two white geckos in a head-to-tail circle

come to find insects which in turn have been drawn to the electric light on the whitewashed wall.

There's the wall to lean against and geckos to watch – their five-toed, spread-out, talented feet. There's her face to memorize; the scent of her he loves to breathe in; her chin to lift; the softness of her mouth to kiss; the slimness of her waist to gentle his hands around; the curve of a hip to follow; the fabric of her dress to raise to find she's wearing nothing underneath.

'We'll be late for dinner,' she says, kissing him on the mouth.

And they are late, for the second time that day, but it doesn't seem to matter much, one or two tables coming empty now for late diners without a reservation. Flambeaux burn in this outdoor restaurant at the edge of the sea where two guitarists play, the sea's blackness their backdrop, a literal drop behind them, three metres down to a rocky beach.

'Greg?' she queries as he pours wine for her, the white of a breaking wave racing in behind her through the darkness. 'Will I see you again?'

'Oh, God, yes,' he says quickly.

'How? Where?'

'I've no idea, Sophie, but – if it's what you want.'

'It is. It's just – our circumstances – the distance.'

He smiles across at her. 'Less than half this tiny planet. Nothing to an astronomer.'

She looks down as a solo hula dancer comes: a long floral dress and a crown of flowers; long strands of threaded shells swaying from around her neck. Greg touches his fingertips against Sophie's forearm.

'We have more time here yet.'

She nods, eyes on his a moment. Tonight and then a day tomorrow and another night before her flight the morning after.

'The dance,' the hula dancer is saying, 'is a story of lovers set in the rainforest by the waterfall.' As she speaks, her hands and body demonstrate the moves which correspond to the story's elements.

'Unless you'd rather give up on it, Sophie.'

'*No*,' she says emphatically, then more softly, 'No. In fact, I'd quite like to adopt some of your practices –' he raises his eyebrows – '–and make you my next – my first, in fact – my first conservation project, my project in sustainability,' she says against the dark sky and sea, as breaking waves roll in and the hula dancer dances her story out, her womanly body in precise and precisely synchronized motion: the sway of her hips – the walk of lovers, her hands inscribing their story in the air, her bare feet rhythmically kneading sand.

Hands touch in the homeward car; hands touch in the annexe bed, facing each other in the dark. Enough love already made that day, they lie at a little distance in silence; enough light reaching through from the veranda to let him see something of her face: an outline of chin and lip and cheek, the curve of an eyebrow to trace his finger along.

'Is it that . . .?' he begins. 'You don't regret our being here?'

Her eyebrows raise, catching a little more light, the tips of eyelashes, too, revealed, but not her eyes, left in shadow still. Minutely, she shakes her head. 'Not for a moment Greg.' Eyelashes blink, once, slowly.

'You seem a little quiet.'

'Just a little sadness at the thought of leaving.'

There's Sophie, then, to gather in his arms, his sated body warm against hers, the snug, tight, perfect fit of her; her weight leaning to balance with his, against him more as she falls into sleep. There's the rise and fall of his body's breathing long and slow, now matching hers, now left behind, now put totally out of phase as he slowly draws his deepest breath to slowly sigh it out again. Thoughts of Ella spring up and he quashes them. He'll sleep in the spare room once he gets home. He shifts his gaze to the window, where lit greenery presses and trails. His eyes close. The warm press of her body in breathing. His face against her hair.

He's coaxed from sleep by her gentle hand cup-lifting his balls, by her thumb's tender slow stroking of his penis, already half-risen to her as he half-wakes, by her buttocks pressing their way towards him, trying to sidle their way beneath him, his sleep-stilled face half-waking to a grin, his mind half-filled with a half-formed thought about something that wants to give voice, only his sleep-blocked brain can't find the route as she guides him onto her, his neck gentled by her hand reaching back to him. He grunts out a half-laugh. He's asleep, for heaven's sake! He's making love to her in his sleep, dream fragments, still: something to do with snow, an image recalled as he lifts his body as directed, just enough for her to slide beneath him, except for the one leg she leaves trailing wide, as he struggles to lend steel to his sleep weakness, willing his arms not to let his weight drop. He soft-grunts a laugh, nestling his face in the froth of her hair to whisper sleep-slurred words in her ear – You don't want to do *that* again, do you? – feeling her buttocks press to him in reply. Half-sleeping, half-slipping, half-missing he tries – another snow-dream fragment as she moves beneath him, making a readjustment of angle – snow at his parents' house – her warmness and readiness make him draw breath as she draws him in – the snow-covered path by the house in Cumbria: a boyhood sliding-on-snow then indoors: the shock of fireside warmth. He draws breath and holds it, holding himself in her, some tide of emotion sweeping through his half-sleep, the thing it's been difficult to let himself comprehend: the shock of finding his manhood wanted.

'You don't want to do *that* again, do you?'

She reaches back an arm, reaches back her head to kiss him. 'Don't mind. Just missing you.'

Oh, *that's* right – the snow wasn't Cumbrian! He was dreaming of the Arctic – pure white snow and the yellowed pelt of a polar bear. He wonders if his weight is squashing her – ought to shift before he drifts into sleep again. Perhaps ought to finish the job in hand.

'I was wondering,' he says.

'Mmmm?'

'What concept polar bears have of green.'

A moment's stillness before he feels her body contract in brief laughter: the nicest of ways to be ejected, he thinks, as he rolls away, rolling her over, gathering her to him, tightly.

'*What?*'

'Only they don't see it for months at a time,' he says, snuggling up.

'What's this, Greg?' she laughs.

'White snow, blue-grey sea, the orange of sunsets and the red of their kill.'

'They'll see it in rainbows,' she says.

'Mmmm.'

'And as part of the spectrum making up the white of snow. Is this relevant?'

'And they'll see it on its own in the thaw,' he says. 'Must

be a very different concept from ours, though, where green equals growth and food and plenty and for them it's the opposite.'

'Is it?'

'In a way – given climate change,' he says, moving his arms to make sure she is thoroughly embraced. 'They need the freeze to get them to their prey species.' Oh! *There*, you see. A little part of her shoulder which could be more completely hugged. 'And because the freeze is coming later, they're not getting enough to eat, which means they're going into winter hibernation weighing less than they need to see them through.'

She lifts her head to look at him. 'Any particular reason why polar bears suddenly?'

He laughs, hugs her close again. 'I was dreaming.'

'Of polar bears?'

'Mmm.'

She tents the covers up and over them, settling her face against his neck.

'And what were *you* dreaming about?' he teases, kissing her forehead and the corner of her eye and the rounding of her cheekbone.

She laughs. 'Can't imagine.'

'Have I neglected you?'

'No! Just being greedy.'

'Might manage a little something now I'm awake.'

'I'd rather not.'

'*What!*' He laughs. 'You were inciting *riot* a few moments ago.'

'Yeah, yeah. Sorry. The mind is perfectly willing.'

'But the flesh?'

She laughs. 'Painful, Greg – If you insist on my spelling if out.'

'Oh, no!' he says, laughing. 'What have we done?'

She laughs out loud. 'I should hope you know *exactly* what we've done!'

'Didn't mean to hurt you.'

'You haven't. We have. Now – *end* of conversation.'

'It's just—'

'Ah *ah*,' she says abruptly, clamping a hand across his mouth. 'End of conversation. I'll be fine in the morning.' And he loves to feel the little fight of her, feisty next to him, in his arms.

'OK,' he agrees, as she releases his mouth, feeling himself fully roused now against her.

'Sorry,' they both say at once, Greg backing off, laughing a little, trying to make himself scarce.

'No, no. I'm sorry,' she says.

'No need.'

'I'll be fine in the morning.'

He rests his head back down, that position they have found for sleep, each curled up, her head tucked beneath his chin. A little silence – Greg wide awake now, making a pretence at sleep: failing as a little laugh escapes him.

'What time do you call morning?'

Hawaii

The lava is darker than the tarmac it has crossed, solidified and rising from a metre-thick edge. It's cracked, this old lava flow, deep fissures revealing fine, dull grey-red layers, but even though it's weathered now, the highway it covers is as nothing. Like a piece of ribbon cut, the road has simply been truncated.

They scrabble up onto the dominant rock and look for their direction across the terrain in front of them – grey-black solid lava into the level distance as far as the eye can see. The slope of the hill is greener some way to the left of them; the sea turquoise to their right. 'We should keep inland,' Sophie says. 'The lava tends to build up into shelves when it hits the water.'

'Not stable?'

She nods. 'Has a habit of collapsing into the sea, especially if people walk on it.'

Although it's quite early, the day is already hot and they walk in silence awhile, the lava brittle beneath their feet.

Greg finds something mesmeric in its patterning and they stop now and then: here where the molten rock has set in curling waves like fabric billowed out; here where it has solidified in rings like the wrinkled skin on cooling broth; here where it twists like strands of coiled rope.

'You've been here before, did you say?'

'Yes. Last time I had some telescope time. Came out with a guide. The flowing lava wasn't far then.' Nearer than the two-hour hike they've been told it will be today.

The rock colouring changes as they walk, the grey-black giving way to paler, younger solidified lava; the paler grey displaying a gold and silver sheen where the formations are younger still.

Looking ahead, Sophie sees an area where the air above the rock is shimmering with heat.

'Over there,' she says, pointing.

'Oh, yes!'

The rock beneath their feet is hot as they approach, heat from the ground easily outdoing the hot day's heat. Not a good time to trip and fall or even to hesitate, Greg thinks, feeling the soles of his boots become sticky if he pauses – even briefly – on the hot recent rock; feeling the skin of his shins demand his leg's retraction, like a hand held too close to an oven. Fissures in the rock look like folds and fissures do at home, only here they belch out heat, and when his eye comes into line, he sees their depths glow a fierce orange. Greg catches Sophie's eye. *All right?*

She grins across at him. *Amazing*.

'Oh, here we go,' she says, pointing a little further ahead, and looking he sees the movement where emerging lava flows.

It's a little like watching slow-motion mercury – a sedate yet inexorable progress, the lava's searing orange cooling within seconds of its coming into contact with the air, darkening into a quicksilver crust, flowing on out from beneath its new skin; lava flowing out over set lava, filling in undulations to set like stumpy, malformed limbs while the body of the thing slides on towards the sea.

'Have you got any change?' Sophie asks, drawing a blank from her own pockets. The coin he passes her bursts into white flare once she's dropped it onto molten rock.

'Richie has set himself a project,' she explains as they walk their way back, skirting even further inland. 'To take images of stars at all the stages of their evolution, so he's wanting to work his way through from nebulae where new stars are forming through main sequence all the way to – well, there are various next stages – white dwarfs, quasars, brown dwarfs – not all of which he will be able to image, of course.'

'Is that where you come in?'

'I have my uses,' she agrees, 'filling in the gaps.'

'It's just a hobby with him, you said, didn't you?'

'He makes his living as a proofreader, so yes the astronomy's a hobby – although that term doesn't do justice to his dedication. Incidentally – did I say he's tetraplegic?'

Greg looks sharply up at her. 'No!'

'He only has movement of his head and neck and some fingers of his left hand. An accident when he was a child.'

'How old a child?'

'He was six.'

Greg lets out breath. A little older than Sebastian.

'I can't begin to imagine how that must have been for all of you.'

'It certainly had terrific impact.'

'I'll bet it did.'

'Anyway – his project on stellar evolution. It's one of the things I set my students to do and he and I were chatting about it and the next thing I hear is that Richie's got it all worked out – what images he wants to take and where he's going to try and find them, and then he's pestering Dad to stay up all night and get started with the telescope.' She laughs. 'He did settle down about it – went into his lower-key, long-term persistence phase. He does have that dogged determination once he sets his sights on something – a real tenacity.'

'In his position – well, I can't *begin* to imagine what it's like to be in his position, but I would guess those are really helpful qualities.'

She nods her agreement. 'Yeah. They are.'

The scrub on the distant hillside is burning at the edge of a slow lava slide a few hundred metres from where the roofs of two houses rise.

'Wonder if they've left yet.'

It's too far away to tell.

'Not the most restful of places to go to sleep.'

'At least at night the glow will be more visible.'

She laughs. 'Well, *that* would be reassuring, Greg.' She tucks loose hair back into its tie, lifting it off her neck. 'There was a whole village here behind us a few years back.'

'Was there?' he exclaims, turning to let his eye run over the wide, empty stretch of lava fields.

'This earth-like planet you've just discovered,' he says as they walk on.

'Solar system that *maybe* resembles ours,' she corrects, rising to his bait.

'How come it hasn't happened before?' he says, through a smile which acknowledges his teasing. 'How come it's only gas giant planets which have been found?'

'It's got a lot to do with the techniques available to us. Planets will reflect some light from the star they're orbiting, but because they don't give off light themselves it's really hard to see them. If a gas giant is orbiting close to its star, though, even if we can't see the planet, we can detect the effect it has upon the star. As the star and planet orbit their centre of gravity, the wavelengths we receive from the star, change. The spectral lines shift towards one end of the spectrum and back again.'

'In a Doppler effect.'

'Precisely. From our point of view, the star appears to be wobbling. If there's a "wobble" – a red-shift or blue-shift – in a regular pattern, it suggests there's a large body orbiting the star. Once you've worked out the mass of the star, you can calculate the mass of the planet and the size of its orbit.'

'And they've all been gas giants?'

'Yes. Earth-like planets are too small and distant from their star to affect them in the same way. And in fact, where we have identified gas giants using Doppler shift, we can be pretty sure there *won't* be earth-like planets in those systems. That's because gas giants tend to form a long way out from their stars. The ones we can detect using Doppler shift have orbits which are very *close* to their star – in other words, they will have migrated in towards the star effectively wiping out anything in their way.'

'Earths, for instance.'

'Yeah – a sort of game of planetary snooker. Anything in the habitable zone is likely to have had it.'

'Is habitable zone as it sounds – an area capable of supporting life?'

'Yes – essentially. A region at a distance from a star where liquid water is stable on the planet's surface. Sometimes known as Goldilock's planets.'

He laughs. 'Not too hot and not too cold?'

'Exactly. Any nearer the star and water would burn off. Any further out—'

'And everything is frozen up?'

'Yeah. It's probably only in the habitable zone that conditions exist in which life can evolve.'

There's an old wall of solid lava to stop and drink more water by – a wall of solid lava to stop and wonder by, this upright structure formed layer by layer by little flows, like the flow of black wax from monstrous candles, until the long wall, twice Greg's six-foot height, was made up piece by little creeping piece. They are silent in the heat of the day, drinking water from bottles that have warmed in their rucksacks, letting their eyes flow over the wall of flows like tree roots, flows like limbs, like elbows and arms ending in club hands. Greg points out the talons of some huge, half-buried bird as Sophie finds the staring eye of an elephant incarcerated behind stone trees where drop-nosed goblins peer and Greg has a sense of Bosch, some gruesome garden of delights. He reaches out a hand to the nape of Sophie's neck.

'Here – let me put some more cream on your shoulders.'

'Am I burning?'

'No, but this heat is pretty fierce. It's extraordinary, isn't it,' he says as he smooths in the cream, 'talking of planetary formation and habitable zones – to think that this place has been so degraded and it hasn't even finished forming itself yet.'

'Hawaii or this planet?'

'Both. Hawaii as an exemplar for the planet, if you like. Here's the volcano busily making new land and already we've wrecked what's here – nearly all the rainforest gone, flora and fauna severely diminished—'

'It seems so rich.'

He shakes his head. 'Nothing like the diversity it once had. Millions of years to evolve. Wiped out in the blink of an evolutionary eye.'

'God, Greg. All too late, then?'

'Probably,' he says, trailing more cream onto her shoulders. 'Worth doing all we can, of course.'

Giant ferns tower over them later as they wander through inland forest, the fern's new fronds tightly curled and twice the size of Greg's fist. There's a tumble of maidenhair fern round the entrance to the lava tube, a delicate fringing before they plunge into the lava tube's darkness, their eyes taking moments to adjust to low light and scale: a wide, overarching space, nature's version of the London Underground, only this tube is cool and musty and silent; lit by spaced-out dim wall lights.

'All right?' he asks, prompted by her silence.

'Sure,' she says, a hand at his waist as they stroll down the gently sloping tube. Her fingers trail along the lava wall, where a huge flow of hot lava once trailed, leaving its cooling tube crust behind. 'Don't much feel like going back to Hilo.'

A family overtake them: echoes of their footfalls and the whispered giggle of teenage girls bouncing off the rock-tunnel curves.

'We don't have to, Sophie.'

'It's why we've headed back this way.'

'We don't have to, though. We could head west again, so long as we get up early tomorrow.'

In time for leaving. In time for flights.

She touches her hand against his arm. 'We don't exactly have much of a track record for getting out of bed in a hurry.'

They do head west, though, turning their backs on the direction of the airport, submerging themselves in a forgetful sea, focusing on the yellow darting of fish and – beach walking – the quiet closeness of each other: words draining; fingers touching and parting as shoulders brush.

They drive on looking for somewhere to stay, finding a tiny village with a wooden pink hotel, three pink storeys high and pink: outrageously and deeply pink, the outer walls and verandas pink, the handrails pink. Inside there's a time warp back fifty years, a shabby grandeur in the heavy dark colonial furniture; in the quality threadbare carpet on the stairs. The plumbing dates back, too, but still it is enough of a shower to loosen salt and sand and volcanic dust. It cannot loosen time, of course, he thinks as he lies on cool linen on the high wooden bed, waiting for her to come to him; watching her moving round the room, a white towel thrown over one shoulder, the whitewashed spacious place a background to her honeyed body, listening to the padding of her bare feet measuring, on the polished wooden floor, the draining seconds passing. She stretches up to draw pale curtains across the high, sunnied window.

'Come here,' he says, his hand reaching out to her.

'Damn it, Jamieson,' she says, letting him draw her to him, snuggling her body close against him. 'Damn it, Jamieson. You're *so* demanding.'

He wakes first as the sun is setting, opening his eyes without otherwise moving, his face again in her hair, the pale, out-of-focus froth, the pale eyelashes on her cheek. How many more such awakenings? In peripheral vision, the curtain billows, breeze-blown through the open window.

South-west Wales

Sebastian looks at the whale on the table. The whale eye is higher than his own. His own eye reflects in the stainless-steel edge of the table and is huge. He tries to measure it with the span of his hand, but when he reaches forward, the eye disappears and moving colours take its place, the blue and red of his shirt reflected. He moves back a little way and the eye in the table reappears and blinks slowly. He wonders what the eye looks like when it is closed and he tilts his head back, looking out under lashes; sees his lashes, huge, reflected like the legs of some spider that's as big as a dinner plate crawling over the edge of the table.

His father had tutted when they turned back the whale's dark skin with its layer of white fat inside like the split-open coconut his father hangs in the garden for the birds. His father had said something Sebastian didn't understand. *So emmy see pated.*

'What does emmy see pated mean?'

'Emaciated,' his father had corrected. 'It means the

whale is very, very thin. You see here?' his father had said, squatting down in front of him, his eye at Sebastian's eye level, bringing a piece of the skin and fat with him. 'There should be six times this depth of blubber.' He had held his rubber-gloved hands a set distance apart to show him. All that space where fat should be. Sebastian had pursed his lips up tight. 'Don't you want to go outside to play now, Seb?'

Sebastian had shaken his head. He's a big boy now. He wanted to be here, inside with the men. Even though he must not touch and he must not *in-ter-rupt* and he must not get in the way, he likes the feel of the men working: Harold cutting up the whale, his father taking photographs of the whale's insides, passing the little plastic bags for bits, the little glass jars with liquid in. He likes the click of the jars as his father puts them in the lit, shiny stainless-steel cupboard with the glass front where the air sucks through.

Sebastian shifts his weight to his other foot, trying to make his tummy feel better, but the whale stink is worse there and he shifts his weight back again, as the moving, blurred eye in the table scrunches up. The unmoving whale eye looks at him and Sebastian looks back. Funny how the eye still looks the same, the long grey head the same, even though the body – he glances along the table – even though there isn't so much of a body any more, just a slithery, glistening mound of – he shifts his weight from foot to foot; looks up at the whale's still eye.

'Don't you want to go outside now, Seb?'

Sebastian shakes his head. He's a big boy now. Not like Moree. Moree wouldn't be able to stand the smell. Moree would be sick at the sight of the blood. Moree wouldn't even come inside. He glances up. Yes. You see. Moree's still outside on the window sill; on the high-up window sill, his back against the glass. Moree's not even looking in.

There's a dewdrop on the end of Harold's nose. His hands are in bloodied rubber gloves. Sebastian watches as Harold wipes his nose on the shoulder of his white coat. And then he does a magic trick. Reaching into the whale's insides he pulls out a packet of crisps! Sebastian feels his face stretch wide, but Harold's face doesn't change. Seb searches it for the look he's seen on the magician's face on the television at the end of the trick when everybody claps, but Harold's face is looking down.

'More?' his father asks, taking the crisp packet Harold passes and – as his father takes it to the sink – Sebastian sees the gold and silvery thing is empty after all.

'*Oh*, yes,' Harold says, and pulls from the whale's insides a carrier bag like the ones they get from Tesco and another one – faded red and all tangled up. Perhaps the whale ate the shopping. Is that what happened? he wants to ask, only his father is wearing his concentrating face. Is that what happened? Like Grandma and Grandpa's dog, who got to the shopping in the back of the car and ate the bread, plastic bag and all.

'Another one from the UK,' his father says, unravelling the polythene and reading the writing as Harold pulls more rabbits from the hat: half a big black bag this time, like the bin bag they put at the end of the drive every Tuesday on his way to school. Then Harold pulls out two clear polythene bags and another crinkled piece of blue all somehow linked together in a string, like a magician's string of knotted silk scarves.

Sebastian rocks from foot to foot. 'Why did the whale eat the rubbish?'

'Hmmm?' his father says, sluicing the polythene bags in the sink, so that Sebastian has to say it all again, though his stomach wants to be very still.

'Why did the whale eat the rubbish?'

'She thought it was something nice to eat, but it's probably why she's so thin and why she died, Seb, all this polythene blocking her stomach.'

Seb says nothing and his father looks across at him.

'I want you to go outside now, Seb. Go down to the shop for me, will you? Take some money from my wallet in the office. See if Mrs Taylor's got some of those lovely apples in.'

He doesn't move apart from rocking.

'Go on, Seb.'

He wants to but he knows the smell will be much worse

further down the table before he can reach the open door and then there is the drain to pass. He looks at it where the pipe from the table ends above the drain hole, dribbling stinking whale juice down. His body is flipped double then by spasm, spewing his own stinking mess to splatter all over the tiled floor.

'Oh, hard luck, Seb,' his father says, peeling off his thin rubber gloves and chucking them in the big bin with the yellow bag where the bits of cut-off whale get thrown, before he scoops Seb up; lifting him high so that he flies out over the whale on the table, lifted by his father's strong hands, over the head and Harold's bald head and the sickening whale mess in the middle and the tail so whole and beautiful still and on out into air that's good.

South-west Wales

'*Went to an astronomy conference last week,*' Sophie writes to Greg in an e-mail from Vancouver Island. '*There was a theorist – does it work like this in marine mammalogy? Having first designed some pretty slick software, some guy spends months with a computer feeding in known information about how something functions and then the computer extrapolates from the known until it comes up with a model of how they think the thing works over an extended period of time, after which it's down to other scientists like me to come up with evidence from the real world – or in my case from somewhere in the universe – in order to corroborate or refute their claim.*

'*Anyway, this theorist was talking about finding earth-like planets in the habitable zone. He's come up with software which models how our solar system with its remaining – Kuiper Belt – debris disc came into being, so that then he can look at snapshots in that process and say – this is what our solar system looked like as it was forming and therefore, if we can find planetary discs which look like this, there's a fair chance an earth-like planet is forming or has formed. When I say what the disc "looks like", I don't mean visible light. This guy has made predictions about emissions in infrared and submillimetre radio waves, and what he did that really made me sit up was to flip through some of his computer model "snapshots" and – Greg – there was one which could have been the image I took for Richie from the James Clerk Maxwell Telescope.'*

'Oh, God,' Greg utters as he reads.

'The hairs on the back of my neck did their standing-up act—'

'I'll bet,' Greg mutters.

'and I couldn't quite find my voice for a moment when I went and casually asked him a few questions afterwards. Anyway, I've calmed down about it since then – a bit at least – it's awhile until I can get back to the JCMT to take more images, so there's no point exhausting myself with the possibilities in the meantime.

'There is still the dilemma about what next, though. Can't get telescope time any sooner. Don't want to wait that long to publish. Don't want to publish until I've got more data. Can't get more data without telescope time. And so the snake bites its tail. A colleague I've taken into my confidence suggests publishing advance notice in the International Astronomy Union Circulars, but I'm really not sure. In fact, with only one not necessarily reliable image to go on, I think it could be professional suicide, plus it would only take some lucky rat with

telescope time allocated ahead of me to read the notice, do the
observations and scoop the prize. Have thought about contacting
the JCMT to find out if anyone has time booked who might be
interested in a collaborative project, or perhaps someone would
let me gatecrash their observation run. My own time is another
problem. Teaching commitments.

'Enough of all that. E-mail soon, would you? I miss you,
Greg. Miss your eyes.'

Sebastian appears to be nesting: gathering twigs and sticks
and mossy bits and little piles of long grass.

'What are you doing, Seb?' Greg calls from where he sits
in the old meadow among the remnants of their picnic.

Seb slides a glance at him. 'Making somewhere for
Moree.'

'Oh, OK.'

The boy goes back to his humming, picking up twigs
from the little pile; adding them to the building circle in the
tree roots by the stream; stopping every now and then to tell
Moree all about it; finger waggling instructions to the space
where Moree apparently sits.

Late, low sunlight slants between old fruit trees, lighting
the globes of dandelion seed-heads so that they glow where
they stand – heads above the meadow grass like lanterns,
lit; so maybe it's something in the quality of light that
makes Greg think of Hawaii – the low sun of that last

evening, walking out from the pink hotel in search of dinner with Sophie and finding, instead, a little art gallery about to close its doors for the night, except yes, the owner said, they could look round. A life-sized shoe made of glass had made her laugh as they peered into the lit glass case to see the sparkling slightly slurred stiletto: surreal glass thing, crystal clear except for the bubbly, blowsy, blue glass bow.

'Wrong fairy tale!' she had protested as he bought it for her.

'Seb's always telling me I get my stories muddled up.'

'I've mentioned it to the doctor,' Ella is saying.

'Sorry?' Greg says, turning his head to her.

'I've mentioned it to the doctor.'

'What?'

'Sebastian's imaginary friend.'

'Really. Why?'

'Because I think it's odd behaviour.'

'Do you?'

'Don't *you*?'

'Not particularly, no.'

'Well, I do – returning to something like that at his age.' She plucks a stalk of grass.

'He's *five* years old, Ella.'

'*Precisely*. And Moree first appeared when he was three. Doesn't that seem a little regressive to you – going back to something he'd dropped when he was a little over three? The doctor said five is quite late for children to come up with imaginary friends and they usually lose them when they go to school and start mixing with other children, so it's *not* the usual pattern.'

'Oh, for heaven's sake, he's a kid. A lot of kids have imaginary friends.'

'Not like this.'

'What are you suggesting?'

'It's not what *I'm* suggesting.' She snaps the stalk of grass in two and plucks another. 'With young children, imaginary friends are often a good sign apparently – role play, exploring social situations through imagination—'

'There you go, then.'

'*But*, at his age, it might be that he's trying to compensate for something.'

'Having a fertile imagination which isn't being sufficiently challenged at school, do you mean?'

'*No*, Greg.' She throws the pieces of grass aside. 'Trying to compensate for some disturbance in his relationships.'

'What sort of disturbance?'

She says nothing, leaving him to work it out.

'What, Ella? Oh, no! You don't mean my going away, do you?'

He sees her mouth tighten.

'The doctor said that your absence—'

'Oh, come off it. He was *much* better this time – when I

came back, I mean. Much less fuss than last time and I do *have* to go away, Ella. It is, after all, how I make my living.'

She leaves another silence. Then fills it.

'Is it? Or is it just that you're screwing someone?'

He cannot help but let his eyes widen.

'Do you really want me to answer that question?'

'I'll take that as a yes, shall I?'

Greg punches out indignant air, sees Seb is sending covert glances towards them. He takes a moment to make sure his next words are calmly delivered.

'What has this got to do with Sebastian?'

'Quite a lot, don't you think?'

'Daddy?'

'Yes, Seb?'

'Can you help me?'

'In a minute, Seb.' Greg looks across at Ella, her gaze set at the field's edge. He picks up his boots from where he's shed them, puts one on and laces it and taking, the second, sees the pattern of the sole is slurred, melted by his walking on the crust of hot volcanic lava. A different crossing ahead of him now, he gathers himself for a leap and makes it.

'Why you should suddenly concern yourself with my sex life when it isn't something you've bothered about for years is quite beyond me, Ella, but the answer to your question is no.' He stands to go and see to Seb, switching grass-seed and

her slander from his jeans. 'No, Ella, I'm not *screwing* someone. It's altogether more meaningful than that.'

Cleaning teeth at Seb's bedtime, Greg feels it's good the subject has been broached. Not that he'd ever had any intention
of secrecy, only a sense of his love life no longer being any of
Ella's business; his return home to sleep in the spare room
merely a physical confirmation of the separateness that's
been the actuality of their mental state for some time now.
Should make things easier between them, in fact, keeping to
separate rooms. More realistic.

'Don't forget to brush behind those bottom teeth, Seb.
That's better.'

And as for the stuff about Moree. Seb's an imaginative,
well-balanced kid. End of story.

Greg catches sight of his own face in the mirror,
browner and more rounded than before he went away.
Something different about his eyes, too – a certain steel of
resolve currently, but – without doubt – since Sophie, there's
been some light or vitality back in his eyes that had been
missing for so long he'd forgotten it could be there.

'All right, Seb?' Greg says, as Sebastian puts the tooth-
brush back in the little rack. 'Let's go find your jamas.'

Towelling dry Sebastian's hair, he thinks about it – how
the light in eyes can come to be extinguished; what it takes
to bring it back. He wonders if it's the same for Sophie,

catching sight of herself in a mirror; seeing some light of their union on her.

'Sit still, monster,' Greg says, trying to brush Sebastian's hair.

And what of the light in Ella's eye, he wonders. You've done a lion's share of childcare while I've been away, Ella – he had said as they came in from the fields this evening – perhaps you should take some holiday and let me see to Seb for a few days. Extend your Wednesday afternoon activity, perhaps.

She *had* looked quickly at him, then.

So that rang a bell, did it, Ella? he'd thought. All those Wednesday afternoons he has noticed. All those hours unaccounted for. All those Monday and Thursday evenings, too, out with the girls he's never been invited to meet. Well, so be it. In the new context of their acknowledged separateness, it's entirely her own business now.

Seb's little body is warm on his knee, solid and toasty and fresh from the bath and Greg wraps him tightly in manly arms and brings his face down onto the boy's neck and says in a deep, monster, whisper, 'You smell good enough to eat and unless you're safely in bed *very* soon—'

He'd hoped to feel the squirm of giggled-panic run through the boy's body, but instead Sebastian gets up, shrugging him off. Daddy being silly again, the set of the little shoulders say, as Seb gets on with the serious business of arranging soft toys in the bed for the night.

If only she'll let it go at that, Greg thinks as he tidies up discarded clothing, then sits on the end of the bed, waiting for Seb to finish his sorting. If only she'll see the sense of it. Parenting for Seb, separate lives lived under one roof. They could do it if she wanted it, too.

He realizes Sebastian has fallen silent and is watching him.

'All right, Seb?'

He's not about to cry, is he?

'Whatever's the matter?'

A little finger comes to point and Sebastian whispers something as tears begin to spill.

'What, Seb? I couldn't hear you.'

He catches enough this time. The finger pointing to guilty father and the words, 'sitting on Moree'.

Greg springs up, looks down at the bed, at the imprint his weight has made in the duvet. 'Oh, God, Seb. I'm sorry.'

'You s-a-a-aat on Moreeeee.'

'I'm sorry. Is he OK now?'

Seb shakes his head. Tears stream.

'Oh, I'm sorry. Can we have a cuddle and make it better?'

Tears stream.

'Hey there, monster,' Greg attempts to soothe,

smoothing down the boy's hair only to be shrugged off again as Seb tumbles out of bed; hurriedly bundles himself along to where his father had been sitting and picks up the invisible – but presumably squashed – imaginary boy. Or they'd always *assumed* he was a boy, but – watching Seb pick him up now, taking him back into bed with him, cuddling Moree tenderly to his chest – from the size and the shape Seb's hands inscribe in air, Greg thinks perhaps they were wrong. Perhaps Moree's a dog after all – or a cat, maybe. Wouldn't quite explain Moree's need for books at school or his wandering off to the sweet shop – but perhaps that's being too literal.

Greg watches and – sensing himself excluded from this cuddle – sits beside the bed on the floor, taking their dragon book from the bedside cabinet.

'Do you think Moree would like to hear some of the dragon story?'

Seb looks down from the bed at Greg; tilts his head on one side to hear what Moree has to say on the matter. Silently Sebastian nods.

'"I can't think how you can have forgotten,"' Greg reads calmly, '"but Nadria is the place where dragons live,' Bethsheba explained as the two dragons strolled through a park, leaving dragon footprints on the snowy path which meandered among sparkling blue-white sunflowers the gardeners had carved from ice."'

There's a shuffle as Sebastian snuggles himself and Moree down. The boy's eyes blink very slowly as Greg cosies the duvet round him.

'"It only takes a few hours to fly to Nadria from here. We should go, you know. Could go this afternoon, in fact.'

'"What about the king?'

'"What about him?'

'"Won't he mind if we just disappear?'

'"Well, yes, he probably will mind. Do the old fool some good, losing us back to Nadria.'

'"Why would it do him some good?'

'"*Why* would it? Well, I should have thought that was perfectly obvious.'

'"The dragon shrugged his wings to show he didn't understand.

'"You don't know very much really, do you?' Bethsheba said. 'Which conclave were you in?'

'"Which what?'

'"Conclave – when you were a pup?'

'"I don't think I was in a conclave.'

'"Not in a conclave? Every dragon is in a – wait a minute. What did you say your name is?'

'"The dragon,' said the dragon.

'"No, your real name.'

'"I don't think I have one of those. The people in Miramba always used to call me the dragon.'

""'Where's Miramba?'

""'The dragon began to feel a bit upset. All these questions he couldn't answer. It had seemed so important to fly the princess home, he hadn't thought about how he might get back again and he really couldn't say exactly where Miramba was. `

""'I'm not sure,' the dragon said. 'I expect the princess could tell us. I just know that it took us three weeks to fly here.'

""'Three weeks! Flying every day?'

""'Every day,' the dragon confirmed, wondering if perhaps he'd said something impressive at last. 'Long days, too,' he said, holding his head a little higher.

""'And before Miramba?'

""'The dragon sighed out a little fire.

""'I don't remember anything before Miramba.'

"'Just then a small girl came along with a big box which she was dragging behind her on a sledge. She looked a bit nervous, the dragon thought, as she stopped in front of them.

""'The Farrins of Castle Street,' she piped up in a rather quavery sort of voice, 'would be honoured if you would – if you would . . .'

""'Accept our gift of fish,' the girl's mother prompted in a loud whisper from where she stood among the ice sunflowers a few metres away.

""'Accept our gift of fish,' the little girl repeated.

""'Oh, *well*!' the dragon began, enthusiastically, only to be flicked in the ribs by Bethsheba's tail.

""'The dragons of Nadria thank you,' Bethsheba said, very formally, the dragon thought, seeing her nod her head once at the little girl.

""'*Really*,' Bethsheba said, flipping the box lid off with her nose once the little girl had skittered away with her mother towards the blue ice helter-skelter. 'I *do* wish they wouldn't send their pups to present the food. It's supposed to be cute, but they always make a mess of it,' she said, pushing the box towards the dragon. 'Hungry?'""

Pausing, Greg sees Sebastian's eyes are closed. He can't be asleep already can he? That hardly ever happens – Seb going to sleep on cue. He waits to see if his voice's cessation causes the boy to wake, but Sebastian doesn't stir from his foetal curl round Moree, hugged, invisibly, to his breast, his little fists twitching in sleep.

'I feel for you about the timing of publication,' Greg writes to Sophie in an e-mail. *'Always a difficult one, especially with something which – in this case literally – sets out to explore new and fiercely sought-after ground. Balancing that desire to be the first to stake your claim (and – given the difficulty of science funding – we do all have to worry about that) while at the same time not giving too much away before the appropriate moment. Let me know how it's going, will you?*

'Yes, we do use computer modelling in marine mammalogy. Spend quite a bit of time fighting with the software myself, in fact. And one of my PhD students – Gina, whose paper I'm supervising – is working on a model to examine the effect of rocket-launch noise on the cranial cavities of spinner dolphins. I have concern about the possibility that the sound might be enough to rupture eardrums or cause brain haemorrhage – as we're pretty sure the naval sonar does. In fact, I've tried hard to divert Gina to working with the sonar issue. With sonar, the sound source is accurately known. The species mostly affected is known and endangered (the Cuvier's beaked whales you saw in the Caribbean stranding) and – perhaps most importantly – the technology is already in use in many parts of the world, so the number of these animals affected is potentially a huge percentage of the remaining population. The one-off rocket launch site may be devastating, but at least the devastation is localized. God – listen to me. I hate it when I start to rationalize evils as if some of them are acceptable. A few dolphins off Sombrero are likely to be wiped out, but – hey – that's not as widespread as what's going on with the sonar, so let's focus on that. Down to resources, of course. It's just not possible to deal with it all. Gina won't switch her focus, though. I kind of understand it. Kind of. She started work on the rocket-launch issue before I went out to Sombrero, so why the hell should she switch now, just because the Caribbean incident happened? Very sensible of her. Wouldn't want to make extra work for herself just because getting results

on the sonar problem would have a much wider and more signifi-
cant conservation application. Might jeopardize her meeting her
deadline. The frustrating thing is, she's Good. Intelligent, diligent
and scrupulous in her way of working within sound scientific
parameters. Just regrettable she's won't see the big picture. I've
told her the Sombrero battle is already lost. The reports our team
submitted have made not an iota of difference to the outcome.
Building on the island is due to start soon, apparently. End of
miniature Galapagos. Bastards. I'm as pleased as the next man
to use satellite technology – to send this e-mail, for example, plus
all the data picked up by my hydrophones out at sea reaches my
computer via satellite. I just wish they'd utilize spare time at
existing facilities to launch the things. Sorry, Sophie. I don't mean
to go on about it. Gina had a tutorial with me this afternoon, so
it's a recently reactivated frustration. No doubt she'll produce a
splendidly academic piece of science.

'Meanwhile, e-mail from Paul to say the navy have
admitted to being in the area at the time of the Caribbean
stranding (difficult to deny it really as Paul got aerial footage of
them on the move the next day which was broadcast on the TV
news report you were in). No comment from them, however, on
what they were doing re use of sonar. Meanwhile, not a single
individual has been spotted from Paul's well-documented popu-
lation of thirty-five Cuvier's beaked whales since the strandings
incident. (On past stats, he would have expected to see two or
three known individuals a week.) As there's no way they could

have got away from the sound source, they are all assumed dead. As their carcasses sink and the water's prohibitively deep there, there's no possibility of gathering proof.

'Big debriefing meeting for me next week with fishing-boat observer teams. Stats to gather and process and forward to some government dept, which – judging by past performance will no doubt totally ignore them.

'Dead stranding of large whale on north-west Welsh coast reported this evening. Fresh, but too big to move. Sounds like an orca. I leave at first light to assist post-mortem.

'So, phew! Sophie – let's hope the solar system you've discovered turns out to be just that. The rate at which we're trashing this planet means a new one is just what's needed, although if we can't reach it so much the better – at least not until we've learned to conduct ourselves – environmentally – immensely better than we currently do. Or who knows, perhaps elsewhere evolution has come up with a far more worthy recipient for its wonders.

'Bunch of third-year undergrads due in week after next. They do me good, all that idealism and determination.

'You do me good, too. It's so very good to have you in my head. Glad to hear you miss my eyes. I miss everything about you.'

South-west Wales

Summer makes time pass more easily. Friends come to stay from Scotland, Ella's friends, so diluting the family soup, making it much the easier to swallow. Summer gives them more space, too, lets them spend hours out of doors, so that Greg and Seb build evening sand-dolphins or go sea-swimming or beach-combing, while Ella goes out with her friends. And maybe it's the easiness of summer that seems to let her accept Greg's staying in the guest room or – when her friends arrive to stay – his sleeping at the field centre and then, of course, he *has* to be at the field centre once the students arrive for summer school: seashore ecology with students from the OU who make a wonderful fuss of Seb.

The summer holiday is not quite so simple and he puts it off, citing the papers he must write; trying to fob Ella off with a couple of family days in Cornwall. He fits in a visit to the National Lobster Hatchery: Seb's finger on the glass tracing the movement of tiny new lobsters. Man helping nature here; ensuring survival for later release and increased stock to be fished. He feels the buzz of witnessing a worthwhile cooperative project: sees the camaraderie of fishermen and the fishery's officer helping each other out, together bringing berried lobsters in, to harvest the eggs to hatch. Ella is not fobbed off. Surely, she says, he could manage a few days away in Cumbria, so they do go to Cumbria to stay with his parents, more people again to dilute the soup, and it's good for Seb to see his grandparents and for Greg to see Seb running in the garden where – as a child – he once ran. So many echoes of the past here: old tennis rackets hanging in the garage; his father's patience remembered, in teaching him to drive. Greg had brought Ella to Cumbria, too, before they were married. His third significant girlfriend. And his mother especially had liked her well-mannered nature; thankful, as she was, that her son seemed – at last – to be over Rachel. *Ella's so much calmer*, his mother had said with scarcely concealed relief.

They had been expected to sleep in separate rooms, of course, when Ella the girlfriend came to stay; an unspoken outcome of his mother's sensibility and anyway, he remembered thinking at the time, they were probably right. Time to take things much more slowly than he had with Rachel. So it was funny to find himself – eight years on – wishing they could once more sleep in separate rooms. But it's not a signal he had wanted to trouble his parents with. And at least the room is twin-bedded. They'll cope.

He supposes later that perhaps Ella felt some history, too, in the house in Cumbria and it was that which prompted her behaviour one evening, coming into their bed-time room. She had caught him undressing, his back to her as she paused in the doorway. He'd stopped his movement momentarily, feeling his blood yet quickened with wine and the whisky nightcap he'd had with his father; feeling her gaze on his naked torso; hearing the door close and the whisper of her nightgown as she walked.

'How's Seb?' he'd asked, busying his hands again; fumbling for something and nothing in his washbag.

'Sleeping,' she'd said, her voice nearer now, so that – without moving his head – he'd looked to locate her, caught an out-of-the-corner-of-his-glancing-eye glimpse of her: the satiny nightdress, pale pink, the shoulder strap fallen from her shoulder. The scent of her, too, had reached him, fresh from the shower: that shampoo she uses.

Keeping his back to her, he'd rummaged in a drawer.

'He's had a busy day.'

'Yes.'

Three months now, since Sophie in Hawaii, the alcohol racing through his blood had sung. *And after all, she is your wife.*

'Greg, if . . .'

Her voice, nearer still – and he had ceased his movement; resting his hands on the chest of drawers; his skin taut with the knowledge of her nearness; another glimpse picked up: the rounding of breasts beneath flimsy-sleek fabric.

'. . . if you wanted to . . . if you wanted we could . . .'

The shock of her hand then, landing lightly on his back, running down to his waist, then gone, leaving his blood further fired.

It need only take a little while.

Releasing some of the breath he'd been holding, he nodded.

'We've had some good times here, Ella . . .'

'We *have* . . .'

In the past he had meant.

He had turned towards her then, leaning back on the chest of drawers, lifting a thigh to mask and ease the growing tightness of his jeans.

'And you're looking . . . lovely, Ella. Lovely.'

His mouth pursed to a wry smile as he shifted his thigh, keeping it raised, one foot resting on top of the other; feeling his hurried blood's fast beat as she swayed her body to him. Drawing himself to his full height, he'd raised his gaze to the beam in the ceiling; his hands holding her shoulders from him.

'It's not what you really want, Ella,' he'd whispered across the little distance.

'But—'

'Not *really*. Is it?' He'd looked down at her, sliding the

narrow strap back up her shoulder. 'I don't think it ever was. In any case, it's not what we do any more.'

Somehow he'd made his way to the door; his gait awkward, ridiculous, round the gripping tightness of his trousers, so that he'd almost laughed as he stumbled out into the corridor, closing the door and heading for the bathroom; alcohol-tumbled back to that time when as a teenager he would do just this in this house: sneak down the corridor hampered by a hard-on, hoping to hell he wouldn't meet his parents as he headed for the shower to let his seed be sluiced down the drain. *Oh, really?* his mother had said, to a neighbour complaining of her own unclean son. *Greg's just the opposite. For ever in the shower*, so that he'd burned a deep crimson, thinking his habit might be known.

It's best this way, he'd thought moments later, at the shower's hot spurt. Keeping to this side of the line. Earning the right to see Sophie soon. It's best this way.

'*I wanted to tell you about Jacob's cabin,*' Sophie writes to Greg in an e-mail from Vancouver Island. '*It's not much, in some ways, an old clapboard place, not much more than one big room inside plus a bathroom with a slightly dodgy shower. It's lakeside, though, and forested and real peaceful. Jacob works in the university department and likes to have the cabin used and aired, and in return a bunch of us go out in the summer and help get the paintwork done. Some of the best times there are in winter, though – being up-island from Victoria, they get more snow and the cabin's warm with the log burner blazing. So, Greg – when can you make it?*

'Some progress of a sort with that new solar system you're so sure I've found. I've been wondering if background sources of light might be influencing the brightness distribution in the ring which could mean that the peak of brightness I've tentatively identified as perturbation caused by an earth-like planet is no such thing. (Sorry to disappoint . . .) An astronomer I know – one of my peer group who's still at Berkeley – has agreed to take some visible light images when he goes to Hawaii to use the Keck next week which might resolve that particular aspect one way or another, unless the background source is a very distant, young galaxy. If it is and it's very "dusty", it might not be visible in the optical at all, in which case I'll need radio data, too. Patience, Sophie. Patience.

'Sure looking forward to Jacob's cabin. (No pressure.)

'xs'

'*Cabin sounds hideous,*' Greg writes to Sophie in an e-mail from Pembrokeshire. '*You know how I hate the great outdoors, especially in less densely populated regions. And then there'd be the company to contend with. Still – anything to aid new planet discovery. Shall just have to bite the bullet. Which dates are you thinking of?*'

*

'Perhaps, when you've finished,' Ella says from the doorway, 'you could come downstairs. I need to talk to you.'

There's the e-mail to send with the touch of a button across an ocean and a continent to wait for her. There's the slope of the ceiling to mind his head on as he goes downstairs to talk with Ella. There's the armchair to sink his body into; her body to notice, sitting upright on the edge of her chair. Ankles crossed. Her face is a mask. There are her words to hear. Simple words. Delivered one by one words, calmly, as she sets out her plan. She does not give him eye contact.

It seems important not to overreact, he tells himself once she's done, though his heart thumps hard. He knows by now how a strong reaction from him only makes her dig her heels in.

'You need to think really carefully about this, Ella,' he manages to say evenly while noticing his hand is shaking.

'Oh – I have, Greg.'

In Flight

'"The dragon had never flown in the company of another dragon before. At first he thought that Bethsheba was teasing him by going so slowly until he understood that she was going as fast as she could in the blustery head wind and – realizing he was bigger and stronger – he took to flying a little ahead of her, shielding her from the worst of the weather while listening to her guidance on direction.

'"After a couple of hours, Bethsheba stopped and hovered in the air and pointed a claw down to where white mountains rose up from the snowy plains.

'"'Nadria,' Bethsheba said. 'The mountain range is at the edge of Nadria.'"'

'Will the mountains in Scotland be white?' Seb's voice interrupts via satellite.

'I'm not sure. They might be, Seb. Are you all packed and ready to go?'

'Mummy's putting the things in the car.'

'And will you snuggle down and sleep on the back seat?' Greg asks, his throat suddenly tight round the words.

'I put Moree and Badger in under the covers already.'

Greg scrunches his eyes hard. Still the tears push through.

'Have you, Seb?'

He should have bloody well cancelled this trip. He should have insisted on going with Ella and Seb or talked her out of it somehow, though God knows he tried hard enough to make her change her mind. He makes himself look out through the cabin window, blinking his eyes out into darkness.

'Daddy?'

'Yes?'

'I don't want to go to Scotland.'

Greg squeezes his eyes tight closed.

'I expect you'll enjoy it once you get there, Seb. And you'll see Grandma and Grandpa.'

'Mummy said we had to find a house to live in.'

'I think Mummy just wants to have a look.'

'But Mummy said we have to find a house. I wish you were coming.'

'We talked about this, Seb. Mummy wants some time with just you, and I expect she'll have a look round at some houses, but it's a holiday really.'

He grits his teeth around what may turn out to be a lie, cursing himself. He's never lied to Seb before.

'I wish you were coming.'

'You'll be home before you know it, Seb, and I'll see you then.' He stares hard out into darkness. 'Hey! Anyway, Seb. This dragon story.'

He listens to the silence down the phone.

'"Soon the dragons saw mountains beneath them, snow-covered mountains in a circle round a valley basin. Flying ever lower and closer, the dragon began to see lights among the trees.

'"Those are the lights of dragon dens,' Bethsheba explained.

'"As they came into land, the dragon couldn't believe his eyes. Everywhere he looked there were dragons: dragons flying among the trees; dragons sliding down the snowy paths; dragon faces peering out of the nearest dragon dens—"'

'Daddy,' Sebastian says.

'"We'd better go and see the MED,' Greg reads.

'"What's the MED?' the dragon asked.

'"It's who, not what,' Bethsheba corrected. 'It stands for the Most Eminent Dragon.'"'

'Daddy,' Seb repeats, and Greg hears Ella's voice, too, in the background.

'Have you got to go now, Seb?'

'Yes.'

'You'll have a lovely time.'

There's a silence and then that little noise Seb makes when he's trying very hard not to cry – that little, rapid breath intake, then there's Ella's quiet voice saying something to Sebastian; the crumpling noise of the phone being handled; the click as the line goes dead.

Canada

At first the forest is dark and dense; conifers men have planted and impenetrable groves of some tall thick-set shrub he does not know; sawn and hacked back to tear a tight path through. They carry stout sticks, though what good they would be he's not sure in this place so far from human habitation where mountain lions and black bears range.

Mountain lions stalk utterly silently.

The knowledge keeps him glancing behind him every minute or so. He must be losing it. Normally he would love this; normally it's what he loves best, in fact, feeling a different, more dangerous, sense of order; his place in the food chain pointed out; staying alive by living on his wits.

It's knowing the boy is in Scotland that's doing it. Not knowing what Ella's decision will be. Not knowing where he stands.

He thinks of Jacob's clapboard cabin by the water; the log burner, hot in the huge stone chimney; the fur of the white-tailed deer on the bed; Sophie's creamy flesh stretched out in the firelight. He had made all things good for her there: all night he had kindled and rekindled her; given his seed to her; brought her to a wept elation and then wept himself while she held him; told her of his fears about Sebastian: a little boy lost.

Sophie turns now from where she walks ahead of him; her eyes gently on him.

'Greg, don't you think we should be finding you a flight home? I'd hate to feel you were here if –'

He shakes his head. 'Ella has to do what Ella has to do. One of those occasions when trying to stop her only makes her more determined.' He prods his stick at the dense under-growth, attempts a smile. 'Could do with getting out of this thicket, though.'

'It gets better. Just here,' she says, pointing to where the narrow path corners. 'Here is the old growth.'

Surely, his reason queries, it can't start quite so abruptly, can it? But it does. It's like walking through a doorway: a huge arched doorway into the old-growth forest; into a towering, calm, cathedral-like space of low light and anti-quity.

The terrain is steep-sided here, carved by a stream and richly banked by deer fern flourishing. Fallen trees, too, are blanketed with dense, mossy, velvet green and then there's the huge, open height of so very tall trees, reaching up to spread their canopy. Cathedral space. Mellow light. They walk on – a contrary sense of being indoors – the softness of forest debris underfoot.

The day is in any case overcast and here a sea fog seeps through trees, gathering on pendulous sage-green lichen, which trails and drops its way down from moss-clad branches. Moist air threads droplets, too, on high spider's webs so that they stretch, revealed, like beaded lace between the ancient trees.

Following the path between massive trunks of Douglas fir, they pass by dells of moss-covered roots to the streaming caw of crow above the canopy and the scuttle of mink at a stream's edge. And there's no point thinking – Seb would love this. Seb is the best part of half a world away and Grandad has bought him a brand-new bicycle, a red bicycle, a red bicycle he's learning to ride without stabilizers, and yesterday Mummy took him ice-skating and he only fell over twice. So swallow the bittersweet and savour the sweet: Seb's having a good time. You could hear it in his voice. A so-far-happy little boy lost.

Sophie has paused ahead of him. She is picking berries from a bush and turns to offer him the small, dark fruit; her fingertips speckled bluish purple where the delicate fruit – in its plucking – has been crushed.

*

There are three tree trunks on the small cove beach, three tree trunks, 200 feet long, stripped by the sea of their branches and bark and tossed back to the land; their blonde, smooth hulks piled high, yet bedded in with sea-swept stones and draped with stems of kelp. The rubbery, smooth-skinned strands of seaweed are the width of Greg's wrist and four, five, six metres long; each ending in a bladdered fist. A few metres out at sea, kelp fists bob, like so many fisherman's floats, only brown, so that it's hard to tell apart the round heads of seals and the fist-floats of kelp the seals and sea lions swim among.

'What will you do?' Sophie asks Greg of Sebastian as they share the lunch they've brought.

'Play it by ear. Ella may have got it out of her system by the time she gets home. No point in concerning Seb with it if it's not for definite. Sorry, Sophie,' he says, 'I'll try and lighten up about it soon.'

She shakes her head in protest.

'It's just that it's been a shock. I didn't expect Ella to take off. Should have seen it coming. I guess it's a case of adjusting.'

'What will you do?'

'Well – I've been thinking – I could always move to Scotland if they do decide to go. Set up home nearby. Be a three-times-weekly Dad.'

'But, your work . . .'

He nods. 'Very much based in south Wales. But you never know, something might come up back at St Andrews. Anyway, it's all speculative for now and meanwhile it's wonderful to be here with you. Oh, look!'

She follows his gaze across the little bay.

'Oh, yes. Eagle.'

'Eagle? Where? Oh, *there*. Beauty.' His eye traces the eagle's glide to tall trees at the sea cliff's edge. 'I was looking at the kingfisher.' He points to where the bird emerges from the water – a fish in its bill. He laughs. 'Whatever next?'

'Bear, I guess,' she says, indicating fresh bear scat further down the beach.

They do see bear. Walking on, a while later, a heavy, fast flurry of dense undergrowth draws them up short. Greg feels the push of adrenalin as he does when diving where there might be sharks. Status shifted from predator to prey. Body ready for flight or fight. The movement is away from them. Away from the path. He grins.

'Must have been bear, don't you think?'

Sophie nods. 'With that amount of noise.'

And then they see him, moving up hill away from them, glossy-coated isolate, the ripple rhythm of his gait, then his pausing, turning curiosity, the raising of his muzzle as he scents them out, before moving on away among trees.

*

"'In a clearing in the forest there was a glow of light. Nearing, the dragon saw a sculpture of a dragon made of ice, twenty feet tall and lit from within by candles placed behind ice eyes, candles inside the big neck scales; a lamp where the dragon heart would beat, a string of candles inside the tail, in the toes, within the length of outstretched wings. The dragon thought his own heart would stop, as his breath did at the beauty of this thing among the trees.

"'There were others. Linked by a trail of lamps the dragons followed along the ground. Proud ice dragons in flight, suspended, lit, in trees. A family of ice dragons, rosily glowing, curled in peaceful sleep. Then there was an avenue of huge, colourful ice pictures, like stained-glass windows lit from behind, telling a history of dragons at Nadria: images of dragon celebration; scenes of men being banished from Nadria; scenes of fearsome dragons in flight, breathing fire down on fleeing men; scenes of dragons slain in their sleep by men with swords, ice stained red; scenes of armies of men arriving.

"'"We're beginning at the wrong end, of course,' Bethsheba said. 'The story reads the other way. First the men arrived. At last we drove them out. The sculptures we saw at the beginning are the finale, in fact. A celebration of our freedom.'

"'The dragon began to understand.

""'Is *that* why the king and his people like to have dragons around? Is *that* why they bring us fish?'

"'Bethsheba nodded. 'By being respectful, by seeing to our needs, the king proves he means us no more harm. By accepting his gifts, the dragons show we will drive them no further. We could of course. We could melt their town in moments. We choose to tolerate them there. And they like to have several of us in their city at all times because – if the dragons all go back to Nadria, it could mean –'

""'It *could* mean we're about to drive them out.'

""'Exactly.'""

'Could we make a ice dragon?' Sebastian asks via satellite.

'I don't think so, Seb. I think, in Wales, the ice would melt. Wales would be too warm for ice. We could make one out of white tissue paper and light it from inside like a lantern.'

'Would Scotland be too warm?'

'I think it would be, yes. It has to be *really* cold for ice sculptures, especially if you want to light them, because the candles and the lamps give off heat.'

He hears voices in the background down the phone.

'I was worried – because I'm a bit late phoning – you might be asleep already, but you're not actually in bed yet, are you?'

'No. Mummy said I could stay up.'

'Well, *that's* good fun. Have you done something nice today?'

'No.'

'What *did* you do?'

'We had to look at *three* houses and it took all day and then Grandpa said we could have an ice cream, but the shop was closed.'

'Oh *dear*. Were the houses any good?'

'There wasn't even a swing. At any of them.'

'Did you ride your new bicycle?'

'No. It was raining. Do you want to speak to Mummy now?'

'I'll speak to her another time, Seb.'

Putting Sophie's mobile back in the rucksack, he sees she is watching him and he smiles. 'You were right about being able to get a signal here. I'm surprised.'

'You're very good with him,' she says.

He shakes his head, comes to sit next to her on the waterproof she's thrown down in a soft, mossy bowl among tree roots. 'Oh – let's disillusion you about that one, Sophie. At best it's repair work.'

'What do you mean?'

He shrugs his shoulders. 'It's very obvious what Seb wants – two parents who love each other living under one roof.'

Her eyes stay steadily on his.

'I *cannot* give that to him. I've tried very hard to, but I can't. So it's repair work. Make-do. Could be a reasonable make-do, too, I think. I mean – I think, as parents, we could still give Seb enough of what he needs. Even if we end up moving to Scotland.' He smiles. 'And then I come crashing into your life. Bastard.'

'*What?*'

'Do you mind, Sophie? Do you mind me crashing into your life?'

'You haven't crashed into it.'

He places an arm round her shoulders; draws her nearer. 'I know it's a bit mad, but we can work it out, can't we? It's a mere nine-hour flight and then maybe we'll both need to be in some other place at the same time, like we had to in Hawaii.'

There's the gentle way she takes his head in her hands – 'Dingbat. Of course we'll work it out' – the sure way she snuggles her face against his neck; the calmness of the forest over them; the piped call of some bird he does not know; the scent of her hair as he rests his head down on hers. There's the rich lush green of the covered tree roots, dense, soft moist growth he reaches out to brush his hand among: familiar mosses and lichens and then tiny plants he does not know. His idling mind overlays the usual ten by ten centimetre grid, starts the usual count of different plant species, six, seven, eight – he sighs out as she leans more weight on him – eight, nine, ten – her closeness – ten, eleven, twelve, thirteen, fourteen – her closeness is intoxicating. He gives himself to it, closing his eyes, breathing her in.

Canada

'Did you see any dolphins today?' Seb asks via satellite.

'No, but I did see a whale after I spoke to you yesterday. A *grey* whale. I'd never seen a *grey* whale before.'

Nearing the end of their walk in the forest, the path approaching the edge of the land again, the sudden, unmistakable punched-out sound of whale exhalation. What! They'd run the last few metres to the low cliff edge, to look down from the forest to the kelp fields just out to sea. They needn't have hurried. She wasn't going anywhere, this huge grey whale, busy circling and surfacing and feeding on krill, her broad, rounding back streaming white with water and ribboned brown with strands of kelp that are nothing to her; their considerable, entangling substance brushed aside with no more effort than his booted foot through autumn grasses.

'Was it a big whale?'

'It was pretty big. They grow to about forty-five feet, Seb – that's about fourteen metres – and this one was fully

306

grown, so I should think she was that sort of length. Pretty big.'

'As big as a bus?'

Greg smiles, remembering that time they'd had trying to gain an impression of the size of things: the blue whale – almost as long as a Boeing 737; weighing the same as sixteen elephants.

'Oh, yes, longer than a bus. Did you ride your new bicycle today?'

'Yes.'

'*Did* you? Without *stablilizers*?'

'Yes. I did fall off, though.'

'Oh, hard luck. Then did you have another go?'

'Mmm. Grandpa holded the saddle, but he did let go sometimes.'

'It just takes practice, Seb. I'm sure you'll be able to ride it all on your own very soon. Are you in bed now?'

'Mmmm.'

'I've got the dragon story here.'

'The bit about the most em-em-nant dragon.'

'That's right! "The Most Eminent Dragon was very old, so old, his scales had gone grey and he didn't fly very much any more. He had a kindly twinkle, though, in rather kindly, twinkling eyes.

""'Hmm,' he said, inspecting the dragon very closely.

'Hmm. How very interesting. One of the Westlanders, I should think.'

'"Do you *think* so?' said a rather portly dragon, also inspecting the dragon. 'Because of the egg collectors?'

'"Shouldn't wonder,' said the MED.

'"What are the Westlanders?' the dragon asked once the MED had finished with them.

'"It's who, not what,' Bethsheba said. 'The Westlander dragons live in the west of Nadria. He thinks they are your family.'

'"My family!' the dragon said, not having thought he might have one of those. But very soon there is no doubt. Flying west with Bethsheba the next day, the dragon found he had really quite a large family. A mother and father and four younger brothers and three older sisters and cousins and aunts and grannies and grandpas and uncles. It was all a bit much for a dragon who – until a few days ago – had never even met any dragons before. But really, there was no doubt.

'"It's Missing!' a dragon who turned out to be his mother cried as soon as she saw him. 'It's Missing! It's Missing. Missing's come home.'

'"So the dragon learned that he had not just a family, but a name, too. Missing."'

'Moree's gone missing.'

'Oh, no! Has he?' Bit difficult to send out a search party, Greg muses, trying not to laugh, imagining the chaos of a search for an invisible, imaginary friend. 'Well, where did you last see him, Seb?'

'In the garden yesterday. I think the eg-lecter might have got him.'

'Do you think the egg collector would be interested in Moree? Usually the egg collector only takes eggs – or very young dragons.'

There's a silence down the phone.

'Moree's not a dragon, is he?' Greg ventures.

'No! Of *course* he isn't!'

'Oh, OK. Well, I think if you go to sleep now, Seb, in the morning Moree will have come home again.'

'Will he?'

'I should think so.'

'Can you read some more story?'

'Tomorrow, Seb. Have you got Badger there?'

'Yes.'

'Give Badger a cuddle then and I'll speak to you tomorrow. OK?'

'OK.'

'Love you, monster.'

He unzips the jacket of his waterproof, slips the phone in the breast pocket of his shirt, picks up the paddle and dips it into water, inky water, so black and slick and still it could be oil. Reflections of clouds and lakeside trees break up, rippling out from where his paddle breaks the surface and where the bow of his kayak pushes through. He does not see the patterning, his eyes instead searching lakeside inlets and island inlets to catch a glimpse of the red of her jacket, to catch the turning slant of her paddle, to catch her where she's gone on ahead of him.

The crawl space beneath Jacob's cabin is deepest at the front, the building stilted level where the ground drops away. Logs for burning are stored in the crawl space – neatly stacked with space left for air to circulate between them and the cabin floor – and he goes out to bring more wood inside, the night air crisp and cold and so very breathlessly still. He has left the flashlight inside and he pauses, taking a moment to adjust to the darkness. Stars burn clear. No moon. There's a glow through closed rosy curtains at the window which sheds a little light, but not where he needs it, so that he feels his way along the side of the building into blackness where the denseness of the forest presses. Beneath the smoothness of the cabin clapboard, his hands find the sharp-cut logs and – in darkness – he fills up the basket he has brought.

It is then he has the sense that – from the forest – he is watched.

A neck-prickling definite.

Picking up the heavy basket, he holds it in front of him and stares out into the forest's darkness, knowing the inadequacy of human eyes. Nostrils flare as if that might be of some use. And it just might. But he senses only the heavy scent of the damp forest floor. He stills himself, utterly. No sound. He thumps his fist twice, hard against the cabin wall. Then listens. Nothing. He must be imagining things – and he picks up a few more logs, then carries the full basket to the front of the building as Sophie opens the door.

'You OK?' her voice calls.

'Ah – there be dragons.'

'Something about?'

'Not sure.'

She brings the flashlight and they scan the beam across the darkness of tree trunks. Nothing else discernible.

'Stars are good,' she says, switching off the torch to let their eyes readjust to the dark. 'There's the one all the fuss is about.'

'In the image you took for Richie?'

'Yeah.'

'Where?'

'You see Cassiopeia?'

'Yep.'

'Follow down this way,' she says, leaning her head against his to line up his sight.

'Oh, OK.'

'It's called Zeta Calliope.'

'Didn't realize you could see it with the naked eye. How far away is it?'

'One of the closest. Only about ten light years away.'

'Oh – is *that* all? So, if we could travel through space at 186,000 miles per *second*, it would only take us ten years to get there.'

'Yeah. We're going to have to *work* on that travelling stuff.'

'Assuming there is something there worth travelling to.'

'That too.'

'How long till you get back to Hawaii?' he asks as they go inside, his footsteps sounding on the wooden floor, she, silent in stockinged feet. He slides the door's bolt home.

'Not long. A few weeks away.'

The fire blazes orange through the fireglass. The light is low. The room warm. He refills their glasses.

'Looking forward to getting on with the project?' he asks handing her wine as he sinks into the sofa next to her.

'You bet.'

'Been doing some prep?'

'Oh, yeah. Telescope time is so precious you *have* to go well prepared and – if you can – knowing exactly what it is you're after. So, yeah, I've been reading round previous papers on the star and its dust ring.'

'Are there some papers?'

'Three that I've found. I can see where I can make complementary observations – in the search for dust-ring carbon emission for example – which may be more conclusive than what's been done already. I need to assess the orientation of the dust ring, too. I'm assuming we're seeing it close to face on because the image is roughly circular, but that may be a false assumption, so I'll be checking out the axes and comparing them with optical data from the star. And then of course I just need to get plenty of images to confirm whether the bright peak that I think is in the dust ring really is there – or not.'

He is silent a time, watching logs flame behind glass; an image in his head, one of the photos of hula dancers he saw at the conference in Hawaii; a montage of a huge yet faint outline of the face, upraised arm and torch of the Statue of Liberty and superimposed over and within it, a so very much smaller and yet more present image of a hula dancer in her flora: a single, tiny figure on a beach, in a floral crown, her arm and floral torch upraised.

'You hope the bright peak is really there, I assume. Well, of course you do. And so do I. It would be history in the making.'

She laughs, curls her body round to face him on the sofa, rests a wrist on his shoulder. 'Phew! Glad *you* won't be reviewing my paper. That *has* to be the most reluctant endorsement ever.'

He laughs, too. 'Sorry.'

'It's just?'

'It's just – we don't have much of a record, do we? I

mean, assuming there is an earth-like planet and assuming we can get to it. Is there someone somewhere working on that?'

Sophie nods her affirmation against her arm, where it rests along the back of the sofa. She lifts a finger heavenwards.

'As we speak, the international space station is orbiting with astronauts aboard, working under the name of the human research facility – not transportation as such, but how the human body withstands lengths of time in space.'

'With a view to transportation?'

'Among other things.'

'And I dare say there are people working on the actual travel bit.'

'Certainly – within the solar system. Not aware of anyone setting their sites beyond that. Plenty of ideas around – light sails, hydrogen collectors . . .'

'But not actual construction of interstellar craft?'

'Not that I know of, but I guess the findings of current work will go to inform the other some day. You were saying – we don't have much of a record for?'

He shakes his head. Gentles the hair from her face. 'Oh. No matter,' he says. 'No matter. Did your colleague come up with the optical images from – where was it?'

'From the Keck telescope. That's Hawaii, too. He did.'

'Anything useful?'

'Well. They showed up three more background objects – light sources – pretty close to Zeta Calliope.'

'Any conclusions to draw from that?'

She grins. 'It's early days, but yes, we don't think they're in a position to affect the bright peak in the dust ring.'

'What did I tell you? It's an earth-like planet. Sophie Douglas making history.'

He leans forward to kiss her and, although they made love all morning, still he feels his body draw particular breath.

'Dinner's practically on the table,' she says between his gentling kisses.

'Uh, uh,' he counters. 'Needs more cooking time.'

She laughs. 'I don't think it *does*.'

'Hour at least.'

He, too, rests his head on an arm he drapes along the sofa's back, his fingers in the softness of her hair; eyes on eyes.

Then he drags himself from her, standing in the low light warmth of this open-plan room; the cooker's warmth, the firelight warmth. He opens the glass and metal door to place more logs inside; his body calmly brimming with the knowledge he will take her soon; she will take him soon. He wedges the logs in, sensing the deep silence of the night: the balm of still-air darkness round the cabin; the uninterrupted depth of forest; the dark half-mile dirt-track distance to the nearest other single cabin – currently uninhabited – the cold, black lake-water's stillness; the old and the ancient starlight reaching earth. He closes tight the fire door.

There's the deerskin she hates to see on the bed to remove for her and drape for now on the back of the sofa. There were deer at home, she'd said, behind the house in the little copse rising from the levels of the prairie fields. All winter, deer would yard up there. Hard winters, foraging on bark and wood. *Why* must you shoot them? she'd little-girl-screamed at the men with dogs, racing out to them across the snow, indoor clothes in the icy wind. *Why* must you? *Why* must you? – arriving only to see the deer brought down, seeing the blood spurt crimson onto snow; delicate legs twitching towards death.

He moves the deerskin from the bed. More wine? he signals with his glass to where she's gone to turn the oven down. She shakes her head.

'Come here, then.'

There's her mouth to kiss; the balance of her body to hold against his; the soft jacket to slide from her shoulders. He knows so well her body now, treasured thing to take from its wrapping; to duvet-turn-down and lie next to in firelight; a treasured text he reads best with his eyes closed; warm, treasured flesh he further quickens with his fingertips. His fingertips. Of one hand. It's practically effortless. A slow fingertip trail lightly up the length of her belly as, naked, she

316

stretches out in firelight. He scarcely touches her, yet feel how – in warmth – she trembles, her breast rising to his fingertip touch in the breath she draws and draws and holds and lets out: brokenly, softly, sighed out; her body turning, pressing to him.

'You don't want me to take you yet, do you?' he says in a whisper against her ear.

'Depends if you want to eat charcoal for dinner.'

He laughs, easing himself over her. 'Are you thinking about food?'

'It wasn't exactly paramount, Jamieson.'

'Only—'

'Don't, Greg. Don't tease me.'

He kisses her frown, kisses closed her eyes, pushes easily on into her – 'Oh Sophie. It's all right. It's all right.' – and he gathers her tightly in his arms and rocks her and rocks her and comes to her coming and his cried out name, his head and his heart and his body full brimming.

He wakes to her waking, to firelight rising round her shoulder, his body curled round her back, utterly relaxed and weighted on the bed, the duvet lightly over them.

'What speed are we travelling at?' he asks.

'What?'

'I was just wondering what speed we're—'

'Speed of the earth's rotation, do you mean?'

'Mmm.'

'Need to know right now?'

'Yep.'

'Not sure exactly what it is at this latitude, but at the equator it's close to a thousand miles an hour.'

He grunts his amazement to the pillow.

'And there was me listening to the stillness of the night.'

'And then, of course,' she adds, turning to face him, 'there's the speed of the earth's orbit round the sun.'

'Which is?'

'Around 67,000 miles an hour and the speed of our sun's orbit around the centre of the galaxy – which incidentally takes 230 million years—'

'Takes *what*?'

'Two hundred and thirty million years to orbit the galaxy once at a speed of over 500,000 miles an hour.'

He groans. 'Oh, *no*!'

She laughs. 'What?'

'These *speeds and distances*. They're just too big to *contemplate*.' He blows out breath, shakes his head.

'I mean it!' he insists, laughing as she laughs. 'At times a few measly square miles of ocean can seem overwhelming when the weather's turning bad and the cetaceans I'm damn sure are there haven't surfaced where I can see them and don't seem to be vocalizing either, but this . . .'

She nods. 'Don't you just love it?'

'It's – stunning.'

She sits suddenly upright, begins to scramble out of bed.

'Less stunning is the smell of burning dinner. Can I interest you in a little charcoal?'

'How could I refuse? You serve up, I'll do the dishes,' he says, helping her slip on the peachy silken dressing gown. 'By which time – by which *time*, we will be 500,000 miles further round the galaxy than we are now.'

'Give or take a few thousand. Could you get some cutlery?' she says, hurrying barefoot to the cooker.

'So – what is it we don't have much of a record for?' she asks as they eat.

'Sorry?'

'You started to say earlier – when we were talking about space travel.'

'Oh, that. Nothing.'

'Don't "nothing" me, Jamieson.'

He smiles across at her bullying. 'Colonialism. Colonization. We don't exactly have a record for low-impact, empathetic colonization. That's all. Hardly news to a Canadian or a Brit.'

'Oh.' She nods. 'It's a horror story.'

'And one that's repeated wherever colonization has taken place.'

She nods. 'It always strikes me when I go to Hawaii –

1 per cent of the population is Hawaiian now; the culture so usurped it's scarcely recognizable. And Mauna Kea – where the scopes are?'

'Yes?'

'Sacred territory to the native Hawaiians. Big dispute about there being telescopes there at all.'

He nods. 'Hardly recommends us for space travel, does it?'

'Think we might displace a culture of little green men?'

He raises his eyebrows. 'Don't you see? Our colonization habits and our degradation of the environment are all facets of the same thing – an acquisitive domination of territory and species – all species – fellow humans and everything else.'

'And you don't think we've learned anything from our past mistakes?'

He shrugs. 'Marginally. Perhaps. I agree there are many instances now of incoming cultures acknowledging the past wrongs inflicted on indigenous peoples and that takes courage – the Aussies, for example, really seem to be striving towards that, even though they know making amends is an impossible task.'

'It's happening here, too.'

'Sure.'

'And. But.'

He shrugs again. 'It's limited. Necessarily. Both because it *is* an impossible task to right such wrongs. Seems to me we can only acknowledge them and move on in a more equitable way. But what really seems limited is the fact that we're *still* inflicting those wrongs. Less on people, OK, but just as much – no, more than ever, in fact – on other species.'

'More than ever?'

'Yes. The number of species becoming extinct is on a very steep rising curve. You know that analogy, if the planet has been around for twenty-four hours, then humans have only been around for the last forty seconds?'

'Yeah. I've heard that and that the impact we've had in those forty seconds has been immense.'

'Immense. Well, it can't go on being immense. The resources for sustaining life on this planet are absolutely finite. There will simply be nothing left to sustain us. And – you know – it's perfectly understandable that we are an acquisitive and dominant species. In fact it's literally natural – a biological necessity to have had those attributes in a survival-of-the-fittest sense.'

'And. But.'

'But now it's different. We're becoming victims of our own success. You know – we have to start to apply our intelligence in a different way now – to balance out those acquisitive and dominatory tendencies – otherwise what have been our tools for survival will become – are already becoming – the means of our destruction.'

'That simple – hey?'

He nods, touching her hand as if to soften the blow of the truism, but she sits back in her chair, deflecting him.

He pushes his plate further onto the table.

'I remember, on Hawaii, you said you felt it's all too late.'

'Yes? Well, perhaps not if we act quickly. Not if we go through a radical shift in thinking and behaviour.'

'Is that going to happen?'

He shrugs. Leaves the question hanging.

'And the work you do?'

'Works towards that shift, of course, and to practical alternatives to damaging practice – in fishing effort, for example.' He leans back in his chair. 'It's barely scratching the surface, though. I mean, there *are* success stories, but really, day after day, I get faced with a weight of evidence which – despite my best efforts and the efforts of people like me – largely gets ignored.'

'So why do you bother?'

He gives a wry laugh. 'Good question. In the hope that there may be a shift of perception. Who knows, we might *just* begin to apply our intelligence to the situation and – if we do – we're going to need objective, scientific evidence to inform the changes. I also happen to believe we don't actually have any right to wipe out a few million other species along with our own.

'You know – there's such a *lack* of holistic thinking. To most of the fishermen I deal with I'm just a thorn in their side

– another suspect scientist likely to suggest no-go fishing zones. And they're right, of course. No-go fishing zones are precisely what's needed.'

'And they can't see beyond their livelihoods being affected?'

'Nope. Which is understandable. Fishermen whose fathers and grandfathers before them were fishermen and fishing is the only way of life they know. But it isn't the big picture and it isn't the scientists who have systematically and very thoroughly plundered cod stocks until – as now – they reach the brink of extinction. I mean, cod reproduce rapidly and spawn *thousands* of eggs at a time, so wiping them out *really* takes some doing. And hey! We've nearly done it. So the government introduce quotas for catches. Which of course is utterly useless. You know – fisherman hauls in his nets, finds cod in them, knows that'll make him over quota, so he dumps them – dead – back into the sea. That's a policy which is *really* going to help fish stocks recover. No holistic thinking.'

He takes another sip of wine. 'And I'm just as bad,' he says, tilting his glass. 'What is this we're drinking?'

'A Chardonnay,' she says, looking puzzled. 'Oh, I *see*. All the way from France.'

'Exactly. Had to be transported across an ocean and a continent before I could buy it in Victoria on the way out here. What was I playing at? Not exactly buying local, is it?'

'And there are some really good Canadian wines available.'

'So I've heard.'

'*And* you transported yourself here. Air travel is the worst form of transportation, isn't it, in terms of pollution?'

'Yep. At least when I get on a plane I can usually justify it by thinking that there's some conservation benefit in terms of the work I do once I arrive, but this time . . .'

'Nothing but lustful self-gratification.'

He smiles across at her. 'Absolutely.'

Canada

"'It was all a bit much – the hullabaloo of a welcome home for a dragon called Missing to a home he didn't know he had. Aunts gave him hot, slurpy kisses, tiny cousins hugged him while treading on his toes, his baby sister got dragon hiccups and Missing was the one expected to lift and comfort her, and all the while, more dragons arrived, friends and neighbours come to welcome Missing home. The great big dragon with handsome green eyes who turned out to be Missing's father beamed. His son! His son! Come home to them.

"'And then there was so much to do. Fishing trips to go on, twenty dragons all together, eating so many good fresh fish and bringing more home for the little ones and for the elderly and for the ice larder store.

"'And then there was the dragon den to build for his sister, old enough to leave home soon. At last! Something useful to do with his fire: no chance here of singeing sails, or burning crops or houses, as he had every time he'd tried to help out in Miramba. For days they worked, a brother showing him how to breathe out careful flame to carve the den from snow and ice. A sleeping den; a living den; a scrubbing-down-dragon-scales den; a kitchen with an ice-store den. Everything had to be just so for his sister, who, Missing thought, knew exactly what she wanted and – in the nicest way – wasn't going to let them rest until she got it.

"'And then – best of all – there were ice sculptures and ice pictures to produce – like the ones he and Bethsheba had seen in the forest. A particularly special use for his fire, once he'd learned to finely control his flame, each family expected to produce an art work for the festival coming up soon.

"'And then suddenly the festival was here: dragon dance and dragon singing and dragon historical parade and feasting and drinking – a festival brew which made him smile and hiccup and positively giggle. I didn't know I could giggle, Missing thought, as he sat with friends and sisters and brothers, swinging together in tree-top hammocks.'"

Greg waits for the interruption which nearly always comes at this point. It does take a second – Seb must be sleepy.

'Can we put the hammock up when we get home?' Seb's voice asks via satellite.

'Well, I don't see why not, Seb. We could pick a nice day and just leave it there for a few hours and wrap up warm and have a picnic in it.'

'With Moree and Badger?'

'Oh! Moree came home then?'

'He was in bed when I woke up this morning.'

'Oh, good. Yes, of course Moree and Badger can come.'

'Mummy says we have to go home tomorrow.'

'That's right. Time to go back to school.'

'Will you be there?'

'Not when you get home, no, but I will be the very next day, Seb. What shall we do? Shall we do something special?'

'Can we go and see the seals?'

'In the boat?'

'Mmm.'

'That would be nice. I expect there'll be some pups still.'

'Did you see any dolphins today?'

'No. But I did see a banana slug.'

'What's a—'

'A banana slug. It's a slug which looks remarkably like a banana. It's the same size as a banana and the same colour as a banana and it's spotty – just like a banana that's really ready to eat.'

So that's what was stalking you last night, Sophie had teased him as he searched the forest floor near the cabin that morning. Stalked by a banana slug. 'You mock,' he'd said, pointing to the evidence he had been seeking, clear and overnight-fresh and perfect in soft mud: the unmistakable crisp outline of the paw print of a mountain lion. 'Told you there be dragons.'

'Is it like a moon?'

'Is a banana slug like a moon?' Greg muses. 'Oh! Curved like a crescent moon, you mean. No. Or only when it goes round corners.'

Packing clothes into a suitcase, Sophie shakes her head at him.

He winks across at her. 'I should go now, Seb. I'll phone you tomorrow and see you the day after and we'll go out in the boat very soon. All right?'

'All right.'

'Love you, monster. Sleep well.'

That evening she places her hand on the side of the telescope, the huge cylinder five metres long.

'It weighs the best part of forty tonnes,' she says, then presses lightly on the scope, so that he raises his eyebrows to see the forty tonnes begin to move to such minimal pressure in the dimly lit dome.

'The engineering of these things.'

'Wonderful, isn't it?' she says, and he's pleased to see her eyes shine after her quietness this afternoon on the drive back to Victoria. 'I love this scope,' she is saying. 'I mean, you don't expect to be able to do anything cutting edge, but I just love it.

'Hey, we haven't got long – the guys from the Spaceguard programme are due in tonight – so let's go see.'

He follows her into the control room with its curving outer wall. 'Let's go see if we can find Stefan's Quintet.'

'Didn't realize you'd laid on musicians.'

'They're *galaxies*. Colliding galaxies,' she says, beginning to thumb through a reference catalogue.

'*Five* of them colliding?'

'Originally thought to be six until it was discovered that the sixth one only *looks* as if it's part of the group.' She drops herself down into a chair in front of computer screens and begins to key in coordinates.

'The sixth one is in the foreground, so to speak – only 35 million light years away – whereas those in the background from our point of view are much more distant – around 270 million light years away. And in fact, of the five, it's only three which are currently colliding.'

'Even so – three galaxies colliding. Are there *billions* of stars in each of them?'

She laughs. '*Billions*.'

Once she's entered the figures, Greg hears the machinery start up and, going back out into the telescope housing, he sees the forty tonnes of telescope move and the sides of the dome draw apart and the whole top of the building rotate to line up on five galaxies 270 million light years away.

'Can't see a thing,' he teases, staring out into the blackness of night that is revealed.

'Dingbat,' she says, coming out to see how the telescope

has settled, disappearing again into the control room, coming back again to let her eyes adjust to darkness to see if there's still no cloud cover.

There's a ping from the control room, like the ping from a microwave at the end of its cycle.

'Dinner?' he asks.

'Image,' she counters, going in to see.

And there they are on the screen. Five galaxies. Their bright-core concentrations of light, their trailing, spiral arms of stars. She points to where the arms of two galaxies are swirling into one another.

'Can you see, here?'

'Yes!'

'This is where it's all happening. NGC7138B colliding with the group and here –' she indicates clumps of stars around the two galaxies – 'is where star formation is occurring as this guy rampages through, so it's an excellent site for the study of star cluster formation and even –' she indicates the elongated arm of a third galaxy affected by the colliding two – 'even the formation of a distinct galaxy, which we think is what's beginning to happen here.'

'I remember you saying in the Caribbean that these collisions are constructive.'

'Oh, it'll be destructive, too – existing stars destroyed, planets destroyed or flung out of orbit – but it's mainly the birth of new stars I've been studying. It's been particularly interesting to look at galaxy collision in submillimetre radio wavelength.'

'Does it give a very different picture?'

'Very. What's not revealed in one wavelength can be much more apparent in another.'

'Pleased with this image?'

She nods. 'Might send this off to Richie. He's particularly fond of Stefan's Quintet and the seeing's pretty good tonight.'

'It seems amazing – for such an old telescope.'

'Well, the new instrumentation means it's much more powerful than when it was built. The new bigger-diameter scopes are much more powerful still, of course – they pick up so much more light.'

He nods. Better receptors. Like last night's mountain cat in the forest around Jacob's cabin. Seeing him clearly as he stood there blind.

He leaves the next morning, taking the Clipper to Seattle for his flight home, and she's quiet at his parting, like she was at the last in Hawaii.

'I'll see you soon,' he'd said, kissing her, leaping onto the ferry at the last, castoff moment, seeing her turn and walk away, seeing her glance back over her shoulder; watching her walking figure until distance took her from his sight.

From the airport he tries to phone Seb, dialling Ella's

mobile number, knowing they'll be in transit now, driving back from Scotland to Wales. He gets Ella's voice-mail. Phone switched off. Annoying – he's never missed phoning Seb before.

With a couple of hours to kill before his flight, he goes to the airport Internet access, glances at the mail waiting, around 150 messages. Situation normal. A week off usually equals around 150 messages. He doesn't open any. Sends Sophie a simple 'I love you'. Then he does go back to the incoming mail to see if there's anything he really ought to attend to and it's as he's browsing that a new message arrives on screen. It's from his father, subject urgent. The urgent need to phone him.

The pay phone doesn't want to take his credit card, so he frets in line at the kiosk for a phonecard and then he only has Canadian dollars.

'You'll take this?' he asks, snapping his credit card down.

'Sure, sir,' and, 'Have a nice day.'

There's been an accident, his mother's voice says, the police have been in touch.

'What sort of accident?'

'On the road.'

'But father's all right – I mean he e-mailed me.'

'It's not your father. It's Ella and Sebastian.'

The sense of things beginning to slow.

'Are they hurt?'

332

'How soon can you be home, Greg?'

'Are they *hurt*? Is Sebastian hurt?'

The muffled sound of the phone being passed, the muffled sound of words being spoken.

'Greg?'

'Dad.'

'Where are you?'

'Seattle,' Greg says, sliding further into slow motion. He thinks about that later. The recognized physiological phenomenon. At times of extreme happening – of danger, or crisis, the human brain activated to full alertness to deal as best it may with each extraordinary detail, so that in its thoroughness, time seems to slow – *there's – no – easy – way – to – say – this – Greg. Is – someone – with – you? No – just – tell – me. They're – gone – Greg.* Time to think – what does he mean gone? Gone on holiday? Gone and left him? – before his father's broken voice says: *both of them; both of them gone, Greg. In a car crash. Both of them.* And his mind takes his meaning, although his father does not say it. What chemical response is it, he wonders later, that gives rise to the sensation he lived through then, triggered by the key word killed that – unspoken – hangs between them, thought to thought across a continent and ocean, via satellite in space – the concept *killed.* It's as if, in slow motion, he blows apart or as if he has been physically hit by something – a sense of the breath blasted from his body, of his head hit from behind, his legs battered from beneath him. *Stay warm, Greg* – his father's voice via satellite is saying, taking refuge in doctor mode – *you must expect to be in shock – I know we are – try and keep your blood sugar up – is there a café?* – his legs battered from beneath him – *Greg? Is there a café near you?* There is. Somehow his legs take him there, his teeth clenched tight, eyes fixed in out of focus, shoulders rigid, breath not coming as somehow he slumps into a chair, muscles trembling. There is a café – with yellow-beigy flooring and girls in red uniform who come to clean the plastic tables as he trembles. He sees the motion of their elbows, the wipe of their cloths in peripheral vision as his eyes fix on the yellowy-beige flooring, its interlocking speckles caught in collision.

They avoid him, the girls with cloths, skirting round the table of this man who sits motionless and without coffee, ashen-faced and staring at the floor.

South-west Wales

Slowly he empties the house of their possessions. He works calmly, methodically: taking neat, ironed clothes from the airing cupboard and their wardrobe, from Seb's cupboard and from his chest of drawers. Placing them in cardboard boxes, he puts them by the back door ready to load into the pickup to take into the city charity shops. There is no laundry waiting in the basket; the sheets on the beds are unused. No scent of them. It was a habit of Ella's. Nice to come home to clean sheets, she'd say, nice to come home and find the laundry done. Ella's mother has the habit too of sending them off with their laundry done – so that even the clothes in their suitcase would have been pristine, had they not been immersed in the river. It was only the clothes they had been wearing that might have held their scent and these had been discarded by the morgue, only a few effects returned to him, bagged in sealed clear polythene: black leather wallet stiff from its wetting; a mobile phone, defunct; an engagement and a wedding ring; a child's wristwatch, working still; a

335

woman's watch stopped at twenty past ten; a dishevelled soft toy badger; a woman's shoulder bag.

Seb's toys next. His hands lift them, put them in boxes; his eyes kept at half-focus. Books from Seb's shelves in the bottom of each box, toys on top. There, in his hands, the smoothness of the globe, the awkward shape of the micro- scope, the child's tape player, the little blue lamp: take off the fantasy-fish shade and pack it with the plastic gun separated by the softness of Badger. He takes the dolphin curtains down. Rethinks the gun. His fingers find it past the fur, throw it in the bin. The jars of shells he takes outside, emptying them at the edge of the shell pit, where he sees the sand is smooth: a blank canvas made in their absence by the weather. White sheet – his mind images and he pushes it aside. It is possible – just – to do this in daylight. Practically impossible at night. He dare not drink. Gives up trying to sleep. A fitful half-hour at three perhaps. Jolting awake. Another fitful hour's half-sleep at dawn. Still the images come. The white sheet against his sheet-white skin, little body, inert husk now, strange, cold replica of Sebastian, remarkable waxwork likeness of a beautiful boy lying on a trolley at a morgue, his head on the stainless steel, the bruis- ing on his temple – *likely to prove to be commensurate with the side-impact of the vehicle hitting the bridge stanchion*, the quietly spoken pathologist had answered. Stone, the police said. Greg had gone to see. The gap in the railing road-coned and orange-taped off. Black trails of tyre rubber heading to the bridge's edge. Great gouges in the tarmac where the midpoint of the lorry grounded and came to rest once the front wheels had gone over the edge, *dangling the cabin over the river*, the police constable explained, eyes downcast, *yes, after the car had been shunted off. The case against the driver of the lorry being considered. No, their vehicle landed in the water on its roof. Yes, the driver of the car almost certainly dead on initial impact. And the boy?* Police constable feet shuffle. *The pathologist's report will take a week or two. The coroner in cases of unexpected death. Toxicology. Alcohol – and drugs to rule out the possibility of foul play prior to the accident. Yes. Police divers. No. Pronounced dead at the scene.* Night images. Ella's face and head and shoulders a shunted mess. He had known her feet, though. High-arching. The sharply turned-in little toe. Red-painted nails. And her hands. The naked mark where the wedding ring had been. Night imaginings. Sebastian on the pathologist's table. Taking the skull apart to see. And as he cannot sleep, he rocks. Sitting up in bed; hugging his knees; the duvet round his shoulders, for hours he rocks: side to side to side in darkness. It isn't what you're meant to do with the dead, scoop them up, but it was done before he knew it, so that the little body in his arms becomes another night image – or sensation, rather – the cold unresponsiveness, little arms trailing back, so that he'd caught hold of one wrist, brought the hand round, held it a moment against his neck, then tucked it between the cold little chest and his own warmth, as if he could warm life into him, his own breath short, *Sebastian* whispered out – the little head flopping, so that his hands had to return to supporting-the-new-baby's-head mode – the full circle flight of years in his hands. Surely not ended. Not yet. Not snuffed out so stupidly and so soon. His feet take him down the dark corridor, to the stripped room where he flicks on the bare light, harsh on the naked walls, little patches of paint pulled off where the whale posters were. The black window reflects his naked torso. He shivers, turns off the light, and it's as he's leaving that his adjusting eyes see the ceiling stars, newly charged by exposure to the brightness of the bulb. He'd forgotten about them. One of the last things they'd done together before he went to Canada: looked up constellations in the new star book, mapped them carefully out on the ceiling, then cuddled up together in the darkness to see Ursa Major, the great big bear and the northern star and Cassiopeia and Cygnus and Orion. No Zeta Calliope. Zeta Calliope didn't figure then and the if-only thoughts come flooding again: if only he hadn't, if only he had, if only he had done differently. Clenching breath round the thought, around the nausea in his belly, he reaches up in the darkness and one by one takes down the stars.

Part Four

In Flight

At three in the morning Canadian time, she gets up from her seat to pace around the plane again. Almost all the other passengers are asleep and she knows she should be, but how many days in the year do you get to see the sun come up over Greenland, the earth's curvature glazed with gold? She presses her face against the cabin window at the rear of the aircraft where stewards murmur behind the closed curtain and a passenger sleeps sprawled out on the floor. There's the golden light ahead and – below them – a jagged whiteness in half-light which could be cloud or could be snowscape. It's not possible to see clearly enough: her neck askew at the tiny window as she leans over the sleeping passenger, and she draws back, facing the fact it isn't just the sunrise that keeps her wakeful or the impossibility of sitting-upright sleep. She wanders back through the darkened plane. Only a matter of hours now.

'*Come late afternoon, then,*' he'd written in an e-mail – his first e-mail for months; a reply, at last, to hers so that she'd stared for long moments at his name on her screen; unbelieving, sensing a corresponding shift in her psyche; connection remade; vacuum filled. '*Come late afternoon, then. If you arrive as the museum is closing, we'll have the place more or less to ourselves.*' Her three o'clock in the morning is his eleven. He'll be at work already. Only a matter of hours now.

The skies are clear over south-west Ireland and she gasps to see the patterns made by the jumble of tiny fields, their shapes so irregular and apparently haphazard. And – a short while later – England, too, seems the same except that the settlements are more frequent.

Only a matter of hours.

London

'*Come late afternoon, then,*' he'd written in an e-mail, cursing himself again for his cowardice, his leaving it again to her to bridge the chasm. '*If you arrive as the museum is closing, we'll have the place more or less to ourselves.*' At the hour it soothes him most, he could have added, when the building is drained of people and the cavernous halls fall silent except for the echoed scrape of watchman's shoes and the echoed clink of watchman's keys.

He emerges from the underground office, along ancient labyrinthine corridors; up and down the seemingly random stairs.

Ridiculous of him to suggest meeting by the iguanodon. Why not just meet in the foyer? There's the skeleton of a dinosaur there also, after all, if it's dinosaur bones he particularly wanted. The iguanodon is well into the exhibition – so much more difficult for her to find. Ridiculous. And revealing of him, too. Revealing of that habit of his of spending moments there, after hours when the halls are empty. What is it when a man finds comfort in dinosaur bones? Overlaying his own hand on top of the Perspex that houses the skeleton of an iguanodon *manus*: fewer digits in the non-rotatable thumb and huge, but in other ways so resembling his own. One hundred and twenty-five million years old. Some unnamed comfort comes; one of several such he doesn't examine too closely; trusting, instead, that if healing is possible, some inherent force will bring it about. He has had to come to this belief, given that he lives still and everything else has failed. Moving to London, for example. He'd never thought for a moment he would ever move to London, but when Iain had said, *Why don't you come to the city for a few months? We're looking for someone at the Natural History Museum and the change of scene would do you good*, he'd taken the step without hesitation as if he'd been planning to all along: accepting the first offer on the cottage; quickly arranging the sale of contents. Bridges willingly, rapidly burned.

He reaches the foyer, looks about for her incoming movement against the outgoing tide.

'I'm expecting a visitor, Charlie,' he says to the uniformed man hovering by the closing-time doors. 'Should be here any second.'

'Right you are, Dr Jamieson.'

Unless, of course, she's in the building already. Unless, of course, she isn't going to show. He glances again across the swell of people; searching out the spume of her pale hair. Nothing.

'*I'm so sorry, Sophie,*' he'd managed eventually to write in an e-mail from Pembrokeshire after the joint funeral was over. '*The most difficult of times. I simply cannot communicate right now. Forgive me.*'

He traces his way to the iguanodon, thinking of the pattern of her e-mailed replies – her concern; her brief messages in the face of his silence – '*Thinking of you, hope things improve for you soon*'; her occasional frustration – '*Couldn't you at least tell me what the problem is?*'; leading to – '*I hope you won't be put out – I phoned your university. Compassionate leave, they said, although – of course and quite rightly – they wouldn't tell me why.*'

From then, it seems as if she made a pact with herself, to e-mail him weekly. Every Friday an e-mail from her. News of her work, more images from another visit to Hawaii; the findings of the black-hole study concluding the definite presence of a black hole at the centre of our galaxy; brief anecdotes about her students; progress with the papers she's working on. For weeks she did it, for months. At times he even deleted them unread; not being able to face what he had done to her. He had read the one, though, she'd sent entitled 'Baby'. '*You remember I told you about Richie's girl-friend, Emily?*' He didn't, in fact. Perhaps in an e-mail he'd discarded. '*Well, the mind boggles at how they managed it and*

*it totally contradicts all medical expectations but – she's preg-
nant! Richie and Emily are going to have a baby! I took some
time off and went home mid-week. The house is positively
buzzing with the news – all the carers who've looked after Richie
all these years are using it as a reason to party – which it is of
course, even though no one can quite believe it apart from Richie
and Emily, who look extremely pleased with themselves, which –
in the circumstances – they're perfectly entitled to. My mother's
pretending to be shocked and makes slightly disapproving noises
about them not being married. God. Who cares? I say. It's nothing short of a miracle. My dad's saying very little, just goes round
humming and smiling a lot.'*

And in another e-mail: *'I've spoken to Paul. He's worried
about you, too – not replying to his e-mails, he tells me, and he
can't get you on the phone. We love you, Greg. You have only to
ask if we can help.'*

Still he couldn't bring himself to write.

*'I've been back up to Jacob's cabin. On my own this time –
or at least I took Herschel, who likes to get his paws dirty now
and then, doesn't think much of the journey, but likes it once
we're there, follows me down to the lake and goes mousing in
the crawl space, curls up on the bed at night and – unlike me –
enjoys the deerskin. In retrospect I shouldn't have gone. I thought
going there might make me feel closer to you, which it did, which
only made it worse, of course, made me feel the lack of you even
more keenly. It must be a major thing that's happened in your*

life, for you to be able to dismiss the closeness we had. Either that or you're not the man I thought you were. I spent most of the time there crying. I wasn't going to tell you that, but perhaps you need to know, just in case you think I'm unaffected by your vanishing act. I cried, Greg. I sobbed. I spent three days sobbing. Poor Herschel. Silly me. It isn't the first time and I doubt it will be the last. I have learned to love you, you see, and I haven't the faintest notion what to do with all that now.'

He hadn't slept after that one, getting up for a run at three, coming back to pace the floor. Still he'd written nothing.

'I dreamt I was sleeping alone at Jacob's cabin and woke in the night to find that the roof around the chimney was being slowly eaten away by fire; the timbers gently glowing in a circle, growing brighter and fading to the wind's rise and fall. I wasn't frightened, just got out of bed to stand and watch the glow like armies with field torches seen from afar, spreading out across plains from some central garrison. I did wonder where they would stop – what there was to prevent them engulfing the walls of the wooden building and I did think I would have to take some action, of course, but there wasn't any sense of urgency and when I looked out through the slowly burning circle, there, so clear and close and beautiful, was Zeta Calliope. So clear and close and beautiful it was breathtaking.'

E-mails soon after the birth of the baby had brought it home to him: the passage of time since he'd seen her, time enough for a boy to die and another to be conceived and born.

'I can't tell you how lovely he is, Greg. And Richie is so very proud. Richie can't hold him, of course, but Emily lays the baby carefully alongside him when he's in bed, crooking Richie's arm and putting the baby where he can hear his father's heartbeat. It has to be alongside. Because Richie has limited use of his diaphragm and intercostal muscles, the added burden of the baby's weight wouldn't be a good idea, but with the baby next to him, it's a bit like he can rock him, Richie says, with the rise and fall of his ribcage. The baby seems to love it, anyway, his toes all lined up along Richie's strongest finger. And Richie obviously adores him, contentment oozing from him at such times as if – for once – he has no desire whatever to move.'

Greg had left a silence still, in which there was nothing from her. Easier and more difficult for him. After the few weeks' gap she'd written: 'I have to wonder where the thoughts I send out into cyberspace end up. Perhaps in your consciousness. Perhaps not. Someone who knows me well called Reinholdt and who I haven't seen for ages tells me it's possible that clinging on to a void can become another form of deflection, perhaps even self-punishment. I don't really know about that, but I do know I've been working with the Zeta Calliope data – an object in space, ten light years away, and it feels so much more accessible, is being so much more forthcoming, than you are, Greg, and I don't think I can do this any more.'

Well. Of course she can't. How could she?

He looks up, sure now she will not come, only to find she's there in front of him, walking towards him, a forgotten, loved familiarity which jars him to the core even as he sees the shock of something register on her face. Of course. The shock of the sight of him: his weight loss; his hair cropped short round its sudden thinning; the gauntness of face that even he has noticed in the mirror. And she the same as when he saw her last – a little tired perhaps – a loved familiarity which jars him hard so that he leaps up from the handrail he's been leaning against, wanting suddenly to escape out onto the city streets. He looks down, shoves his hands into his pockets, half turns away, turns and paces back to her, a glimpse of her eyes: especially bright. He feels the lightness of her hand on his arm, jolts a hand to her shoulder, tilts his frowning face to the ceiling, keeping his forearm's distance, practising hard the trick of inner distancing as he does now, daily, with everyone and everything.

'Shouldn't I have come?'

He opens his eyes to the ceiling. Struggles with breath.

'Of course you should.' His hand's pressure on the nape of her neck. His forearm's distance. His gaze over her head. Holding breath now. Releasing it a little at a time.

'Listen, Jamieson,' she says, moving to one side of him, slipping an arm through his, beginning to walk him back the way she had come. 'No offence to the dinosaurs, but it's been a long flight and I could use something with a little more meat on its bones.'

He feels better once they're out on the streets, another trick of distancing he's practised these several months: letting the city occupy his senses, stopping his eyes with its vertical planes of buildings and billboards; filling his ears with its endless dissonance of endless traffic; letting it press near him with its body of people and the comfort of concrete: solid, predictable beneath his pacing feet. He sees more people in five minutes on the rush-hour tube than he would have seen in months in Pembrokeshire. Or rather – when he first arrived, he didn't *see* people, just let the blur and push of humanity move his life along with theirs. It was only after a few weeks that he'd begun to rest his eyes on faces, to feel wonder, even, at the genetic diversity of what he saw, the range of colour of skin and hair; the differences in height and breadth; the diverse range of facial bone structures.

All right until his gaze lands on a little boy.

This is how Greg is mugged on the streets – the knife blade plunged deep into his gut by the little boy sitting on his father's knee; the little boy taking giant steps up the stairs; the little boy riding on his father's shoulder. He'd handled it badly that first time on the tube, doubling up round the blade in his belly; moaning out even; so that people gave him wary glances and a woman got up and moved away from the suspicious, distasteful figure he presented; not realizing it was he who had been assaulted.

And now, here's Sophie. He stops his pacing where they must cross the road and glances at her as the signal sounds for pedestrians to walk.

She'll be gone again before he knows it.

It's too early for the English to eat and – apart from the man in the corner with a newspaper – they have the hotel bar to themselves – polished floorboards and Victoriana; potted ivy and aspidistra – and they eat soup in silence and it could be difficult, only she's hungry and the soup is good, so that it's good to see her enjoyment of it.

'How long are you over for?'

'Ten days. I've got an observing run for a few nights and then some spare time.'

'Jodrell Bank you said, didn't you?'

'Yeah – do you know it?'

He shakes his head. 'Know of it.'

'Big radio telescope. Seventy-six-metre dish for collecting long-wave radio frequencies. *Well* outside my normal field, shan't have a *clue* what I'm doing.' She smiles. 'Especially as we're using it as part of Very Long Base Interferometry.'

'Which is?'

'Using radio telescopes in different countries to observe the same object at precisely the same time, so that, in effect, you end up with a telescope roughly the size of the northern hemisphere.' She smiles again at his widening eyes. 'You have to be spot on with timing and then spend ages putting the information from the scopes together and hope to hell all of you pressed the right buttons at the right time and that everything was working OK, otherwise the whole thing is messed up and you've sent four astronomers to four different countries for nothing.'

'And the object of study?'

'Colliding galaxies again. A pair this time and not my project. I just let myself get involved with this one.' She looks down at her hands breaking bread, then back up at him. 'Well, as someone once said to me, Greg – the science is a perfectly legitimate reason to be here, but . . .'

He gives a grim half-smile. 'Just sorry to be such a wreck.'

'It's quite a change, but hey –' she smiles – 'haggard kind of suits you.' She puts the bread down. 'I'm just so sorry about what you must have been through.'

He draws deep breath. Now's the time to tell her, then. 'Ella and Sebastian—'

She touches a hand on his arm. 'I know, Greg. I know what happened to them.'

He lets out fast breath. 'Do you? *How* do you?'

'Paul phoned me a few days ago.'

'Ah.' He'd worried about that – the unfairness of Paul knowing when she didn't. 'I hadn't told him, Sophie.'

'I know.'

'One of my students went out to—'

'To do some fieldwork with him and she told him. I know. Listen – could we get out of here?'

He'd warned her his flat would be a bit of a mess, but it isn't. Not enough in it to make it a mess. Scruffy, he could more accurately have said. Paintwork slapped over cracks. Chipped money-in-the-meter gas fire. Third-hand furniture. His few things are, in fact, scrupulously tidy: laptop set up neatly by the phone; a line of books on the shelf above; three neat files.

'Could I take a shower?'

'Of course. Run the hot first. Coffee when you come out?'

'Lovely.'

While the kettle boils, he listens to the sounds of the shower; the sounds of someone else in his flat. A first since he moved here. And not just someone else. It's Sophie. All the way from Canada to see him.

She'll be gone again before he knows it.

The grounds have mostly fallen to the bottom and gently he presses down on the plunger, seeing a slurred reflection of his face as she pads into the kitchen behind him. Turning, he sees she's wearing his big bath robe; a towel, too, draped over her shoulder. Her wet hair is in ringlets. Memories of beaches. He looks to the floor; turns back to the counter to pour her coffee.

There's a scrap of back garden – utterly overlooked – and French doors of a sort which open inwards. He's placed the sofa a few feet back from the open doorway so that they sit inside, unseen and looking out. The cacophony of traffic noise flooding over buildings is let in more loudly through the open doors. Lowering sun lights the tops and backs of houses opposite. The shrubs in pots have revived since he's been here. Still, he usually thinks of it as seedy, only somehow she makes it homely: the girl next door, feet curled up on the sofa, come round for coffee and chat, except it's astronomy she talks of – galaxies colliding and stars new born and how it seems more and more likely that there *is* an earth-like planet round Zeta Calliope, a dust profile she's made of the disc producing a remarkable similarity to the dust profile of our own solar system.

'Written it up yet?'

She nods, talks of the nerve-racking waiting game: the paper put forward for publication in *Nature*, currently being peer-reviewed – and while he listens, he watches her, the loved animation of her face, and against his strongest, distancing will he feels it: the goodness of having her near again.

*

Faces turn to watch her as they walk into the restaurant. He'd forgotten that – how faces turn to her. Their table overlooks the Thames, where the summer sky drains of colour. For the first time in months he notices the moon. And as she's drinking, he risks drinking too, another first in months, as they talk of his work at the Natural History Museum – Yes, he answers, it's only a temporary thing for him, although already he's been there longer than he thought. Yes, the strandings project – data collection of stranded whales, dolphins and porpoises; coordinating the collection of the carcasses for delivery to the pathologist, or at least the collection of samples. Yep – it's pretty busy – 600 cases this year to date. Yep – the phones have to be monitored at weekends, too. Some public speaking to do for them soon and then there's a piece of software he's working on in his spare time and some papers to finish writing up.

'And your PhD students?'

'I'm still supervising their work.'

'Oh – good!'

'Didn't want to let them down.'

'And the by-catch survey?'

'End of contract. Written up. Sent off.'

'But the work at the field centre?'

'The university found someone to fill in pretty quickly. They insisted on holding the job open for me, so my replacement's on a temporary contract for a year, but . . .' He shrugs.

'When's the year up?'

'February.'

'Will you want to go back?'

He shakes his head. 'No. There are some ends not quite tied up. The prosecution of the driver who caused Ella to have the accident is the big one. He's being done for dangerous driving. Case is due to come up in a couple of weeks.'

'Do you have to be there?'

'I don't have to go, no. The CPS are making the prosecution. My being there wouldn't make any difference. I may well go, though. See justice is done.'

'It must be nearly a year since the accident happened.'

He nods.

'A few days before nine, eleven, wasn't it?'

'Yes.'

The night house empty of them: the TV's flickering in the darkened bedroom, repeated images of the Twin Towers falling. Again and again they ran the footage. The neat, lethal scything mirroring his own skyline.

'I'm sorry,' she says to his silence. 'I shouldn't have—'

'No, it's . . .'

'Why don't we order dessert and think about the good news.'

He smiles across at her. 'There's been some of that?'

'*Bound* to have been.' She laughs, sounding dubious.

356

'Well, there's Sam, Richie's boy.' She looks down. 'I know in the circumstances . . . it must be difficult to be pleased for . . .'

'No. No. Of course it's wonderful news.'

'Well, I think it really is.'

'Do you know Emily very well?'

'Yeah. We've all known each other since we were kids. I really like her. She was the one who stuck by Richie when he went back to school in a wheelchair. She's a year younger than him and even then – aged five – she was a force to be reckoned with. I mean, the school were really thorough about making sure Richie wasn't bullied, but they needn't have worried too much with Emily around. I don't mean she's aggressive, not remotely that. The opposite, in fact – she's so *calm*. Richie says she has a steady way of looking at you that cuts straight through the crap and I know what he means.

'They kind of lost touch for a while – or didn't see so much of each other when they went to different high schools – and then Richie went through a really tough phase as a teenager when he refused to go to school at all, but Emily's mother is a nurse and she became one of Richie's carers and Emily would tag along sometimes after school and would go and chat to Richie once her mother was done with him. I remember she would always bring him something. Something she'd picked up outdoors. A single flower, a bunch of berries, an icicle—'

'An *icicle*?'

'Yeah. Brought him an icicle once. Put it in a glass and watched it melt amid lots of whispering and howls of laughter.' She smiles. 'None of us could quite see the joke – still can't for that matter – but, hey, who cares so long as they were having a good time. I guess we all thought they'd grow out of it, especially when Emily went off to university, but it seems they didn't. She's been so *good* for him. And he is for her too. They're practically inseparable. *And* she's helped him find the motivation to do a degree.'

'Oh, that's *brilliant*.'

'Yeah – we never could persuade him, which always seemed a shame, because he's so obviously capable, but Emily's gone one better – increased his self-esteem and confidence, I suppose, so that he wants to study now for his own reasons, not just to please other people.'

'Excellent, Sophie.' He pours more wine for her. 'Well, OK, I've got some good news, too.'

'Yes?'

'You remember the Sombrero project I worked on.'

'The rocket-launch site?'

'That's the one – except it *isn't* going to be a rocket-launch site after all. They've abandoned all plans.'

'Oh, Greg! Your environmental-impact assessment—'

'Had *nothing* whatever to do with the outcome. Well, it did make Rocket-launch Man look elsewhere in the world for a while – you know, if there's going to be too much opposition in one place, go somewhere else.'

'Path of least resistance.'

'Precisely, which would, in fact, have been just as devastating, because all the other sites he looked at had equally fragile ecosystems.'

'All well away from human habitation, I suppose.'

'In case of launch failure, they have to be, yes. Anyway, the thing that finally clinched it was that the guys at Cape Canaveral were able to accommodate the extra business.'

'You *said* that all along, that the thing could happen from an existing facility.'

He nods. 'So – a triumph of commercialism rather than an environmental success. The positive outcome for the ecosystem is the same, of course.'

'A bit like the old-growth forest we were in.'

'Yes?'

'There's a mistletoe which invades the wood and renders it commercially unviable.'

'And that's how come the forest we were in is still standing?'

'That's it. Part of the last 2 per cent left.'

'Oh, well, *that's* good news, then.' He shakes his head. 'There's good news about the US Navy's sonar, too.'

'Yes?'

'They've just published a report—'

'Only recently? They've taken their time, haven't they?'

'—with considerable input from dear Gordon, which acknowledges naval involvement in the event and cites their use of sonar as a probable cause of the strandings.'

'Well, that *is* something, Greg. So presumably they'll stop using the system now.'

She sees him pull a face.

'Ah,' she says, 'silly me. I'm being logical, aren't I?'

'Nasty habit. Or at least, I would guess the navy's logic works differently, something like: they haven't spent millions of dollars developing the technology only to discard it because of a few dead whales. But there is a court case coming up – conservation groups alleging that the navy are in contravention of wildlife protection laws and have failed to make a sufficiently comprehensive environmental-impact assessment before using the gear.'

'Will it stick?'

'It certainly should. In the meantime there have been more of these associated strandings.'

'Oh, *no*.'

'Afraid so, but at least the conservation laws are in place in the US, so in time the courts should be able to do something – unlike here. That's the not-so-good news. The British military have just gleefully announced a 160-million pound investment in similar technology.'

'So the same thing is going to start happening over here?'

'I think it's inevitable, and without such rigorous laws to contain it . . .' He raises his eyebrows. 'One step forward, six steps back.'

She laughs at him as he twice fails to hail a taxi. 'Pathetic,' she jibes, as the second cabby drives past. And Greg laughs his protest as she steps dangerously out, only the next taxi stops for her and she negates his comments with the raise of an eyebrow, opening the door and bundling him in before her, sliding along the seat towards him, till her body contacts his and his arm has little option but to round down over her shoulders.

'Sophie, I . . .'

'*Greg*, I've been awake for thirty hours. It's the least you can do.'

And he can tell from the way her weight relaxes that she does soon doze: beautiful woman, giving herself to his safe-keeping, warm against him in the back of a taxi in the night-time heart of the city.

Though it never entirely stops, the sound of traffic noise outside his apartment thins over night; the sweep of lights on the ceiling becoming less frequent through the heavy, drawn curtains.

'Are you serious?' she'd murmured when he told her he was going to sleep on the sofa. 'Is there,' she'd said, in his arms in the darkened hallway, leaning – sleep-drunk – against him, 'is there someone else, Greg?'

'No, Sophie,' he'd sighed not knowing how to say he senses his body damaged now; he senses his body no longer whole. 'My libido . . .' he'd faltered.

'Gone on vacation?'

He'd grunted wry laughter in her hair. 'Bloody long vacation.'

'Well – sure you must sleep on the sofa if it's what you need to do. Sure you must,' she'd said, only so forlornly that he'd walked her across the room, sleepy from the taxi still, to lie beside her on his bed and hug her back to sleep, wrapping a single cover round her body in the warmth of the night.

She sleeps still, as he lies wakeful and he wonders what it is to have her here: her weight once more against him; against the gaping Seb has left. He had thought he would never again hold her. Never again.

From the street a car horn blares, countered by another. She stirs and he uses the moment to resettle his arm beneath her head; listens as her breathing steadies back into the rhythm of sleep.

London

She wakes to his movement in the room, seeing him in sepia: feeble dawn-light through dark curtains. There's the sound of a drawer drawn slowly open. Her eyes open enough to register *He's wearing shorts – must be going for a run*, before she falls to sleep again.

He buys oranges and croissants on his way home; leaves coffee to stand while he takes a shower. No sign of her, so he goes through to find she's brushing her hair at the bedroom window in the house's only hour of direct sunlight. Bare-legged, she's wearing a shirt of his.

'I took a shower while you were out,' she says walking over to him. 'Borrowed a shirt.'

'Suits you,' he says quickly kissing her head, before turning away.

'Couldn't believe it when I woke up in yesterday's clothes. Did we both fall asleep in our clothes?'

'We did.'

'Haven't done that since – since a student party. Woke up fully dressed in someone's bath. How was your run?'

'Oh – it let me know how unfit I've become.'

'Not done much lately?'

'No.'

The blue of the shirt makes her eyes more blue as the sun inscribes a gold outline to her hair. He turns away.

'Breakfast by the French doors? The sun reaches there, too.'

'Lovely,' she says, following and then stopping. 'It's so poignant, Greg, seeing this.'

'What? Oh. Yes.'

She's stopped to indicate the box on the chest of drawers. Cardboard shoebox. Or boot box, more precisely. A box for brand-new walking boots. Tiny size. For a child of five years old or so.

'I didn't keep the boots. Ella made such a fuss about the extravagance when I bought them, I felt honour bound to let some other child have the use of them. It's just a few things of his.'

'Can you bear to show me?'

He shrugs.

'Only not if—' she says to his hesitation.

'Yeah. I – there isn't much.'

The *Strombus listeri* takes up much of the space. 'His favourite shell,' Greg explains, taking it out of the box.

'Did that shell I went to Customs about in the Caribbean ever arrive?'

'Ah, yes.' He gives a grim smile. 'It took them rather a long time to process it. Postman arrived with it just as I was setting off to Scotland for the funeral.'

'Oh, God!'

He nods. 'Curious timing.'

'And to *Scotland*? The funeral was held in Scotland?'

'Yes. They're both buried there. Ella's parents wanted to take her home.'

'And they didn't think home was with you?'

'Evidently not.'

'And was that all right with you?'

He shrugs again.

'It seemed really important to them and – well – as it's turned out, it probably made it easier for me to move away.'

His hands lift out a grey-black soft toy; its face misshapen, blunted by repeated cuddling.

'This is Badger. Badger got put in one of the boxes for the charity shop and then it was the devil's own job to find which one he was in when I decided . . .' He puts Badger down on the chest of drawers. 'Well – they'd spent a lot of time together.'

'Greg, we don't have to do this if—'

'No. It's OK. There's not much more now. A few photos . . .'

Encased in a clear plastic wallet. He places them aside.

'You've seen some of those. Oh, and the dragon story.'

'I remember.'

'This is our original – with Seb's drawings.'

He passes it to her and gently she turns the dog-eared pages.

'And this is one of his school books. The journal they all had to write every week at school. Ella and I both get a mention, of course as does Moree – the imaginary friend – who, for all I know –' Greg laughs – 'who, for all I know, might be lurking in the box here somewhere.'

She sees his eyes are bright with tears. 'Greg, I'm sorry. I . . .'

'These were the *real* curiosity, though,' he says, taking the last things from the box and handing them to her. A piece of paper, thick, handmade, with elaborate handdrawn script and then a scrap of vellum with the same script and the curved edge of a small cross of ancient design, some parts with gold illumination.

'I don't understand.'

'Neither did I. A rather tweedy gentleman – in his late sixties, I should think – called at the cottage a couple of weeks after the funeral to give them to me; saying how much they all missed Ella and what wonderful work she'd done.'

'*This* was her work?'

'Apparently it was.'

'You didn't know she'd been doing this?'

'No. I would never have known if he hadn't called round. I mean, I knew calligraphy had been part of her MA. I knew she *could* do this kind of stuff. Obviously these are just the offcuts, the roughs, trial runs. She'd been working on the main piece for months apparently. I went to see it. It's an extraordinary thing, Sophie – I mean amazing – dense, dense tiny script on a large piece of vellum about two feet square in reds and black and sepia, passages from the Bible, all interwoven in the shape of a Celtic cross with illuminated decorative sections. Months of work. The calligraphy society asked if they could hold on to it for a time. They've still got it, in fact. She'd entered it for an exhibition last spring and there's another in spring next year in the Midlands they want to keep it for.'

'I wonder why she didn't tell you she was doing this.'

He shakes his head. 'I'd noticed her time unaccounted for.' Grunting self-ironic laughter, he says, 'Rather assumed she'd taken a lover.'

'Perhaps she had. Perhaps the guy who came round . . .'

'I wondered that, but I don't think so. He was so very much older. And, anyway, he wouldn't have come round, would he?'

'Might have been curious to meet you.' She tilts the vellum to better light. 'This is such painstaking and specialized work, Greg.'

'Apparently she was hoping to become a fellow of the Society of Scribes and Illuminators. Apparently this type of script is known as the foundational hand – all derived from a manuscript that's in the British Library – and being fluent with it is one of the SSI's requirements – apparently.'

'She hadn't told you any of this stuff?'

'Nope. It was down to the total stranger to inform me about this facet of my wife's existence.'

'I don't understand why she didn't tell you.'

'Me neither.' He takes the pieces she passes to him and puts them back in the box; packs the other things away on top of them; places the lid on; smiles briefly. 'Come on. Coffee will be going cold.'

'What happened to the dragon?' Sophie asks as she sits peeling oranges by the French doors.

'At the end of the story?'

'Mmm. Seem to remember something about him finding his huge family and didn't he sculpt ice?'

'I read that bit to Seb from Jacob's cabin.'

'You did.'

'Oh, well – Missing went missing again. Found his huge family a bit overwhelming, so he went off to live with the dragon artists in the forest for a few years, fine-tuning the use of his fire to make ever more beautiful sculptures.'

'And was that the end?'

'Nope. After a while he decides he wants to go off on an adventure again, see a bit more of the world, see if he can find any more dragons who were taken by the eg-lecter – that's the egg collector to you and me. So every day, Missing flies lots of laps round the forest to get himself fit, and one day Bethsheba flies over to join him and she's carrying the princess. They'd been thinking the same – about going off on an adventure.'

'Ah. Dragon telepathy.'

'Absolutely. So that's what they do. Set off together to do some exploring.'

'And *that's* the end?'

'Yep. Thought it left room for a sequel – "Further Adventures of Missing, the Dragon." Didn't quite get round to those.'

He hesitates in his pouring of more coffee, eyes unfocused as he thinks again of that last phone call from Jacob's cabin, trying again to remember Seb's last words to him and the very last words he said to Seb. Again he fails quite to recall. Sophie might remember. She was there in the room, wasn't she?

'I don't know much about the process of grieving,' she is saying, and, looking up, he realizes she's been watching him.

'No?'

'At least not in the usual sense of the word. I guess – with

Richie – we all grieved after the accident. We had, in effect, lost him. Lost the Richie we knew anyway.' She offers Greg the plate of orange segments. 'I remember my mother saying he's lucky to be alive. And we all looked at each other, none of us quite sure if she was right.'

He places coffee on the low table near her, takes more fruit from the plate she's placed on the sofa between them, turning his body to face her.

'I do know about blame, though,' she continues.

Her eyes blink slowly, her gaze resting on his. He makes out the corner of her mouth, flickering to a small smile.

'I didn't even tell this bit to the shrink.'

'You went to see a psychiatrist?'

'Psychiatrist. Psychologist. We tend not to differentiate. Anyway, yes, I did. I wanted some objective insight into why I always mess up with relationships.'

'*Do* you – always mess up?'

'Have done until now.'

The flicker of her smile again.

'It *was* useful. I stopped going – partly because you can overdose on that stuff; partly because Reinholdt had done a good job – really helped me gain a new perspective; partly because he'd given me enough for me to continue the process for myself and partly –' she raises her eyebrows – 'partly because I didn't want to go wading around in stuff about Richie's accident.'

She gives a little laugh. 'Reinholdt was *extremely* good at needling stuff out of me. Precisely his job, of course. But, hell. I've thought it through enough over the years.'

He says nothing, watching her face.

She shakes her head. 'It is so *ludicrously* ironic the way Richie got hurt. I mean, there really *aren't* many trees in the Canadian prairies, but we had some in our backyard by a stream. Three big trees – their trunks close together – and my father built a tree house, kind of slung between them. It was easy for me to climb up the rope ladder – I was older – but Richie needed my help up the last bit and it was as I was reaching down to him one day that he slipped and fell. Simple as that. Caught his foot in the ladder, which meant he went down head-first and landed on his face. It was summer and the ground was rock hard, but even if it hadn't been . . . His body flipped right over his head.'

Greg frowns his eyes closed at the image.

'He broke three cervical vertebrae and severely damaged his spinal cord.'

Greg lets out breath. 'I didn't realize you'd witnessed it, Sophie. God. *Appalling* accident.'

'Worse. Appalling *preventable* accident.'

'In what—'

She brings her hand up between them. 'Before he fell – I had his fingers more or less in mine. Only I couldn't quite be bothered that day. Usually we played pretty well together, but that day I had my seven-year-old thoughts somewhere else, really wasn't paying attention to my pesky little brother, and why ever couldn't he manage without me, anyway? He could make enough noise, for heaven's sake, always puppy-dogging me around when sometimes I wanted to be on my own.'

'An accident, Sophie.'

'Yes, Greg – but I had his fingers in mine when he slipped. Just another half-inch of effort, just a moment's better concentration.'

He sees her mouth close tight round her words.

'We all felt blame, of course. My father for having built the tree house in the first place. My mother for not having banned Richie from using it or for not being there as he *was* using it. *I shall never forgive myself*, I remember her saying – no, not saying, *sobbing* that evening in the hospital. Again and again: *I shall never forgive myself*. While all along I knew my much greater guilt – my much greater *fault* – in it.'

She pauses.

'So you see, I know about blame.'

'And you're saying –' his throat feels tight – 'you're saying I blame myself for what happened to Ella and Sebastian.'

He feels her fingers lightly on his shoulder. 'I've been wondering if you do.'

He frowns, placing the orange segments he'd taken back on the plate.

'Well. Of course I do,' he says simply. 'Of course I blame myself. I *am* to blame. They would never have *gone* to Scotland if I . . .'

'If you hadn't taken a lover. If you'd stayed within the marriage.'

'Yes.'

'There's your sense of self-blame, then,' she says. 'And, if it goes the way of mine—'

'Yes?'

She sighs. 'Self-forgiveness doesn't wash.'

'Oh – tell me about it, Sophie. Listen. Is this supposed to—'

'The nearest I've got to it is a recognition of extenuating circumstances. Perhaps I shouldn't have been asked to take responsibility for Richie. Perhaps – at seven – I couldn't have been expected to have an understanding of the possible danger or to have the concentration or the physical strength to . . .'

He passes the flat of his hand over his short cropped hair.

'Yeah, well, thanks, Sophie, but at thirty-seven, thirty-eight, I think it could be fairly said—'

'At thirty-seven – at any age . . .' She pauses, doubling her legs up onto the sofa. 'Tell me, Greg,' she continues quietly, 'this marriage you say you should have stayed within. All your needs were being met, were they?'

'What do you mean?'

'Your needs – intellectual, emotional, sexual – they were all being supplied by the marriage, were they?'

'That really isn't the point, Sophie.'

'No? Well – you're the mammalogist, but it seems to me –' She sighs again. 'It's not something you *invented*, Greg – the desire, the *compulsion* to have those needs met. It's a – well, it's a universal, biological given, isn't it, which we also happen to have formalized into a cultural expectation. You know – isn't supplying each other's needs one of the things marriage is supposed to be about?'

From somewhere higher up the building, feet sound, descending stairs.

'Where do I fit into your list of infidelities, Greg?'

'*What?*'

'Where do I fit? How many women had there been during your marriage – apart from me?'

'*None*, Sophie. Zero. Zilch.'

She tips her head on one side. 'Doesn't exactly sound profligate.'

'Oh – and that makes it all right?'

'I'm just saying it seems to me your behaviour was *reasoned* – and *reasonable*. So unless you think marriage *should* be vacuous or stifling or crippling, or unless you think you *should* have just walked out and left them to it, I think your behaviour is something you really *don't* have to beat yourself up about.'

Her fingers trace the spare line of muscle at his shoulder through the fabric of his shirt. 'I should have thought the grief part is plenty hard enough without . . .'

He nods his head, eyes tight closed; then looks down, focusing on the fabric of the sofa: short, tufty, worn at the front edge of the cushion here. He looks back up at her, two seconds outgoing eye contact to channel his words along.

'He died as the dolphins do,' Greg hears himself say, and even after these eleven months, he hears the tone of amazement still ringing in his voice.

'He *what*?'

'He—'

'No! I mean I don't understand.'

He looks aside.

'The car they were in ended up in a river,' he says in monotone now. 'Seb was unconscious before it hit the water.'

'You got hold of—'

'The pathologist's report. Yep, well –' his eyes blink recognition of irony – 'with my job I read them all the time. The point is, Seb didn't drown. He suffocated. Enough depth of water in the upturned vehicle for his head and shoulders to be immersed. Dry drowning. Just like the dolphins. Well, *easier* for him, in fact,' he amends, his face flinching. 'Being unconscious, he wouldn't have known anything about it. No evidence at all of him struggling to get out.'

'*Jesus*.'

He nods acknowledgement of her reaction while practising inner distancing from it; from the image of Seb unconscious in the car and inner distancing from himself now; from this wound; from this gaping where Sebastian has been ripped out, so that he stills himself, stiffly, keeping his breath short.

'And Ella?'

He shakes his head this time. 'Even quicker for her. She took the impact from the lorry.' He shakes his head again. 'I *couldn't* contact you, Sophie.'

'Greg, that really—'

'I *couldn't* just say, hey! Sophie! I'm unencumbered now! No kid! No wife! Come on over!'

'Listen.' She picks up the suddenly obstructive plate of oranges, slings it onto the low table so that she can shift herself nearer to him, curling her body into the hollow his resting arm makes against the back of the sofa. 'Not contacting me is something else you don't have to beat yourself up about. I *don't* know much about grief, but it's easy to imagine it takes time and that maybe other things have to slide for a while.'

He presses two fingers hard against the bridge of his nose, nods his head against them.

'Well, Sophie, you imagine more accurately than I did. There was me thinking if I just got straight back to work, if I just *did* the things I would normally do, then everything would slot back into place.'

He presses fingers harder, forbidding tears, diverts himself to focus on the rounding of her shoulder, untouching, within his body's space.

'But it didn't happen like that?'

He draws deeper breath, leans his head down to hers.

'No. Well – for a few months it appeared to. Took a few months before everything finally came crashing down.' He shifts his head away again. 'Better now. Here in London.'

There's the deep rumble of a lorry passing the building and his feet feel the slight shudder of the floor. He ventures eye contact and she brings a hand up to cup the side of his face.

'God, but we know how to have fun, don't we?' he says, letting some weight fall into her hand.

'*Don't* we? *And* you've got another problem,' she says.

He half-chokes a little laugh, rests his head against hers. 'I have? Another one?'

'Mmm.'

'Go on, then.'

She draws back to look at him. 'I'm not about to give up on you.'

Her train leaves a couple of hours later and they walk together to the tube station, through the clamour of mid-morning traffic, past shops where the shaven-headed hairdresser works on a woman's abundant hair and the high-class butcher, blood smear on his cheek, eyes Sophie between the window-hanging pheasants. A fire engine siren screams, then shuts off as it passes them, halting at the street-side supermarket, pressing pedestrians together as firemen hurry into the unburning building.

Once clear of them, Greg asks of her observing run, which starts at Jodrell Bank tomorrow, and she talks – through the traffic noise – of this evening's task of getting herself acquainted with the unfamiliar kit and then her hours won't be so bad in the days that follow: radio wavelength observations available twenty-four hours a day; plus the placement of the object of study and the other three tele-scopes involved means her run will finish at one o'clock every morning. A doddle, relatively speaking, so long as she can get up to speed with the technology.

Two horses emerge from a narrow alley crossing their path: one tall, an old hand, moving steadily; the other wild-eyed, led as well as ridden, the delicate dished face of a sea horse, dancing scared.

'And then back to London?'

She glances at him. 'I was thinking of going up to Scotland. I have some relatives there.'

'*Have* you?'

'My father's family. Two brothers and a sister. Haven't

seen them since I was little.' She glances a smile in his direction. 'Did wonder if you might want to come up with me.'

He touches a hand briefly to the nape of her neck.

He smiles, sighs quietly. 'I dare say I'm owed some time off.'

At the mainline station, he puts her luggage down on the platform – big hug before she gets on the train and it's then she feels the gun in his pocket and – still holding him – tosses back her hair, broadly grinning – *aha, then* – whispered in his ear – *so you* are *pleased to see me* – and he grins, too, tilting his face up in the cavernous place – *splendid timing on my part* – softly laughed once he drops his face again to her hair as the guard blows the whistle.

London

Bodies on the beaches of France. Messages reach him. Numbers rise. Twenty. Fifty. One hundred and fifty. In the underground office he pushes back his chair. The red phone rings. Bodies on the beaches of Cornwall. Twenty-four this week. It happens sometimes. The pair-trawlers operate in the Channel and soon after they empty their nets big enough to hold thirteen jumbo jets, the by-catch carcasses wash up on either shore. He takes details of this Cornish latest. Makes phone calls to arrange collection.

More bodies on the beaches of France. Two hundred and thirty-five the end of the working day website says. Three hundred and ten the next day lunchtime update tells him. Silly figures. Three hundred and eighty-six. Mostly common dolphin.

'That'll be a misnomer if it goes on at this rate. It's been a while since there were quite so many. Wonder how our colleagues in France are coping.'

'Very well, I should think. They've had enough practice. I might go across and give them a hand anyway.'

Iain raises his eyebrows.

'I've got a few days off,' Greg reminds him.

'Thought you were going up to Scotland.'

'I was.'

He doesn't want to call her from the office, so he takes his mobile out onto the street, finds he's let the charge run down; finds a pay phone. There's silence down the line once he's told her. Traffic rumbles past and he presses the handpiece to his ear in case he's not catching her words. But there's nothing. He stubs the toe of his shoe against the phone-box casing. Red paint. Call girl calling cards, twenty or thirty stuck aslant on the board behind the telephone-like votive offerings at a roadside shrine.

'Sophie?'

'I don't know what to say, Greg.'

'I *have* to do this.'

'Do you?'

'I can't go on . . . *hiding* in the city for ever—'

'Is that what you're doing?'

'Yes. I think it is. It seems to me it's what I'm doing. I can't do that for ever.'

'Come to Scotland, then.'

'Or I could, in fact. That's the problem. I *could* just go on being here. In a way it would be *much* easier to forget about going to France, but then I'd look round and find a few years have passed and I'm still *here*, still using the city like – like armour or camouflage. Don't you see?'

There's silence down the line.

'Sophie, I've realized for sure in these last few days, I *love* you and if I'm ever going to be close to anyone again—'

He hears short breath down the telephone – tries to catch the tone of it.

'Mixed messages, Greg.'

A woman peers in through the glass, ramming home hints about the length of his call. He turns his back to her.

'I just have to go to this incident in France to . . .' *to see if he can hack it any more*, he fails to finish. 'Since Sebastian,' he restarts, then changes tack once more. 'Yes, I *could* just meet you in Scotland.'

'But you're not going to.'

He toes a cigarette butt on the floor.

'It might just be another way of hiding.'

'And going to France isn't?'

'Oh, no. No. No. That's facing stuff. That's the point.'

Needing to know if what's left of him can deal with that kind of situation any more. Needing to know if every dry-drowned dolphin from here on in can only ever be an utterly disabling reminder of Sebastian – dying as he did. The ones in

Pembrokeshire had become that. Tony bringing home the body to the cooler – the moment of breakdown for him.

'Listen, Sophie, I really can't do this on the phone—'

'It doesn't seem as if you're offering any other way of doing it.'

'We could meet in London on your way back through.'

'Will you be back by then?'

'Probably. I think so. It depends.'

Another phone silence.

A red double-decker pulls in to the stop, its engine idling two feet from the phone box. He shoves a hand across his open ear.

'Sophie?'

I'm sorry Greg. I have to go now, he just manages to hear her say.

'Sophie, I need you to *trust* me on this.'

I have to go now, he thinks she says, as the engine thrubs and the phone clicks back to dial tone.

London

Hyde Park has a light swell running and spinner dolphins ride the city skyline as waves come in the darkness, catching him off guard; the sea of seated people there before him; picnic rugs and bubbly in the dark and unsteady decking beneath his feet. Hunting seal pups, the killer whale beaches, crashing spray twelve storeys up the high-rise.

'Watch out, mate!' a voice calls as Greg lurches with the swell and stumbles to sit where he is on the grass.

'I'm so sorry,' he says, and the ss slur as the orchestra crescendos and another orca powers from the water simultaneously on two huge screens placed high against the night sky.

It steadies the motion, sitting. The waves lessen. He'll never find his colleagues, anyway, among the crowded thousands and besides he'll see them soon enough, at work tomorrow when they'll want to know all about how it was in France. In the self-intimacy of his alcoholic haze, gingerly he lifts the lid off the images. *Coped with it did you? Cope with it, now, can you?* Five hundred and three – the count as he left. Spread out over many kilometres of coastline, but the beach he worked on held most of them; his first sighting of the grey wall, not registering, not computing; so that he'd relived the grey wall of lava on Hawaii, only this wall was a holocaust wall of carcasses; more than a metre high, many metres long and stinking; those dolphins not already putrefied going for post-mortem; six pathologists working outdoors on tables, white-gowned and gloved, moving among the grey rocks and grey weather and the grey of cetacean skin, among the browns and pinks and reds of innards. He'd joined them, collecting, packing samples; among the carrying of carcasses; more washing in with the waves; more being brought in by truck. They weren't even remotely Sebastian. They were what they were. By-caught dolphins. Their stomachs full of mackerel and sprat. Pelagic fishery target species. Beak injuries or the avulsion of a fin. Scratches from fish spines inflicted as the catch was hauled in; post-mortem fractures: bones broken as their bodies jammed the winching gear. Some individuals slit along the length of their bodies in the fisherman's false hope of sinking the evidence. By-caught dolphins.

He slips the bottle from his pocket; tips his head back to swig more whisky, sees a jet in the sky. It won't be hers. Wrong direction and hers left yesterday. He, still in France. Another swig. A devil's mask now in the city sky. A devil's mask from two miles down, bioluminescent, long-toothed monster. *Hey, monster! It's a deep-sea monster!* He hugs Sebastian to his side, feels the boy snuggle warm. *Wow! Look, Daddy! A spaceship!* Camera panning a sea-creature body – bioluminescent pulses like lights at spaceship portholes. Alien, from black water two miles down, hanging in the city sky. Seb snuggles. The pain in his side. Another swig. He feels his mouth do some pursing thing as his eyes frown tight. It's *there* the wound. The left side of his torso, from hip to chest and shoulder. Some two-mile-down, luminous thing darts – like an asteroid – across the sky. *Quick! Bring in Spaceguard! Warning of a Near-earth Object!* The one that spelled the end for the dinosaurs would have missed Earth altogether, she'd said, if it had arrived half an hour later or half an hour earlier. The burn of whisky is warm in his throat, spreads its comfort down that wounded shoulder where Sebastian used to snuggle in sleep, warming up that wounded hip, where Sebastian used to sit in carrying. *Oh, look, Seb!* Common dolphins, team-working bubble nets to corral prey while gannets dive, the flying, swimming boundary blurred. Then out onto the surface of the ocean, seeing common dolphins leap, hundreds of them travelling together, God, so good, after the days he's just spent, to see them well and whole, and he sits up, actual breeze on his face, only to sway down with a wave again to fretless bass and flugelhorn; to an image of the brimming moon; to the sudden pulse of a fishes' shoal mirrored by musicians' arms. White lights twinkle round the screens like stars. *It was on the last of 3,000 days in the field that we came across a sie whale.* The man himself again at the end. Attenborough. The sea breaks into a storm of applause. And we won't let him go. We won't. We won't let him go from this Blue Planet Prom in the Park. A storm of applause. Greg too moved to move. Hugging one shoulder tight and his knees. Alcohol-warmed. Wildlife warmed. People-caring-enough-to-be-here warmed. Thank-God-there's-an-Attenborough-in-the-world-warmed. The storm rages round him. His body shivers. The ache in his side. The tears in his eyes. Cold bum damp from the dewed ground.

'*Dearest Sophie,*' he writes in an e-mail. '*It's going to take some forgiveness, I know, but I hope you can find it in you to forgive me. What a rat, hey? Bunking off to France. I have some definites now, though, as a result of that trip which I wouldn't have if I hadn't gone to France. I'll be moving out of London soon. I don't know where to yet. I know I want to keep working with bio-acoustic-related software. I know now I still want to combine that with fieldwork, too. Plus I'd like to continue to work with students, not least because I like them, so that means affiliation with some university or other. And I know all of it has to be conservation-related. There's such an urgency about that now and I find I grow ever less tolerant of marine biologists who haven't woken up to that fact yet. Anyway, really that's most of the type of work I was doing in Pembrokeshire, only I know it won't be Pembrokeshire this time. So – somewhere else in the world. I thought – if I am forgiven – you might want a say about where in the world that might be. E-mail soon, will you? If only to tell me to make it as far away from Vancouver Island as possible.'*

For a week there's no word, ten days, still nothing. He thinks of how it must have been for her. The closeness at Jacob's cabin, then not just days but *months* of nothing from him. Crossing a continent and an ocean to see him; only not seeing him – or only for less than twenty-four hours – while he went chasing off on some mission he didn't even properly explain. He jumps from his chair to pace the thin carpet. God! He's been a *bastard*! And then his e-mail to her – not exactly an apology, was it? He goes to the bedroom for jogging bottoms and trainers, gets himself out on the street – the route he's worked out, four miles for now, trying to link pockets of green. Even given his lack of fitness, the parks fly by. And whatever have we done to the air, he thinks as it rasps his throat, turning his snot black. Coming back sweated, he throws himself down at the computer again, e-mails her one word: *'Sophie . . . ?'* Within moments her reply: *'Reinholdt has tutored me well, Greg. I'm thinking about it.'*

For days, nothing more from her, then this.

'I've been asking around at the university. As you know,

there are quite a few different gatherings of orcas (well, OK, you'd use a different term from gatherings – pods, isn't it?) in the seas off Vancouver Island – the ones you wouldn't go out and see when you were here. Someone from the Marine Bio dept confirms your sense they are overwatched. Apparently there are large numbers of whale watch boats in Victoria harbour now and some of them go out three times a day. With private boats going out, too, there have been up to seventy boats watching in one area at one time, plus about forty kayaks. There's a problem, too, he said, of orcas habituating to humans with one individual in particular seeking human contact. There's been work – and legislation brought in – to prevent this. I understand the killer whale northern residents and the transient pods (pods, there you go) are categorized as threatened, while the southern residents are endangered with numbers in all populations decreasing. A heavy build-up of pollutants has been identified on post-mortem.

'Boat strike is a problem with the resident killer whales, which are both hit by the bows of boats and caught by propellers. There's work going on to assess the affect of noise pollution here. It's thought that some of the orcas are deaf at certain frequencies due to their overexposure to noise and they simply don't hear the ferries coming.

'Fish-farm acoustic harassment devices are known to be displacing killer whales and probably white-sided dolphins, while farm-borne parasites are being linked to the decline in wild pink

salmon – an important prey species for many cetaceans in that area.

'There's also been a study of hybridization between Dall's and harbour porpoises, which – I'm told – is happening frequently off southern Vancouver Island and is thought to be an indicator of environmental stress, as is the declining number of harbour porpoises.

'There was something else, too – oh, yes – Big Concern over the North Pacific Right Whale – very small population now, apparently – threats include ship strike, entanglement in fishing gear, habitat degradation, noise, coastal development, pollution, reducing food supply, climate change . . .

'I guess you knew most – if not all – of this stuff, but hey – even to me it sounds as if there would be enough conservation work here for you to get your teeth into, if here is what you are contemplating. Whether you'd get a work permit is another matter. My source tells me a history of work with bio-acoustics might swing it if the work falls within certain parameters. I didn't know enough about your specialism to be able to give him details, but if you want to talk it through with him, I can put you in touch. Not that they have a vacancy at present.

'So you see – I said I wasn't about to give up on you and I haven't – yet. Reinholdt has tutored me well, though, so I have now managed to work out for myself that I am deserving of the love of a good man – a category I had put you in, Greg, right up until the France vs. Scotland escapade. ("Rat" hardly covers it.)

Claim some of those extenuating circumstances if you like and I'll listen, but you're going to have to give me some pretty convincing reasoning before I can get round to that forgiveness you talked about.'

In Flight

From six miles high, the sea – in sunlight – looks smooth like flawless, finely pored skin. He rests his head at the cabin window's edge, letting his focus slide into blur: grey and white and silver and blue. He sighs, his eyes heavy. He might doze in a while.

'Water, sir?'

'Oh. Yes. Thank you.'

The flight path map is back on the screen. The little icon of the aeroplane poised midway between landmasses.

It hadn't taken him long, in the end. The visit to his parents had been the most difficult part. He'd jettisoned so much stuff when he left Pembrokeshire; he had only to jettison a little more in London to leave himself with the minimum of gear he needs for his work: the laptop; the set of disks; a hydrophone; a theodolite; a few books; plus a few clothes. He can always pick up more dive gear once he gets there, if he needs it; once he knows whether or not he's going to settle. He settles back in his midway seat. Of all the changes, of all the upheaval, it's a part he allows himself to like as, indeed, he always has: travelling light.

Ella's work on paper and the scrap of vellum he'd sent to her parents with details of where they could see more of it. They might want to take a trip down to the exhibition in the Midlands. A holiday or pilgrimage.

The visit to his parents had been the most difficult: leaving the *Strombus listeri* with them in the garden of his own childhood; the loss of their only grandson written in their eyes and now this loss of their only son that their only son is inflicting on them.

He'd strolled empty Cumbrian beaches with his dad, who was putting a brave face on things; going to the local with him for a lunchtime pint before going home to the roast his mother had spent the morning cooking, not letting on it's not what he eats any more and hasn't been for years.

'But it's your birthday on the eighteenth,' she had protested when he'd told her his departure date, as if it being his birthday somehow precluded him from going.

He raises the water to his lips and drinks. Thirty-nine today. Midway. Well, more than midway, quite probably.

He does doze, wakes to a stiff neck and Venus in an orange sky. Evening and morning star that's not a star at all. *She's* such *a hussy*, Sophie had said of Venus at a Jacob's cabin sunrise, so that he'd raised his eyebrows and waited for more – *Always flaunting herself, pert and shining, lounging around on the lakeside beach* – and he'd laughed; hugging her tightly to him. *That's not very scientific*, he'd teased; hearing her laughter pressed against him.

'Could you fasten your seat belt, sir?'

At Toronto his plane is delayed and he waits in the airport lounge, looking out at the grey of heavy rain tinged yellow by the pall of pollution trapped beneath cloud. It's a long delay, extending into night: fitful sleep on lounge seats, waiting for the next announcement, which comes – three hours more yet.

Stars are fading in a morning sky by the time they're under way again. Bleary-eyed, he looks out at them, thinking of that thing she'd told him in the warmth of their bed in Jacob's cabin – of how elements are forged in stars once the hydrogen is all used up – a thermonuclear progression through the periodic table until – in the collapse of massive stars; in supernovae explosions – elements are flung far into space, to gather in dust clouds, to begin again to coalesce into stars and dust discs and planetesimals and planets. *You wouldn't be here, otherwise*, she had said. *Did you know that?*

That our bodies are stardust?

Mmm. Life couldn't have happened without the forging of elements in stars, she'd said, her hand on his belly, so that he draws quick breath at the memory of it.

I think Missing would call that a particularly wonderful use for fire, he had said.

394

She had laughed, her lips against his ear, his manhood in her hands, her voice mimicking the Brit: *Ah, yes – a particularly fine configuration of stardust.*

There's the rattle of the steel trolley.

'Tea or coffee, sir?'

He chooses water.

Daylight reveals the landscape below and although he'd expected prairie, although he'd expected agri-business, still, the sight of it all – shrouded in darkness on his last flight – is a shock: the scale of it. Several hours' flying at – what? – 500 or 600 miles an hour – and still the rigid grid of fields prevails. Or you couldn't really call them fields, could you? Fields suggests hedges, doesn't it? A relief of hedgerows and trees and copses, whereas here there are none. Eight hundred and eighty-four metre squares, she'd said, the boundaries marked by dirt roads or main roads or the railroad or where a farmer ploughs one square up to the very edge of the next. In all those hundreds – no, *thousands* of miles – he sees scarcely a tree. Sometimes rivers snaking through the flat terrain have to be ploughed along, or sometimes a classic ox-bow lake curves across a couple of squares so that plough lines have to follow. Otherwise the rigid grid persists.

Wherever will the wildlife have fled?

To the north, he supposes, those that can withstand the cold.

He gives himself to reading. Her paper again, finally published in *Nature*. The celebration of a solar system similar to ours, the dust-disc perturbation likely to indicate the presence of a rocky planet – only orbiting too close to its star, after all, to be within the habitable zone.

Tucking the journal away, he pulls out papers from the university and the dog-eared dragon story is pulled out too. He checks himself from checking his watch.

'Did your little *boy* do that?' the woman sitting next to him asks, seeing the child's drawing of the fire-breathing dragon and the name 'Sebastian' in a child's haphazard hand.

'Yes. Yes, he did,' Greg says, tucking the thing quickly under other papers on his knee, giving himself quickly to re-reading about the university: their projects and resources – needing to make sure he's got it straight before meeting members of the department in a couple of days.

He dozes again, wakes in time to see mountains rising, their west-coast shoulders rising high to shrug off the grid's imposition. They'll be in Vancouver shortly where he must change planes for the journey's last leg.

The transfer is quick this time and he is soon airborne again, looking down on the beauty of forested islands – seas and countries he barely knows.

Not long now to Vancouver Island.

'*Hate to say it,*' he'd written in an e-mail to her, '*but the seas around Vancouver Island don't have a monopoly in marine biological crises which need dealing with. I really could go any-where in the world, Sophie, and find more than can be coped with. I guess – if I wanted to give myself an easier time of it – I could go to New Zealand. They seem to be ahead of the game there – relatively speaking – a greater awareness and better application of conservation strategies. So again – the science is a perfectly good reason to be in VI, but . . . you're the reason to be there specifically – a unique reason; my love for you a unique reason.'*

Not long now to Vancouver Island.

Not that Sophie will be there to meet him.

'I'll be in Aus when you arrive,' she'd written in an e-mail to him, *'Nothing personal, Greg. A family holiday, no less. There's been so much change at home with the arrival of baby Samuel and Emily living there now. And the other thing that's changed is that my parents have decided they want to do some travelling and Richie has said he wishes they would – it would leave him some peace and quiet and when are they going? – only could they make it soon, please and for quite a while! So they are. They're going to Australia for a month and they've asked me to go with them. So that's why I won't be in VI when you arrive, Greg. Bad timing, I know, but it could be good healing time to spend with my parents and we need that, the three of us.'*

It's not bad timing, in fact, he thinks, as the little plane banks steeply to come into land. It will give him time to establish himself – find somewhere to live, buy a car, get to know the marine biology people, follow up leads he's had of possible work there for him.

And it's good, too, that she's had time in Australia, he reflects, thinking of the e-mail he'd picked up in Toronto.

'OK – so it's a bit fanatical, visiting telescopes while I'm on holiday, but it's a good thing to share with Dad, and Mom doesn't seem to mind. Parkes is like the Lovell at Jodrell Bank – a huge radio telescope. This one was in the right place to collect the images from the Apollo 11 mission when the rotation of the earth meant the US scopes went out of range, so if you saw those TV pictures, you saw at least some of them courtesy of Parkes. There's a printout in the hallway – NASA sent as a thank-you – of the heart rates of Armstrong and Aldrin at the moment they stepped out onto the moon. I think even Mom was impressed. Difficult not to be – the dish on its edge when we arrived – fanned out over the tree-lined drive like the tail of some monstrous albino peacock with the sun through its feathers.

'And then we went to the Warrumbungles. I'd always wanted to see 2df. It's an instrument on the Anglo-Australian telescope which can collect the light from 400 objects simultan-eously within two degrees of field. A robotic arm positions the 400 optical fibres ready to make an observation, while the symmetrical other half of the instrument is already observing. By the time the observation is complete, so is the setting up of the first half and the instrument rotates through 180 degrees so the whole process can start over. They've got software on site which can *analyse the data and so with 2df they're able to observe and analyse the spectra from thousands of objects in one night! One of the things these guys have been working on is a survey of galaxies – they've mapped over 220,000 now, measuring the red shift and consequently the speed at which the galaxies are travelling – terrific and increasing speeds – the galaxies all zipping away from us as the universe expands.'*

He smiles to himself as the plane comes into land, thinking of her enthusiasm, thinking of her, thinking of seeing her again fairly soon. Two or three weeks and she'll be home. He'll be able to take more time this time. Court her, even. Court the forgiveness she hasn't yet granted; court the continuation of their closeness. Some simple, straightforward gesture to start with: Darcy's perhaps, for dinner on the waterfront, an evening stroll along the harbour, watching the float planes come and go.

Acknowledgements

In order to fictionally represent some of the subjects of study being considered by contemporary astronomers and marine mammalogists, it has been essential to research current actual events. While there is no link whatever between my totally fictional characters and any existing persons, the science and issues with which Greg and Sophie concern themselves are closely related to those in the real world. I am deeply indebted to the following people for their kind willingness to share their wisdom. Throughout the text, the knowledge is theirs and any remaining errors are assuredly mine.

In – or relating to – the United Kingdom

Roger Bamber – Consultancy Leader, Department of
    Zoology, Natural History Museum, London
James Barnett, Bob Bulgin and Arie den Hollander – British
    Divers' Marine Life Rescue

Kelvin Boot – Head of Education, National Marine
Aquarium, Plymouth

Judith Crowe – Spinal Injuries Association, London

Rob Deaville – Research Assistant, Institute of Zoology,
London

Defra – Sea Fisheries, Milford Haven, Wales

Bill Dent – Astronomer, Royal Observatory, Edinburgh

Devon and Cornwall Police

Sarah Dolman – Whale and Dolphin Conservation Society,
Australia

Members of the Exeter Astronomical Society, especially
Howard Donaldson, Joyce Hedges, John Ruddy and Liz
Thompson

A. D. Goodson – Chief Experimental Officer, Underwater
Acoustics Research Group, Loughborough University

John Goold – Development and Academic Manager,
Institute of Environmental Science, University of Wales,
Bangor

Jonathan Gordon – Sea Mammal Research Unit, University
of St Andrews, Scotland

Monica Grady – Head of Petrology and Meteoritics, Natural
History Museum, London

John Hingley – Fisherman, Brixham

Lindy Hingley, OBE – Brixham Seawatch

Jonathan Lovell – Researcher, Institute of Marine Studies,
University of Plymouth

Colin MacLeod – Beaked Whale Research Project, Glasgow

Phil Midgley – Hatchery Manager, National Lobster Hatchery, Padstow

Tim Naylor – Head of Astrophysics, University of Exeter

Mark Simmonds – Director of Science, Whale and Dolphin Conservation Society, UK

Trudy Ward – General Manager, Duke of Cornwall Spinal Unit, Salisbury

Stephen Westcott – West Country Seal Group

Rob Williams – Sea Mammal Research Unit, University of St Andrews, Scotland

Phil Yates – Clinical Neuropsychologist, Mardon Neuro-rehabilitation Centre, Exeter

In – or relating to – Canada

David Balam – Space Guard Canada, Department of Physics and Astronomy, University of Victoria

Martin Beech – Assistant Professor of Astronomy, Campion College, University of Regina

Christine Erbe – Fisheries and Oceans Canada, Institute of Ocean Sciences, Sidney, British Columbia

Doug Johnstone – Research Officer, Millimetre Astronomy Group, National Research Council

Cheryl Miller – Royal Astronomical Society of Canada, Regina

Vance Petriew – Royal Astronomical Society of Canada,
    Regina
Colin Ranson – Volunteer Park Warden, Vancouver Island
Glenn Sutter – Curator of Ornithology and Human
    Ecology, Royal Saskatchewan Museum, Regina
Pamela Willis, MSc – Simon Fraser University, Burnaby,
    British Columbia

In – or relating to – the east Caribbean

Karim Hodge – Associate Executive Director, Anguilla
    National Trust, Anguilla
Roland Hodge – Director of the Department of Fisheries
    and Marine Resources, Anguilla
Dr Floyd Homer – Wildlife Consultant, Anguilla National
    Trust, Anguilla
Lighthouse Keepers, Sombrero, Anguilla – especially Head
    Lighthouse Keeper, Donald Lloyd
Jim Stevenson – Global Programmes Officer, Royal Society
    for the Protection of Birds, UK

In – or relating to – the west Carribean

Ken Balcombe – Earthwatch Marine Mammal Scientist,
    Bahamas Marine Mammal Survey

Alessandro Bocconcelli – Operations Director, Centre for
  Marine Science Research, University of North Carolina

Liz Clark – Earthwatch Volunteer

Alessandro Frantzis – President, Pelagos Cetacean Research
  Institute, Greece

Leigh Hickmott – Marine Mammal Scientist, UK and
  Bahamas

Darlene Kettern – Senior Scientist, Woods Hole
  Oceanographic Institution, Massachusetts

Naomi Rose – Marine Mammal Scientist, Humane Society
  of the United States

In – or relating to – Hawaii

Harry Abraham – Maui Ocean Centre, Hawaii

John Davis – Astronomer, Joint Astronomy Centre, Hilo

Martin Duncan – Astronomer, Joint Astronomy Centre, Hilo

Frossie Economou – Manager, Computer Services, Joint
  Astronomy Centre, Hilo

Andrea Ghez – Professor of Physics and Astronomy, UCLA
  (www.astro.ucla.edu/research/galcenter)

Mike McCartney – Astronomer, London

Robin Phillips – Support Astronomer, James Clerk Maxwell
  Telescope, Hawaii

Rob Wilder – Pacific Whale Foundation, Hawaii

In – or relating to – Australia

Michael Burton – Astronomer, School of Physics, University
    of New South Wales, Sydney

John Reynolds – Officer in Charge, Parkes Observatory,
    Australia Telescope National Facility

John Sarkissian – Operations Scientist, Parkes Observatory,
    Australia Telescope National Facility

Relating to New Zealand

Mike Donoghue – Relationship Management, Department
    of Conservation, Wellington, New Zealand

Especial thanks to the following who have – over a considerable period of time – tolerated my questioning, giving so generously of their time, thought and invaluable expertise:

Andy Adamson – Head of Operations, UK Infrared
    Telescope, Joint Astronomy Centre, Hawaii

Ijahnya Christian – Executive Director, Anguilla National
    Trust, Anguilla

Diane Claridge – Earthwatch Marine Mammal Scientist,
    Bahamas Marine Mammal Survey

Jane Greaves – Research Astronomer, Royal Observatory,
    Edinburgh

Paul Jepson – Veterinary Pathologist, Institute of Zoology, London

Rod Penrose – Strandings Coordinator (Wales), Collaborative UK Marine Mammals Stranding Project

Richard Sabin – Curator, Mammal Group, Department of Zoology, Natural History Museum, London

Nick Tregenza – Secretary, European Cetacean Society

Fred Watson – Astronomer in Charge, Anglo-Australian Observatory, Coonobarabran, Australia

My thanks to Nicky Hursell, my editor at Pan Macmillan and to my agent, Simon Trewin, for their constructive editorial input and to Frances Fraser, Mary Jacobs, David Rivington, Christopher Southgate, Roz Webb and my mother for such considerate supportiveness.